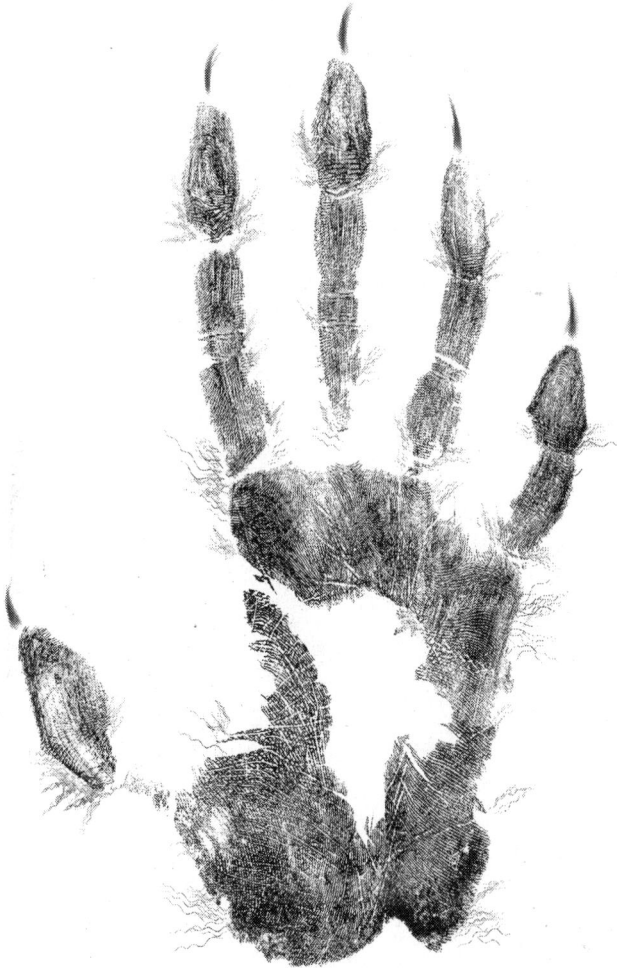

Visit us online anytime at johnpeterjones.com
Follow on twitter @JPeter.Anim

ISBN-13: 978-1502969798

ANIMALIS

By
John Peter Jones

For Kaitlin

1
Born to Fight

"Come on, kid," Gillian said. "Your guts aren't made of jelly-fish! You're not your daddy. Are you? Are you a coward? Huh, you a coward? Huh? Coward!" He struck as if beating a primal drum. "Coward!"

Jax's head shook with each blow. The taste of blood blended with the scent of pine and western hemlock trees floating in the crisp autumn air. Jax squeezed his eyes shut, blocking out the fuzzy crowd of officers swirling around him.

"You can do better than this, Minette," the staff sergeant overseeing the test said. "The enemy doesn't play by the rules."

Jax could barely hear him over the sound of his own breathing and the hammering pulse in his head. It was supposed to be against the rules to strike the head. *They're going extra hard on me,* he thought. Pushing to bring out his full potential. His test was turning out more like a fraternity hazing ritual. He tried to imagine if everyone certified to pilot orbital pods had gone through this, but the punches breaking past his arms and hitting his face kept interrupting him.

Jax's ears began to burn red. He wasn't his father. He wasn't a coward. *I'm winning this fair,* Jax thought. *Even if he's breaking the rules, I'm not giving up. I'm winning this fair.* Jax bent his chest forward, coming off the ground and closer to Gillian's knee. Then, with a burst of strength, Jax twisted his hips and shoved Gillian's knee off his stomach. Freedom! Jax whipped his legs around Gillian's waist, arched backward and pushed his head out of Gillian's reach. His feet locked together below Gillian's ribs.

Gillian smiled and continued to strike Jax's thighs with his elbows, but now at least Jax's vitals were safe. He took a moment to catch his breath and let his vision settle. His face was cold with sweat, and his hands shook, fueled from adrenaline.

Gillian's smile was wrong; *why does it look like he's pitying me?* Jax thought, *I've outplayed him.* The smile faded as Gillian brought his elbow down with a sickening smack into Jax's groin. Jax hadn't even thought to protect that area—it was so far below the line dividing the acceptable from the unacceptable in a fight—but just before the blinding flash of pain, he realized his horrible mistake.

Pain. Pain. Pain.

It was all Jax as aware of. Everything was pain for the first five seconds, then Jax realized his eyes were still open, mindlessly staring at Gillian and the crowd beyond. Somehow he had managed to keep his legs locked around his opponent's waist.

Gasps, chuckles, and jeers came from the small audience. "Do it again!" someone called.

The pain was unbearable. Jax's head rolled back in agony. Before he squeezed his eyes shut, he focused in on the one familiar face in the crowd. His friend Hank lifted his chin from its hiding place below his collar.

I'm okay, Jax told himself. *It'll have time to heal later.* He wasn't sure, but just thinking it helped bring his focus back to winning. He fought past his body's urge to curl up and pulled himself back off the ground into a seated position. Every movement dug the pain in deeper, but he kept going. His hands reached out to grab hold of Gillian's head.

"Come on, kid," Gillian moaned. "Don't go lookin to me for help up. You're gonna make me feel bad." He pushed Jax's hand away. "I wasn't sure wether you had anything down there. I mean, we gotta check, right? Hey-"

Jax finally had a hold and quickly swing his right leg over Gillian's shoulder next to his neck. Now Jax had his legs locked together again, with Gillian's right arm and head trapped between them. The smile didn't come back onto Gillian's face.

Using Gillian's own bulging bicep against his neck, Jax would cut off the blood being pumped to his brain until Gillian passed out or tapped out. If Jax could just … put enough … force into the squeeze without succumbing to his own pain.

A distant part of Jax's mind could feel the twisting and shaking of Gillian trying to pull himself free. Jax held on, and kept holding on, but with each passing moment, it became clear that he didn't have the strength left to finish the choke.

"Time!" Through the tiny funnel that still connected Jax to the world, the voice of the staff sergeant signaled the end of the fight. "Good fight, gentlemen."

Jax flopped back onto the grass and finally let the pain curl his body into a ball. He couldn't hear what else was going on around him; the pain drowned out everything but his subconscious mind and the memory it dredged up.

"You expect to get anywhere in life if you let that sprained ankle stop you now?" his father had said, his patience run dry.

Jax could see the memory more clearly as the pain settled. His father's robotic arm knocked the basketball out of Jax's small hand and started dribbling it down the indoor court. "I guess I've already won." His father shot the ball from the three-point line. The sound of the ball sliding easily through the net echoed around the room.

It was playing out like it always had; Jax hadn't wanted to play and his father had become frustrated and angry. Jax had stumbled to catch the ball and felt a sharp sting. Jax remembered sitting with his leg tucked against his chest, holding his throbbing ankle. He could already feel it swelling. The tears in his eyes flooded his vision, threatening to spill over and run down his eight-year-old cheeks. Seeing his father make the shot, though, turned Jax's fear into rage, and he stood abruptly. Pain arced from his toes to his skull.

His father had just retrieved the ball, and at the sound of young Jax rising, he now waited in silence. Everything in Jax's watery view seemed a blurry blob. He could have let the tears drain away, but the distortion formed a shield, and all he wanted now was to be protected. His teeth clenched with each step as he ran to the door of the rec room. *I'm not going to let it stop me!* he shouted in his mind, *I'm not going to quit, like you did,* but he was not going to stay another second with his father either.

After what might have been five minutes lying on the ground, with thoughts of his past swirling around him, Jax noticed a gloved hand hovering above him. Gillian stood before him with a wide smile splitting his face.

"Not bad! You've got something, kid—really got something. No one takes a hit like that and keeps fighting. Sorry you had to be the one to feel it. But believe me, this is not going to be a fight I forget."

Jax tried to hold onto the words while he brought himself back to reality. The jeers from the crowd had disappeared, and as he took hold of Gillian's hand, he even heard some light clapping.

"That was good, Gillian," Jax managed to wheeze out. "You fought dirty, just like an Animalis."

Jax drooled a bit of blood as he spoke the last word. His intended insult and drops of red disappeared into the dark shadows amongst the grass. He clumsily pulled his hand out of his glove and put pressure on it. While he had been consumed by the pain, all he had wanted was to get away from this mad group of people pretending to be his enemy, but now he might stick around long enough to get a few more pats on the back.

Gillian turned away and joined the group of officers gathering behind him. Jax noticed Hank had left the group and was standing by his side. It was a relief to have someone next to him who was really on his side. Hank was about to speak when the staff sergeant cut him off.

"Did that help? Crying about the rules like the army brat you are?" the staff sergeant said. "When your enemy's breaking international law, all that matters is maintaining control. Every attack from the Animalis gets more brutal, and now they're right in our back yard. Are you ready for that? For an attack in your home town? This certification you're applying for isn't for kids, brats that just got out of bootcamp. You think any hatch-pop is routine? If you board a plane when you're not ready, you're gonna kill yourself and your team. It's all about staying in control. Even when the odds are stacked against you, you have to stay in control." The sergeant narrowed his eyes at Jax.

Jax's cheeks began to burn. He nodded as he looked up at the tall sergeant. There was plenty of time to make the sergeant eat his words, calling Jax an army brat. Jax was going to be a hero. He was going to help people. He was going to be remembered. He was going to be the soldier that the Animalis militants cowered before. They'd pray to whatever strange animal god they had for Jax not to destroy them. The sergeant was just mad that Jax was applying for pod pilot certification so young. Or mad that the sergeant's twin brother, Felix, had earned the certification and not him. Maybe he was jealous, but maybe the he was right. Maybe Jax *was* too young. He hadn't controlled the fight; not as much as he had wanted to.

Since high school graduation and full adult status came at sixteen, it wasn't rare for a seventeen-year-old to be in the army. But the number of skill certifications and qualifications Jax had was above average. He should have done better in the fight. Was he wrong to think he could be a hero?

He resisted the urge to throw up as the pain in his groin continued to cut through him. Where did he go wrong in the fight? How did Gillian get him trapped so vulnerable on the ground? Someone had called his name.

As the crowd started to break up, Jax scanned the faces wondering which one it was he had heard called his name during the fight. "*Jax … Jax … Jax …*" He had caught the voice floating above the crowd, not as a chant, but as a whisper. He had twisted to find its source. At the time, the faces of the small crowd—remote specks within his consciousness—had continued to watch the fight. No one else had seemed notice it. And there was something else … black and white, swirling together, trapped behind bars. He had seen an image of a yin-and-yang, but now … it was like a dream quickly fading.

Then he had been slugged in the face and sent tumbling to the ground.

"Your results will be sent to you in a day," the sergeant said. He turned to Hank. "This your boyfriend, Hank?

"No. I've known Jax a long time," Hank said. "You can be sure that my notes for his certification will be entirely encomiastic."

The staff sergeant nodded with an empty smile while his eyes shifted back and forth. *Reading the monitor's interpretation of what Hank had said,* Jax knew. Hank would have been offended with the dumbed down version the monitor offered: *encomiastic means good.* Jax watched the sergeant's eyes light up with understanding. His smile widened and he slapped Jax on the back before turning to leave. "Yeah, at least it was an encomiastic show," he said.

Jax began walking back to the Hornet and Hank fell in beside him.

"Sometimes I wonder if we're in the hands of the staff sergeant, or his monitor," Hank remarked.

"What do you mean?" Jax asked. Once they were clear of the officers, Jax spread his legs wider, walking with a humiliating gait.

"He's just doing what he's told," Hank said. "His monitor keeps his whole life nice and tidy for him, telling him when to get up, what to eat, what words to say. It has a constant video feed going, so why does he even need to hold onto memories?

He'll forget ninety nine percent of his life, as the days float away like the last smoke of a dying fire. How can someone say a day has value when they don't even remember what happened? Maybe he'll forget that you pretty much lost the fight. But, then he'll have his monitor to tell him what he saw. His monitor will take that responsibility." Hank had a worried smirk with his chin still hidden below the collar of his barely regulation copper leather coat. His eyebrows shot up as he met Jax's glance.

"Yeah. I noticed that, too," Jax said with a wince.

"See? You should have used my Vicarity Suit. The darn thing is flawless, Jax. If you could just see it work. Heck, if the Captain could just see it work. I could control another soldier remotely as they board a plane, while I'm still on the Hornet! I wouldn't want to control you, though, you've got instincts that are far beyond me, but Felix maybe."

At the end of the sparring field, the path turned and joined a road running through the middle of the small base, passing the armory and storehouse. Jax tilted his head up to gaze at the launch shaft of the base's airport disappearing into the clouds. It was used to sling space planes almost to low orbit, saving thousands of pounds of fuel. It was a magnificent sight. The honey comb pattern of the beams started wide at the brightly lit base and rose up to a slender point a thousand feet in the air, like a giant had pinched the metal and dragged it into the sky.

The view was cut off as they entered the hanger beside the launch shaft and continued walking toward the Hornet. The barracks, the mess hall, the officers quarters, and the command center were all part of the Hornet—a monstrous space plane with two pod bays, four turrets, and room to house forty men.

"It's hard to know either way, though. Maybe in their eyes,

you did win," Hank said, breaking the silence. They started ascending the stairs into the Hornet. "After he hit you in the groin? That earned you prodigious credit."

———

It was late. Jax should have been in his bunk, but he couldn't sleep. He stood in the hall in front of the pods. The walls were smooth and white, radiating a soft light from diodes spread throughout their surfaces.

He could see his reflection in the window to the vacuum chamber of the first pod. The face looked confident. Jax's crisp, strong features and thin brown eyes looked older than most seventeen-year-olds—with their unwearied faces. This was just the start of his military career, but he had been pushed forward because of his physical abilities, and his commitment to never quit.

Jax was a good complement to Hank, ever since they'd first met in middle school. Hank needed a protector, and, with the poison of everyone around Jax pretending his father wasn't a disgrace, Jax needed Hank's honesty like an antidote.

Hank had blazed through academy and straight into a commanding position as warrant officer. In high school, Hank was the one planning pranks to reprogram the walls of the school to play movies, and Jax was the one that climbed onto the roof and found openings in the skylight to get in at night. Hank had even found a way to hack the city traffic control, and subsequently sent all of the teachers' cars to a meat-packing plant instead of the high school one day.

A glowing orange box appeared in the air beside the pod door. He gave a mental gesture to his retina monitor and watched the message expand to be read.

9-25-2093: Jax Minette. After careful review of your enrollment records, and having evaluated your test with high marks, your request to fill the position of pod pilot aboard the Hornet under the command of Warrant Officer Hank Schneps and Captain Jesus Hernandez has been approved. Call sign Catcher 6. Report to Officer Schneps at 0400 hours.

Jax let out his breath slowly, and the glass window clouded with moisture. He took another deep breath and smiled.

When he turned to leave the hall he would now be reporting to regularly the pain of the fight returned. Each step sent a stab into his stomach. *Like old times,* he thought. Him and Hank. They would send a tremor of fear through the ranks of the militant Animalis.

2

Animalis

"Let me be clear. If you don't make it out in thirty minutes, you'll blow up with the rest of the plane." On the wall, colored diodes and microscopic electromagnets rearranged to form a vivid, textured replica of Captain Hernandez's head and torso. The wall moved like an animated Roman relief sculpture in full color.

Jax couldn't help looking at the scar disfiguring the captain's left ear. Hernandez's bare scalp glistened, reflecting the light emanating from the walls around him in the cockpit of the Hornet. War and stress had etched the years in lines across his face.

Jax stood in the pod bay hall, facing the vacuum chambers beside Hank, with the other two pod pilots, Maven and Felix, a short distance away.

Jax glanced at the window beside the captain's image and caught a glimpse of the last clouds in the sky disappearing below the Hornet, starting to catch fire from the sun peaking over the horizon. As the plane rose higher, the deep blue of the sky shifted to black.

Jax smiled despite the constant ache from the fight with Gillian. He was here, shooting up into space and getting his first mission brief from the captain himself.

Somewhere in the plane, a valve hammered open and sent

a hollow echo through the floor and into Jax's feet. The quiet hiss of the electric motors died. He could feel the liquid-fueled rockets rumble to life, ready to launch the Hornet through the last thin layer of atmosphere.

"This cargo plane is ancient," Captain Hernandez continued. "When they first started hitting the shaft in the fifties, they were pieces of junk. It looks like this one's lost its maneuvering thrusters, making reentry impossible. We need intel if we can get it. Data logs, everything so get in and out fast. If it has any of its original paint left, they burn green in ozone. Big, beautiful explosions."

"Only thirty minutes?" Felix interrupted. "How close are we to even being orbital?"

The captain waited in silence once Felix had finish speaking. Felix opened his mouth slightly, then closed it again and rocked back on his heels, away from the wall bearing the image of the captain's face.

"We need the encrypted logs from the computer," the captain continued, "and any other bits of data that can be recovered. Warrant Officer Schneps …"

"Yes sir," Hank said.

"You're authorized to board the plane and take anything from the computer you can get. Our scans are being blocked, but, from the modifications, looks like a rat Animalis is on board. No effort will be made to assist or evacuate. Is that clear?"

"Yes, sir. Valuable information is always worth the risk, sir," Hank said. He saluted the captain, then Hernandez's grizzled face disappeared, and the wall rearranged into its normal, flat, surface. Hank let his hand drop, and his eyebrows scrunched.

Jax was surprised the captain hadn't corrected Hank. He should have just said, "Yes, sir," and left it at that.

With the captain gone, Felix turned to Maven and clapped his hands together. "Aw, a rat hole! Isn't that just what gets you out of bed in the morning? I can smell it already." He feigned a large whiff in the air, then walked to the west wall, which folded away to reveal a rack of spacesuits. Hank interrupted him before he took down his suit.

"Felix, Jax has this one," Hank said.

Felix scowled and glanced from Hank to Jax. His expression brightened. "That's right," he said with a grin. "Jax is now officially certified to pilot. Heard you fought Gillian last night and didn't do half bad!"

Hank grabbed his own suit off the rack and started stepping into the bottom half. "It's going to be tight," he said. "I wouldn't trust anyone else more than you, though. Are you ready for your first flight?"

Jax waited for the words to echo through his mind again so he could make sure he had heard them right. "Yeah, yes," he said. "Yes, definitely."

Jax hurried to the rack of suits. He lifted both halves of a suit together, but lost hold of the legs, and they clattered to the floor. He left them there and started to pull on the torso piece. Training, learning, expecting, waiting for a real opportunity to make a difference. And here it was, him in control, flying through space, retrieving … data. Maybe not the world-changing mission he was waiting for, but it still fed his sense of purpose.

Jax pulled up a menu in his own retina monitor and navigated to the military training information on Animalis encounters. He had read most of it, and had gone through a series of training classes designed to prepare him for encounters, but this was his first operation.

While Jax read, the three others continued to chat.

A list of articles appeared in Jax's vision:

Rat Animalis Disease Prevention

Rat Animalis Recent Attacks

Rat Animalis Neurology and Psychology

…

Jax robotically put the pieces of his suit on and fastened them together. He scrolled through the list of articles till one caught his eye—*Signals a Rat Gives before an Attack*—and pulled it up:

While this document aims to give you the tools that will help you recognize a dangerous situation before it develops, it is impossible to know with certainty that an Animalis is not about to become aggressive. Studies from within the Animalis detention center over the past thirty years have led to a compilation of common behavioral cues that each species of Animalis gives.

"And," Felix was saying to Maven, "you think it's the wrong test for pod pilot certification? You want it to be more like the ASVAB? Please no. I went through that torture ten times and barely passed! I had this one question: you have twenty-nine colored apples, then you take five out, now there's a 25% chance of getting green so how many green apples do you have? What is that? Are we supposed to be fortune tellers?"

"Fighting is what we work the hardest to avoid," Maven said before Jax's attention returned to reading.

> Unlike Predator Animalis, rats do not usually attack the neck area. In most cases, only legs, tails, and lower backs are bitten. However, when a rat is territorial, their attacks become deadly, clawing and biting at the stomach, genitals, and throat with a vicious ferocity.
>
> A rat Animalis will almost always turn to violence if a situation suddenly changes, or if they are put into a new environment. Be cautious if the rat is experiencing a situation it might interpret as dangerous.

"This is the last place you want to be if you're trying to avoid a fight," Felix said, laughing.

"My favorite teacher in grade school," Maven said, "taught that intelligence is stifled by violence."

Jax found himself losing track of his place while reading. Snippets of the conversation were drawing his attention. He skipped to the next points of information:

> ... Rats will almost always attack intruders ...
> ... Avoid eye contact ...
> ... Avoid sudden movements ...
> ... Do not approach a rat, or any Animalis, that becomes cornered ...

"We're all here for different reasons," Hank said. "Jax, we've got to go. Twenty-seven minutes and we're hot cinders."

Jax glanced to his left. Hank was at the pod bay, with the door already folded open. Jax closed the browser, quickly locked his helmet in place, and pulled down a laser rifle from the rack beside the suits. He was glad he had missed the conversation. While he liked Maven, and wanted to take her side just to aid an underdog, he couldn't agree with her. The fight had been exhilarating. Waking this morning, after taking a few pills and putting on the bandages that his health monitors had recommended, he was as happy as he had ever been. Singing in the shower, dancing while he brushed his teeth, even sending a quick message to his mother that things were going well for him in the military.

"Sayonara, comrades," Felix said. Before the door folded shut, he called out, "Hank, if you die, can I have your stuff?"

"Jax."

Jax felt a chill run up his spine.

"Jax," the voice said again. The sound echoed through the walls and floor, entering his ear as a whisper. *"Protect us, Jax, and we will protect you."*

Hank bent to call through the last gap in the door: "Come on, Felix, you know I've already willed all my patents to your brother." Before it closed, Felix's smile broke in a look of honest disappointment. Hank straightened up and grabbed Jax's shoulder. "Come on."

The electric buzz in the air that accompanied the voice was gone. Jax wanted to ask if Hank had heard it, but there was no time. Maybe it was the meds Jax had taken to recover from the fight. He slapped his own face a few times and followed Hank through the vacuum chamber and into the pod.

After strapping themselves in, they waited for the *Hornet* to reach orbital speeds. Jax had a countdown going in his retina monitor, ready to launch out into space as soon as it reached zero. A second countdown ticked off just above it:

24:32

That timer told him how long they had until the rat plane burst into flames. It was going to be tight, but as long as Hank could get the information fast enough, they'd make it. *Heroically*, Jax thought as he eyed the main timer:

03   02   01   00

Just as Jax felt the weightlessness of orbital freefall, he launched the pod. Cameras ringing the pod captured a complete view outside and fed the video into Jax's retina, giving the illusion that the walls were transparent. The sun blazed over the eastern horizon of the massive Earth below them. An ocean of twinkling jewels riding on waves of ghostly transparent satin covered the rest of the view. The blackness was more beautiful than Jax had imagined. Even the pod simulator, which he had practiced in so many times, didn't come close to showing the range of depth and color that surrounded them. It was stunning. Massive formations of swirling teal and magenta gasses seemed close enough to touch.

Jax rotated the pod and found the rat plane, highlighted by the computer. It was a medium-size space plane, two hundred yards away, designed to carry twenty tons of cargo anywhere in the world within an hour. It was drifting now, just above the atmosphere of the Earth, unable to use its rockets for safe reentry.

"Here we go," Jax said, pushing the throttle.

Numbers ticked away, showing that they were moving closer to the plane, but everything around them seemed to stay still and permanent. It was an anticlimactic moment, stealing away some of the mystique of flying in space.

"Hank," Jax said. "Did you … "

Hank stopped reading from his retina monitor to look at Jax. "Yes?"

"Did you notice anything weird just before we got in the pod?"

Hank leaned back and closed his eyes, thinking. "Well, the pod seemed fine. I didn't see anything misplaced." He opened his eyes. "But you hesitated for a moment in the vacuum chamber. Is that it?"

"Yeah," Jax said, still not sure he should tell Hank about the voice. "I thought I heard someone. Not from my radio. I thought they said my name, something about protecting them. You didn't hear anything? Not even a whisper?"

Hank shook his head. "Just Felix, but he never whispers. You heard words? How clear was it?"

"Pretty clear, kinda like we're talking now. It felt like there was an electric buzz in the air. And I heard it before, during the fight."

Hank sat looking at Jax for a long moment, his eyes moving in and out of focus. Delving into his vast memory, Jax knew. "Sounds like one of the strange things in life, the whispers of the angels, songs of the seraphs. Mysterious. I've heard of people hearing voices before, like the flutter of a moth beside your ear, with a warning or a prophecy. Then again, you are at the prime age to show signs of schizophrenia."

"Great," Jax said, reading his retina monitor's blurb about the syndrome. "Schizophrenia."

"I'm only kidding. I would let you know if I thought you were schizophrenic."

Jax gripped the joystick firmly, hoping that he wasn't putting them both in danger with a potential psychotic breakdown in the realm of possibility. He felt fine though.

"You said it wanted you to protect them? More than one?" Hank asked.

There had only been one voice. "I think just one, and it said it would protect me." Jax watched Hank's eyes narrow while he thought. "But I took Advil this morning."

"Hearing voices from a pain killer? I've never heard of that. Let me know if they speak to you again," Hank said. "Did they tell you how you'd protect them?"

"No."

"Fine. I'm glad you told me about it. From what I've read, which isn't very much, there's a fifty percent chance something big is going to change in your life." His attention shifted to the air in front of himself. "Here, I wanted to show you this."

A prompt to join Hank's retina projections appeared in Jax's vision. When he accepted, he and Hank could see the same illusion floating in front of them. It was a rotating 3D rendering of a naked unisex mannequin with what looked like paper thin octopus tentacles wrapped around it's body.

"That's the Vicarity Suit," Hank said.

Jax watched the model rotate, examining the geometric pattern covering the body. A tag beside the model said the straps were completely transparent. "That's all there is to it? Brilliant," Jax said.

"Thanks."

"It's so simple," Jax went on. "You said it could control someone's body though? This looks more like a fitness tracker."

"No, it'll control the body," Hank said. "Here."

The 3D model was replaced by a video. Jax kept watch on the approaching cargo plane while the video played: "Vicarity Suit, using electric frequencies to block normal nerve impulses and replace them with impulses sent from a remote host." The video showed a frail looking man, reminiscent of Hank, with a plastic mouthguard, gloves, and a helmet on. The strands of the suit became highlighted in radioactive purple, reaching out from under his clothes in the same pattern that had covered the mannequin. Another man, this time a husky fighter-type, was shown reclining in a chair wearing a headset labeled NeuroReader. "Diodes along the fabric connect to every muscle set, giving the NeuroReader full control over the-"

"You highjack the nervous system?" Jax asked. "I know you've already thought of this, but what's the difference between this and a robot avatar? You'll still have to have a permit, right?"

The video showed the reclined fighter imagining a martial arts form, and the frail man moved in sinc. "For 1600 United Credits, you can print the Vicarity Suit at any print shop..."

Jax looked at the suit with new appreciation. It was a lot of money—as much as his new yearly salary. Hank had created something special.

"Sure, it'll be banned, or regulated in a year of two, but it's not for now," Hank said.

"The captain's okay with it?" Jax asked while the video continued to play.

"I've started warming him up to the idea."

A memory clicked in Jax's mind, and he did a search through his monitor's transcripts.

"Valuable information is always worth the risk," Jax repeated Hank's words back to him. "I noticed that, but didn't figure out what you were trying to do."

Hank nodded. "Hernandez knows it's always risky to send in men."

"So the next step is to equate your value to the value a mission has," Jax guessed.

"Glad you can see it for what it is," Hank said. The video of the Vicarity Suit playing in Jax's retina monitor ended abruptly. "Change of subject. There's a new arena fight video. This one is unbelievable."

"I don't want to see it, not after the last one you made me watch," Jax said reflexively.

"We'll watch it when we get back," Hank continued. "As your commanding officer *and* your friend; you have to watch this one."

"Whatever you and the rest of the world see in those videos, I don't," Jax said. He decreased their speed with light bursts of counter pressure as they neared the disabled cargo plane.

Arena fights—Two Animalis fighting to the death. Not just to the death, but till the loser was devoured. Or worse, till the body was thrown into the crowd of Animalis watching in the stands, and they devoured the loser. The Animalis were still mostly animals, and animals needed to hunt. It was better than Animalis hunting on the streets, as long as you didn't have to watch it. Hank treated it like a delicacy that Jax had to try a few times before he developed a taste for it.

The distance to the cargo plane decreased in Jax's retina

monitor until the pod reverberated with a metal clang and jerked to a stop. Jax's first flight was complete. Now they were coming to the unknown part of the mission. Without being able to get an ICT scan of the plane, they really didn't know what they would find inside. There could be a dozen Animalis. Jax had to focus, so he pushed the thoughts of the arena out of his mind.

"For the computer to go into recovery mode, we'll need to get into a panel at the front of the plane," Hank said. He opened the door of the pod. "Plane must have oxygen; there was no pressure loss."

Through the opening, Jax could see bits of plastic debris floating in the air. Emergency lights were flashing. Jax's ears were filled with a slight ringing that fluctuated in and out of his audible range. The ceiling was low for a cargo plane, only about ten feet high according to the retina monitor readout, and the doorways were five feet tall. The hallway widened in the middle at the hatch they had entered. Jax noticed bolts and adhesive tape holding panels together along the floor and walls. Each panel was a different color, and some were entirely different composites of metal. The whole plane was a patchwork quilt of metal and machinery. The adhesive tape stood out like a bold *DANGER* sign. Was that the only thing keeping the air inside the plane?

Incredible that we aren't being sucked into space, Jax thought.

Hank held up a small ICT scanner and passed it over the opening, scanning the plane. After a moment, Jax received the information. Hank had run the scan through a program that created an easy-to-follow map of the plane. Little icons floated above rooms and crates.

Hank held his hand out to block the door. "Hold on."

Jax had already expanded one of the crate icons as Hank had

spoken. It expanded to reveal its contents: *Weapons.* Tactical, long-range laser rifles. Jax expanded more icons. Rifles, pistols, shock sticks—the whole plane was loaded with military-grade weapons. The mission had a new layer of complexity. It was illegal. They had to be Animalis militants willing to die to protect their payload. Jax could have a shootout. Blasting holes in the walls, sucking the plastic debris out into space.

He readjusted his grip on his rifle.

"I've sent the information to Hernandez," Hank said. "If he wants to abort and detain, he'll let us know. We hold until then."

Jax exited the icon information and scanned the rest of the map.

"He's close to the cockpit," Jax said. "And look at the compartment he's in. That's a telltale hiding hole. That rat is scared for its life. He's not coming out of there."

After another moment the captain's orders to continue the mission came. Hank reluctantly flipped his palm up and gestured to the door. "After you."

Jax went through, grabbing hold of a handrail beside the hatch with one hand and gripping his rifle at his hip with the other as his body floated into the open corridor. Once Hank had joined him, he closed the door to the pod and locked it with his retina monitor.

It would be Jax's job to clear the way for Hank to get to the information. Assuming he was right about the rat, it would be an easy job.

Jax pushed off and started floating down the hall. He pulled the rifle up and watched the patchwork metal drift by through the sight. Everything was quiet, making Jax's breathing blare like a megaphone. Chunks of plastic bounced off his helmet as he went. He pushed off the ceiling to avoid a thick bundle of tubes and cables crossing the upper half of the hall. When he landed at the end of the hall he checked the countdown:

17:45

Hank hit the wall beside him. He opened the door to the cockpit. "Keep an eye on him," he said, pointing to a section of floor paneling that was missing, "I'll be out in a bit." Hank floated in.

Easy—stay and watch the hole. But as Jax waited, his subconscious mind filled with the conflicting information he had heard about the Animalis, trying to prepare him for a possible encounter. He had seen plenty of videos of Animalis. Of course there were the violent and disturbingly brutal videos of the arena. In Jax's mind, they confirmed that the Animalis were as unpredictable and unthinking as their animal counterparts. Then there were the videos of Animalis acting like humans, and sometimes super humans: working complex jobs, learning new languages, and most surprisingly, teaching other Animalis similar skills. The behaviors were likely mindlessly programmed into the Animalis through training, and if left alone, the Animalis were sure to revert back to normal animal behaviors.

Deep in Jax's subconscious, where his life decisions had been affected, loomed the constant news updates about militant Animalis attacks. Bombings, maulings, and even gunfights in which humans were killed. Were the Animalis smart enough to organize and execute these plans themselves, or were they being led by a human-run terrorist organization, or had the creation of the Animalis been more complex—ticking genetic time bombs to serve some unknown cause?

"They're not animals, they're weapons!" Jax had often heard his dad say, usually followed by a curse. "Expecting them to behave is going to get people killed. Round them up, tag them all, neuter the whole lot of them; we must have absolute control over them." His father rubbed his replacement arm whenever he talked about the Animalis.

While Jax's subconscious mind sorted through the information, his conscious mind was running through scenarios of the rat attacking him. When the rat crashed through his glass helmet and bit into his face, he had to correct his imagination: *No, it'll go for my stomach, not my face.* He re-imagined the rat coming out of the hole, staring at him with evil, bloodthirsty eyes, then scurrying toward him across the floor with frightening speed. He slowed down the action as the mouth of the rat widened to bite into his stomach. To avoid blasting a hole through the wall with his rifle, he could drop his elbow down on the snout instead—*Maybe a move Gillian would try*—or he could float back into the air to match the line of the rat's head, then wrap his arms around it like an alligator wrestler. *Or kick its throat hard enough—*

A movement from the hole brought Jax's mind back to reality. Nothing had come out, but Jax could see a large tube undulating back and forth near the opening. *Just keep it away from Hank,* Jax kept telling himself. It was an old pink tube, covered in some kind of rusty-brown crud, and short, thick, wiry hairs. And spidery blue veins—pulsing.

The tail.

Leathery pink skin covered in splotches of freckles. The undulating stopped for a moment, then the tail slid away from the opening.

Jax could feel his heartbeat jump.

The blackness shifted, and the eyes of the rat now stared out at him. Yellow, feral eyes that seemed to glow with the reflection of the light.

It'll stay in its hiding hole, Jax told himself, but his muscles were tightening for a fight.

The lights flickered and came back on. Jax risked looking into the cockpit to check on Hank.

"Got it. Computer is entering recovery mode," Hank said. His voice had come from the cockpit and Jax's helmet speakers.

"Hurry it up. The rat started moving—WOW!" Jax verbally leaped when he had turned back to watch the hole. A streak of vapor flared on Jax's helmet; it was right in front of him, nearly bumping its chest against the tip of Jax's rifle.

Up close, the Animalis looked surreal. In gravity, it would have stood upright at about four and a half feet tall. It was like a human, but the proportions were all wrong: head was too big, arms too short, legs too thick, spine too long. And yet every feature had the same design language as a human's.

The hands had opposable thumbs, thick knuckles, bulbous fingertips, and pointy little claws where fingernails should have been but they could still manipulate any tool that human hands could. The neck could have been an extension of the chest. It was thick, muscular, and covered with hair that poked out from under the collar of its thermal jumpsuit. Instead of the shoulders coming up and out like a human's, the rat's came forward and down, along the side of the rib cage.

But its face was where any resemblance to human beauty ended. The head was almost identical to its rodent relatives. The long, bent snout of a rat. Two large front teeth. Ears the size of baseballs. Fur that was glossy and black. But the eyes were the hardest to look at—yellow, expressionless eyes. They gave no hint to the creature's thoughts or emotions, so Jax assumed it wanted to kill him. The image of the teeth breaking through his glass helmet and biting into his face repeated over and over in his mind.

"You alright, Jax?" Hank asked, followed by a sound of movement coming from in the cockpit.

Keep it away from Hank. Aside from the teeth and claws, the rat wasn't armed. Jax spread his arms wide to block the doorway.

"I'll handle it. Stay on the computer," Jax said. "Get back!" he shouted at the rat. He pushed his head forward. He had to make sure that the rat wasn't about to get territorial. "This is my space. We are from the United States Army, aiding in border patrol operations."

"What is this, human? You shouldn't be here," the rat said. The dry lips stretched with large movements, revealing the two jagged front teeth. A growl punctuated its speech. "Don't touch anything. On my plane, and you think this is your space? Confused, it must be confused, insane. Don't touch it. Computer wants a week for repairs, but we know the computer is stupid. Are you here to do what the computer tells us to do? Burn up with the plane?" It held itself from drifting away by gripping a section of tubing that crossed the ceiling. In its other hand was a spool of the same adhesive tape that was holding together most of the plane.

"I can't let you pass." Jax continued blocking the door. "We'll only be a few more minutes, then we'll leave you to your plane." Maybe it was pointless to reason with the rat, respecting authority wasn't common.

The rat moved. With a quick jerk, it flung itself down from the ceiling. Jax acted nearly as quickly, pulling his knee up to protect his vulnerable stomach and pulling the nozzle of the rifle back to point at the rat.

But the rat hadn't been going for his stomach.

"Don't go near our pod!" Jax yelled.

The rat was already sailing down the hall, back toward where Jax and Hank had come in. Jax knew it wouldn't be able to get through the door lock, but the rat could be trying anything. If it managed to cripple the door, or block it, they were all going to burn.

Jax flung himself forward down the hall. According to Jax's retina monitor, the rat was almost thirty feet ahead of him, already halfway through the plane, where the door was located. As Jax watched through the sight of the rifle, the rat dragged its hand along the ceiling and came to a stop. Jax checked the countdown while he followed after it:

11:13

When Jax reached to get past another mass of cables on the ceiling, he vaulted off of them, increasing his speed.

"Hank? Progress? Tell me you're on your way out of there," Jax said through his helmet mic.

"Close. Five more minutes and we're gone. This computer is almost defunct, but it's bending to my will," Hank said.

Jax reached to the ceiling and began slowing his momentum. The rat wasn't near the door. Now crouched against the ground, it had opened another section of floor paneling and was reaching inside, muttering to itself.

"Meryum would say, 'Karl!'" The rat's voice rose in pitch. "'I can't raise these pups without you. Why didn't you think of them before your plane broke down?' But I would say, 'Meryum, I found what broke. I just need some time to myself. I can get along by myself. I am very good with my hands, Meryum.'" The rat came back out of the floor, carrying what might have been a spacesuit, but it looked puffy and bloated.

Jax stopped in front of the pod door and held his rifle ready.

The rat pulled on the suit, using its teeth along with its hands, biting and pulling, twisting and ruffling the billowing fabric until it had nested inside. It *was* a spacesuit after all. It was an ancient design, and the thermal layer had obviously decayed to nothing. The rat had probably filled it with random bits of junk to re-insulate it.

It reached back into the hole. "Ah, my cutters. There they are."

Jax tightened his finger down against the trigger, ready to put a hole in the rat if it came back up with a weapon.

But it didn't. As its hand retracted from the hole, Jax could see the slick plastic banana shape and glossy glass tip of a laser tool, just like the one strapped to his own waist. Once the floor panel was back in place, it flung itself left, to the tail of the plane, where it disappeared from view.

Jax checked the countdown:

09:23

He moved to where he could see the rat again. He saw a flash of light and heard the sharp crackle of metal popping under the tip of the laser tool. The rat had begun cutting into a wall panel.

Something chattered and squeaked near Jax. He turned and found two eyes watching him from within a large cage secured with the rest of the cargo. It was not an Animalis. These were the blue eyes of some … ferret-like animal Jax didn't recognize. It was long and slender, about two feet from head to tail, with delicate white fur drifting weightlessly. And then Jax noticed a second creature like the first, with equally beautiful black fur, scurrying around the cage that he hadn't noticed before.

"Hey, rat!" Jax called out, returning his attention to the situation. "What are you doing? What is that you're cutting into?"

The rat pulled the laser back and jerked his head to look at Jax. "I'm making my plane work," he said. "Engines need coolant, so I'm getting them coolant. I can fix it. I always fix it. It can't be fixed, but I'll fix it. Computers don't know how to fix it." He turned back to his cutting and lit up the laser again.

Some of the plastic debris floating in the cabin began drifting past Jax to the tail of the plane. Something was creating a wind current, and Jax was pretty sure it wasn't a fan.

"Hank!" Jax said, feeling the tug of the wind now. That wind current was an air leak. The rat had just cut a hole through the shell of the plane. "The rat is depressurizing the plane. Things are going to start freezing fast."

"Thirty seconds," Hank said.

Jax checked the time:

06:47

There was another loud squeak. Jax turned to look at the creatures and found them clinging to each other. Black and white, swirling together, floating in the middle of the cage. The way

30

they held each other reminded Jax of a yin-and-yang symbol. He froze at the thought.

It all seemed so … familiar. Then it hit him.

During the fight. The vision—or dream—and the voice.

One of the creatures was watching Jax. The teeth were chattering together. The poor things would soon be dead. No thermal layer to keep out the cold, no air pressure to keep their blood from rapidly expanding into a boil, no oxygen to keep their vital processes going. They would only last another minute or two, unless Jax could get them into the pod, where atmospheric pressure could be restored.

He leaped forward, compelled by the dream-like memory that these creatures needed to live. The tip of the laser tool lit up in his hand while he slung the rifle over his shoulder. *Hank is going to have a fit.*

Jax went for the door latch of the cage, quickly cutting through and swinging it open. He reached in and gently pulled the tail of the white one. Now that he was close, Jax could see how large the creatures were, probably reaching two and a half, maybe three feet long from head to tail.

"Don't you dare bite me," Jax whispered to the pair.

"What's that?" Hank said. "I'm done. On my way."

Jax fought the wind current, pulling himself along a tube that ran along the ceiling to the door. The countdown was getting dangerously low:

05:50   05:49   05:48

He was nearly to the door when the lights went out. The yellow and orange flash of the emergency lights had been

31

cut, and the blackness outside of his retina monitor was absolute.

"Jax, power? Ah, dang it!" Hank stopped himself from cursing. "Lights!" A beam of light came streaming down the corridor from Hank's suit.

Jax quickly switched his own light on.

"Watch your speed," Jax said.

Hank was falling too fast through the hall. Something had happened to him; he was too far away from any of the walls to slow himself down.

"It's the suction," Hank said. "Abominable rat. Jax, grab my hand!"

Jax moved. He had to keep a hold of the tube, or they would both tumble to the end of the plane. His mind bypassed his other hand, which was holding the two suffocating ferrets, and his only other option was his feet. Jax stretched his body out.

"Grab my foot!" Jax said, and he felt Hank's hand hit his boot.

It was no good, Jax's legs were knocked away before Hank could get a grip. Hank tumbled passed, spinning now from hitting the boot.

Jax hesitated, but he knew what he had to do. The ferrets were getting in the way.

He started to let go of his grip on the tail.

"Umph!" Hank's light stopped a few yards down the hall.

"Hank! What's going on?" Jax held onto the tail. He twisted his body to shine the light down the hall. The wind had stopped.

Hank emerged from the darkness being pulled along the ceiling by the rat.

"Human, getting in the way. Getting into trouble." The voice of the rat was quiet in the thinner atmosphere.

"Jax! It's got me. The rat's got me! Get me away from it!"

"Scrounging around my plane. Quit wiggling! I'll get you to your pod."

Hank was still moving closer. Jax checked the countdown:

04:22

A militant Animalis couldn't be trusted. Why would it care to save a human? They were all about to burst into flames anyway. But, Jax might still be able to save the ferrets, if he decided to believe the rat and went for the pod now. He still couldn't shake the feeling that they were important.

He took the risk: pulling himself along the tube while he opened the pod with the retina monitor.

When he got to the door, the rat had caught up to him. Its puffy marshmallow body bulged and curved, grasping the ceiling with three limbs while carrying Hank's weightless body.

"Jax, what are those things?" Hank asked. "We're not taking anything with us."

Jax pushed the ferrets through and then took Hank's hand. "I know this sounds stupid, but they feel important. Some dream—or déjà vu."

"Not going to happen—not on *my* mission," Hank said. His eyes shot back and forth, reading something in his monitor. "They're not even animals, Jax. The computer can't find a match from the scan. What if they're an unknown species of Animalis?"

"What?" Jax hadn't thought to check the icon the program had generated for the creatures. It was a horrible thought, bringing unknown, possibly dangerous animals onto a military plane.

Jax checked the countdown:

02:52

They were going to be hitting atmosphere very soon, heating the pod and the plane to unbearable temperatures. If the rat hadn't sealed the hole it had made, the heat would easily pour into the plane and incinerate them all.

"The voice. I think they have something to do with the voice. I'm supposed to protect them, Hank." Jax pulled himself into the pod. "If they are a new species, that could be big news for science. We could be sitting on some—what'd you call it?—prolific creds."

"That's ridiculous." But as Hank said it, he climbed into the pod. "And it's 'prodigious.'"

As the door closed, Jax looked out to see the rat one last time, but it had already vanished into the blackness. Jax commanded the pod to pressurize with air. When the ferrets had come in contact with the interior of the pod, they had lodged into a nook between the chairs.

"Launching," Jax said.

With a jolt, the pod detached from the plane. Jax could see its exterior now, glowing orange, creating a trail of excited atmosphere behind it. He pulled the pod up, fighting to escape the death dive, forcing their bodies against their chairs.

They had made it. As they continued to rise out of the atmosphere, the glow around the pod faded.

The countdown ticked off its last numbers:

19   18   17

The two of them looked down in unison, the prospect of watching the plane explode was too alluring.

11   10   09

Jax frowned. These were the last moments of the rat's life. Scurrying around, muttering to itself, so convinced it was going to fix the problem. Jax wasn't even sure the thing had been self-aware. But then it had helped them, pulling Hank back to their pod, and Jax felt sorry that it had to die.

05   04   03

The plane was still falling, carving a beautiful streak across the sky. Dropping farther and farther away. The hull of the plane would soon pass three thousand degrees Fahrenheit. At any moment, the expanding pockets of air in the metal would burst, causing a chain reaction that would instantly rip a hole through the plane and into the fuel tank. The intense temperature would ignite the entire supply at the same time, creating an unbelievable fireworks show.

00

They waited.

"Wow, what did the rat do? His engines are showing active again," Hank said.

"No, that's impossible," Jax said, but he actually felt hopeful. It was strange, he realized, to hope for an Animalis to live.

Jax had one of the pod's cameras zoom in, and he saw the

blue flames coming from the plane's jets. He marveled at the rat's tenacity. It looked like it was gaining altitude again.

"I would have lost a lot of money on that dumb rat," Hank said. "The computer said the engine coolant line was gone. That's a repair you can only do from the outside, with a new hose, and about three hours of labor."

But from the way the rest of the ship was put together, Jax figured the fix was probably far less than Federal Aviation Association standards.

"Yes, sir," Hank said. "I'm receiving the trajectory now." Hank was staring a few feet in front of himself. "No … No, that's plenty of distance, but our pod is right in the line of fire. … Yes … Yes, sir." He turned to Jax. "Throttle your starboard thrusters for about three seconds." Hank's attention went back to watching the rat plane gain altitude.

Jax hesitated. *Line of fire?* Were they going to have the *Hornet* shoot down the rat plane? Jax raised his hand, ready to hit the thrusters to get out of the line of fire. But he didn't want to. The rat hadn't attacked them, and probably would have cooperated with any demands the captain had made. It might have been close to US airspace, but it wasn't trying to enter it. International law dictated that lethal force was reserved for military combatants. It was one thing to let the rat plummet to its own demise, but completely different to shoot it down without exhausting nonviolent measures.

Hank started to open his mouth again, but stopped. He was watching Jax. "*Now,*" he mouthed.

Jax had to throttle the thrusters; it was mutiny not to. *Chain of command, orders are to be followed …* It had been carved into the very core of his brain during boot camp.

You aren't the one shooting it down, Jax tried to tell himself. *Let whoever pulls the trigger on the Hornet take the blame.*

Hank pushed Jax on the arm; his eyes were intense. He nodded to the thruster controls.

But Jax couldn't do it. He pulled his hand away from the thrusters.

In a flash of movement, Hank threw his weight on Jax and contorted his body in front of him. His arm shot out and slammed down on the thrusters. The two ferret creatures squeaked and hissed, with the force of the pod rocketing to the side and clearing the path for the laser beam.

"Clear!" Hank said.

Jax looked up and saw the turret on the front of the Hornet light up. The tip glowed white hot, and the molecules of ozone in the laser's path radiated light as the laser fired. He turned to look at the rat plane. It had moved too far away for Jax to see, but he could tell about where it was by the stream of vapor that had formed from the ozone condensing and releasing the energy the laser had left behind.

But there was no explosion, or burst of debris. Jax had stalled too long, and the rat plane had moved out of range. The laser had certainly hit its target, but with several miles of atmosphere getting in the way of the beam, it had lost too much of its concentrated energy to do any damage.

Hank spoke again to someone in his helmet. "No, the pod doesn't have enough oxygen to stay in orbit for more than twenty more minutes. ... Atmospheric re-entry is very costly. We might have to purchase a whole new pod ... Yes ... Yes, sir." Hank waited with his eyes closed when he had finished speaking. Then he turned to Jax with a solemn expression. "Alright, I don't know what you were thinking, Jax. Go ahead and return to the plane for docking."

Hank lifted himself off of Jax, but slapped the back of his helmet hard. Jax felt his stomach sink. What was he thinking? He could actually be executed for what he had done. Was he willing to trade his life for the rat's?

Or worse, he could be dishonorably discharged and sent home.

3
Dicipline

"I—" Jax stopped himself. With a light click, the seal released and he pulled his helmet off. He waited a few more moments as Hank did the same, effectively cutting off the microphones that would have recorded their conversation.

The pod had latched onto the company jumper, and the two of them were stalling before opening the hatch. Even the two ferret-like creatures were quiet and unmoving. Jax had expected them to start scurrying around the pod once the orbital weightlessness had ended, but for the most part, they had stayed out of sight behind the two chairs.

Beyond the pod door, Jax could imagine the captain waiting for him. In his mind, Hernandez's face was contorted with rage. Would he give Jax time to explain himself? Could Jax justify his actions somehow?

Or will he send me home before I even open my mouth?

Jax was the one stalling. He watched Hank burn through information in his retina monitor, his eyes shifting in seemingly random directions like he was an insane person. Hank was busy with something. *Writing his last will and testament,* But that wouldn't require any eye movement; the words would have been easily dictated as he thought them.

"I'm taking the blame," Jax said. "They can't bring you down with me, and—"

"Yes, you take the blame," Hank said, cutting him off. "But it's because you were the one that found this information while I was busy trying to follow the captain's, admittedly ignorant, orders."

A prompt blinked in Jax's monitor, linking to a document. Jax scanned through it:

> … arrive in Port Hedland, Australia …
> … the cargo of the two planes …
> … explosives. Narasimha will provide the targets …
> … all evidence will vanish …

"Is this real?" Jax asked. "This was in the rat's computer?"

It was outrageous: the Animalis militants attacking Australia? It was the one place that had opened their arms to receive the Animalis! There had been rumors that they would begin attacking North America next; that was the reason the border patrol had been reinforced by the US Army. It couldn't be Australia.

"It was." Hank reached for the door. "And it's a good thing you stopped us from blowing up his ship and making them scatter back into the woodwork. We might still have a chance to actually do some damage if we—Ahhhh!" Hank jerked his body out of his seat.

Jax heard a hiss, and the white ferret creature ducked its head back behind the chair.

"It bit me, Jax! Your stupid thing bit me!" Hank backed up against the wall, holding his side.

Jax released his harness and moved in front of the gap the creature had come through. Now even his choice to save the ferrets was backfiring on him. They weren't even grateful that their insignificant lives had been spared.

There was a knock at the pod's door.

"Warrant Officer Schneps?" said a grizzled, accented voice.

Jax felt a cold chill filling his stomach. Hank had some kind of plan brewing with what they'd learned. The computer's information still hadn't settled into Jax's mind. He wasn't sure if Hank had fabricated the document, or if they had really stumbled across secret Animalis plans. He would keep his mouth shut for as long as he could, go along with whatever Hank was scheming, and do exactly what he was told to do.

"Let me do the talking," Hank whispered.

———

"What do you plan to do with this soldier?" Captain Hernandez gestured to Jax like he was a maggot. "Insubordination is unacceptable."

The captain's physical presence was intimidating. Jax felt an electric charge in the air—a weight to the moment that a wall screen, no matter how realistic the representation was, could never reproduce. The pod behind the three of them was closed, with the two animals still inside, and Jax and Hank still held their helmets under their arms. They stood in the vacuum chamber with the captain as the *Hornet* descended back through the atmosphere.

"Nothing," Hank said. His voice was confident.

"If you're incapable of keeping your soldiers in line, you'll be stripped of your command." Hernandez leaned closer to Hank, lowering his voice: "It needs to be ground into every man and woman that thinks they can wear one of those uniforms. Orders are not given as a suggestion. The organization of the military is strictly maintained because the people who are burdened with the responsibility of making decisions have to know with one hundred percent certainty that their decision will be executed."

"This soldier may have prevented us from making a bigger mistake," Hank said.

Jax kept silent but cringed at Hank's audacity to speak back to the captain with that much confidence.

Hernandez straightened with a scowl. "What do you mean?"

"I had given Jax permission to review the information retrieved from the computer …"

The captain's nostrils flared at this reported breach of need-to-know protocol. But Hank kept talking.

"And when we were on board, he came across two never-before-seen animals. They don't match anything that is known to science—animal *or* Animalis." Hank watched the captain's eyes in silence. "This is more complex than just cutting off one shipment of weapons."

Hank looked back at the pod door. "There. You see that?"

Jax turned along with the captain and saw the white creature's head sniffing the air around the window on the pod door. Now that they were on the plane, in the presence of the captain, the creature looked more like an infestation than some important scientific discovery.

Captain Hernandez grew so big that Jax thought he was on the verge of erupting. "You brought an animal on my plane?"

Hank kept going. "Two, sir. But what Jax found in the data recovered was much more disturbing than these animals."

The captain raised his head, looking at the air three feet in front of himself.

"That is the document that highlights what was discovered," Hank said. "The Animalis are not planning to attack the States, like we all thought. Their next target is going to be in Australia, somewhere in Port Hedland." Hank waited a moment while the captain scanned the document.

"What does this have to do with these two animals?" Hernandez asked while reading.

Hank lowered his voice: "They may have the ability to create new forms of life."

The captain stopped reading and looked at him.

"Check for yourself; they are completely new to science," Hank said. "And it's impossible that they have just now been discovered. They were *created*, and the only explanation is that the Animalis now have the same technology that created the Animalis in the first place. It could be the Ivanovich Machine!"

Hernandez folded his arms and let out a breath weighted with lost patience.

Jax had never heard of an Ivanovich Machine, and couldn't tell if the captain had, either. The way Jax had always understood it is there hadn't been any special technology used to create the Animalis. It had been the work of hundreds of scientists working in secret for nearly a decade at the beginning of the twenty-first century—a deranged Russian billionaire named Romanov, throwing aside every moral objection to achieve his insane vision for the future.

But the captain wasn't stopping Hank. "Proceed," he said.

"With the protection clause in the United Nations Security Council's resolution ten-nine-seven-five," Hank said, "all participating members of the body—Australia included—are required to foster efforts made to maintain normal societal functions.

"There is a precedence," Hank went on, though the conversation had officially gone beyond Jax's understanding, "for a US Army unit, or company, to pursue hostile combatants into an obliging country."

"The Australian military won't be needing any help from us," Hernandez said.

"Then they will be the ones to gain control of this weapon," Hank said. "It *is* a weapon. One that changed the face of the earth the last time it was used. Think of that power, captain. Do we want to lose our chance? Right now is the opportunity to go in, while-"

"While Australia is forced to oblige," Hernandez finished.

Hank watched the captain's face as he thought about it. Jax was amazed to even see him considering it. If Hank was actually trying to convince the captain to act on the information, it was real. The documents and the threat to Australia were real.

"I had the foresight to leave the rat's computer with the appearance that it had blocked me from accessing its encrypted data," Hank said. "The rat is sure to divulge that he was boarded by the army, and that we took the two animals, but it is unlikely that they will change their plans knowing that the computer wasn't hacked. We have a real chance to get one step ahead of the Animalis militants."

After another moment of thought, the captain sighed. "If you are unwilling to decide how to keep your own unit in line, I will take it upon myself to choose a course of disciplinary action—for the *both* of you." The captain looked back at the door to the pod again and said, "Get those animals contained and ready for medical to sedate."

Jax and Hank saluted. The captain returned the salute, and left.

Hank just stood there, with his hand still held to his forehead, staring blankly into space. The echo of the captain's boots seemed to hang in the air. Jax wanted Hank to say something, some lighthearted joke that would show everything was still going according to plan. But he wasn't speaking, and his face was growing pale.

The captain wasn't going to send them home; Jax was confident of that. He had been paranoid to imagine that he would. He shouldn't even have been surprised that the captain would ignore Hank's recommendation to bring the war to the suburbs of Australia. That was a decision for a general at least. But the threat of being kicked out of the army still loomed in the possible future, twisting Jax's gut with a sickening nervousness. And then there was the idea that the Animalis had created the two ferret creatures using this Ivanovich Machine. Jax still didn't know what that might mean.

Quietly, Jax began to undo the seals of his spacesuit. He stepped out into the hall and the closet door folded open. When he turned back and looked at Hank, he was still frozen in place, though he had lowered his salute.

Say something, Jax urged himself, but nothing was coming to mind. He finished pulling off his spacesuit and hung the pieces up in the closet.

"Hey," Jax finally had it. "Are we going to watch that arena video or what?"

Hank blinked, and seemed to shake himself free from his

daze. "You're actually going to like this one," he said, and his signature smile lit up his face again.

———

"What's this you're watching?" Felix asked, poking his head through Hank's cabin door. "Aw no," he said after watching for a moment. "The decapitation video? Again?" He stepped into the room and moved beside Hank. Maven stepped through behind him and folded her arms.

Jax wasn't excited to watch the video and adding decapitation to the description made him want to reach to the wall and shut it off. But he wouldn't, because somehow these horrific videos made Hank feel better.

"Way to spoil it," Hank whined. "Jax hasn't seen it yet."

"That croc is at the top of my nightmare list," Felix said. He sat down on the cage Jax had printed out to hold the two mystery animals. "Look at how its eyes roll back into its skull when it goes to bite."

The relief-like images on the wall moved as fluidly as if there really were two tiny Animalis attached to the wall. With sections of the wall extending up to four inches away from its normal flat surface, the video demanded everyone's attention. The floor of the recreated arena sloped up slightly, adding to the illusion of depth for the two Animalis to stand on. They seemed almost puppet-like and silly—impossibly realistic dolls circling each other—but when they struck, it was with a savage violence.

"Maven, have you seen this one?" Felix asked.

She shook her bobbed black hair. "No." Her eyes weren't on the wall screen, but on what Felix was sitting on.

Felix followed her eyes down and immediately jumped up. "Whose squeaky little devils are these?"

"They're not mine," Hank said. He stepped away so that Felix could examine them.

"I thought they were going to die on the rat plane, so I rescued them," Jax said. He kept glancing back at the arena fight, both to let Hank know he was still watching it and because the motion of the tiny figures on the wall activated his protective instincts. He didn't want them jumping off the wall and attacking someone. Impossible, but instincts were hard to reason with.

The two Animalis were equally matched in size, five foot, 140 pounds. The crocodile stood on its hind legs and wore a ragged, tan jumpsuit. Its little eyes glistened, and the thin vertical slits of its irises gave no indication of thought or emotion. The thing was evil and—Felix was right—nightmare worthy. With a quick hop, it backed against the wall of the arena and huddled as the ram threatened it with its large horns.

"Can I hold one?" Felix asked, already undoing the latch of the cage.

"Absolutely not," Hank said. "I'm not giving those things another chance to bite me." Hank pulled up his shirt to show the little bandage on his hip. Hovering in the air beside the bandage was an image taken of the puffy, red skin where he had been bitten.

Hank moved farther away from the creatures and folded his arms. It looked like he went back to watching the wall screen, but Jax could see his eyes shifting around to invisible retina monitor menus.

"Are they minks?" Felix asked. "I wouldn't mind a coat made of this. Softest thing I've ever felt." He managed to pass his finger over the white one as it scurried by in the cage.

"You're going to keep them?" Maven asked.

Jax shrugged. "I don't think the captain would allow me to—"

"Your commanding officer won't allow you to," Hank interjected, still pretending to watch the fight. "And they're not mink. My dad used to run a mink farm, and they're smaller than these things."

Felix laughed. "So it was your momma that got all the nice mink coats."

Hank was still turned to the wall screen. He closed his eyes and shook his head.

"They're a new species," Jax said, getting the topic off Hank's mother.

Jax glanced at the wall again. The crocodile had managed to bite onto the ram's foot and was fluctuating between pulling it and being pulled by it. With a good kick, the ram got loose and scrambled to its hands and knees. When it had its footing, it charged the croc.

"Here it comes," Felix said, watching the wall now.

The croc ducked, and the ram barely missed gouging it with its horns. It lost its balance and went headlong against the wall of the arena. The ram scrambled but couldn't get up.

Jax's stomach was starting to tingle with dread. Dozens of horrid scenarios of the ram's head being ripped off were bombarding his mind.

The ram still couldn't stand, and now Jax could see why: the two horns had lodged into the floor.

In a flash, the crocodile dove and bit down on the ram's leg again.

"When did this happen?" Hank said to himself. He scowled. "Today?"

The tone of his voice drew everyone's attention, but Jax could see that Hank still wasn't paying attention to the arena match.

"Huh? This video is from weeks ago. You know that," Felix said.

The crocodile began to twist and then roll, contorting the Ram's neck.

"No, guys, I was just on a news site: there's a new video from the arena," Hank said. He moved to touch the wall screen. "It's human." Hank cut off the croc-ram match and navigated to another video.

The group grew sober. Hank stepped back as the video started to play.

A rhythmic *Boom! Boom! Boom!* came from the stands surrounding the arena. The Animalis were chanting something: "Na-ra! Sim-ha!" it sounded like to Jax. The two combatants were released from their cages on either side of the circular arena. On one side, the cage folded away to reveal a man. He looked disoriented and disheveled. The brown hair on his head was clumped, and he had an unkempt beard starting to grow. Stains covered his now dysfunctional clothes. Red ringed his irises, indicating that his retina monitors had been removed. And on the opposite side of the arena, a cage folded away to reveal a lion.

Or lioness, Jax decided.

The lioness obviously hadn't been mistreated like the man had been. She looked groomed and tidy, with dark gray clothes. There was no mane around the top and back of the head, just speckled, golden fur. As she called up to the crowd, her teeth were exposed. They could have been sharp, human teeth, except for the large canines. Relaxed, soft-looking hands hung at the end of her muscular arms. The tail was only a foot long, maybe cut short, but now fully healed. Her movements were slow and calculated, assured of victory.

"I can't believe this," Felix said. "They still can't stop these things? That should be our top priority: taking out this arena."

Jax nodded in agreement. The few times that the Animalis had put humans into the arena had been outrageous. It was unthinkable that they had gotten away with it before, and that it still hadn't been stopped.

On the video, the man was scrambling at the wall. He jumped and flung his arms up. But it was useless, the fifteen-foot high walls were smooth and unscalable. He turned and flattened his back against the wall.

The lioness slowed. Her posture lowered, ready to sprint.

The man's muscles contorted, pulling his face into a horrified gasp. He was too scared to do anything. Too scared to move, too scared to fight back.

"I can't watch this," Maven said. The door to the cabin folded open and she stepped out. "Excuse me, Captain," she said before leaving down the hall.

They all turned to see Captain Hernandez standing in the doorway. Hank leaned away from the wall and unfolded his arms. Jax glanced at the floor and animal cage, before remembering he wasn't in his barracks about to get an inspection. Felix gave a brief wave.

Hernandez was about to speak, then saw the video playing on the wall. Hank moved to shut it off.

"As you were," Hernandez said, stopping him. "I'm glad you're watching this. It's something that we all need to be reminded of." He lifted his leg to step into the room. "May I come in?"

"Yes, sir," Hank said.

Jax moved to give the captain space, but there was nowhere to go. He tried to straighten up even more, but there was nothing he could do to feel more comfortable with the captain so close. Once Hernandez was in, the door folded closed, and the room felt even more tiny and cramped.

"This is one of the leaders of the militant Animalis mentioned in the documents you retrieved." The captain nodded to the lioness on the wall. "At least, as far as we can tell."

Her muscles were a coiled spring, ready to fire at any moment. Against the wall, the man seemed to have regained his composure. He stepped away from the wall, raising his fists. That must have been what the lioness had been waiting for. She burst into a sprint.

"I've reconsidered what you suggested earlier, after a conversation with the admiral," the captain said to Hank.

On the screen, the man's resolution evaporated. He turned and ran, squeezing his eyes shut. The lioness was almost twice as fast.

"There is precedence, but only for very small units," the captain said. "So I will be sending several small units to attempt to prevent these Animalis attacks. Hank, you are to be one of those units—you and Jax—along with three other small units from our company. All working independently but under my supervision."

"Am I in one of those units, sir?" Felix asked.

The captain looked at Felix as if he were just noticing him for the first time. "No."

"You're not sending the whole company?" Hank asked. Then, "Why us?"

The captain frowned. On the wall, the lioness had tackled

the man. Jax saw a flurry of movement as the man struggled wildly in her grasp. Small retractable claws had extended from her fingertips and were now anchored into his skin.

"You—" the captain said, then stopped. "I'm giving you an opportunity to correct your earlier mistakes. I will not expect you back in my presence without, at the very least, the contents of that plane destroyed."

Jax felt ready to put up a salute in a heartbeat. It seemed almost too good to be real, the chance to really make a difference in the conflict. Even more, standing together there while packed into the tiny quarters, Jax felt like he was part of a conspiracy—and the plot was to strike at the heart of the enemy.

Hernandez stepped back toward the door, but then stopped as it folded open. "And I need you to look into the possibility that the Animalis are creating new animals. The rest of the details will be in the orders I'm sending out shortly. Since this assignment isn't strictly adherent to convention, I've arranged for a dear friend of mine to transport your unit. Her name is Hurley Grimshaw. She …" He looked down, seeming unsure of himself for a moment, which took Jax by surprise. "She was in the area, and I … Well, she always loved visiting Australia." He shook his head, looking almost angry with himself. "Ms. Grimshaw is somewhat of an animal expert and has agreed to take a look at these animals you've brought on board."

"Yes, sir," Hank said.

Before the captain turned down the hall, he held onto the frame of the door. "Make sure that Ms. Grimshaw is kept safe. And, if you could, let her know that I would have gotten in contact with her sooner, but all I have is that ridiculous Animalis rescue message bulletin she runs."

Jax brought his hand up to his forehead before the captain turned again. Hernandez matched the salute without straightening his posture, and left. Jax just stood there and blinked. The captain was putting his trust in Jax again, even after he'd gone against orders. He wouldn't let him down this time, not again. Jax had given himself to the army, and he couldn't put himself first again. He nodded to himself. There were others to think about.

On the wall, the muted screams of the man had died down. The lioness now stood in the center of the arena, fawning to the crowd. She finished waving, bent down to the man's mortified face, opened her powerful jaws and bit.

4

Atticus Five

According to Jax's retina monitor, the lady he was eyeing as likely being Hurley Grimshaw stood five feet, ten inches tall. Jax kept himself from smiling as he took in her appearance: slippers, a mass of curly red hair tied in the back, a pound of metal bracelets dangling and twinkling on each wrist, and wearing a thick, billowing blouse and pants his mother would have complimented. What surprised him most, though, was that she didn't look a day over twenty-five.

Jax rechecked the location in his retina monitor. In civilian clothing, he and Hank stood in one of the outdoor terminals of the Buffalo New York Airport, where the *Hornet* had landed for their rendezvous. This was where the small private planes sat, in between patches of lush greenery that broke up the sidewalks. Jax again took note of the fifth plane down the row, which was being prepped for takeoff. This was where Grimshaw was going to be. There was the plane, and there, if Jax had her pegged correctly, was Grimshaw.

She waved.

"That's Hurley?" Jax asked.

Hank shook his head and put up his hand to return the wave. "Our captain is a mystery. The way he talked about her, I was imagining a grizzled ex-wife he was trying to bring back into his life."

"Maybe this is his daughter, or a niece," Jax said. But even as he said it, he recognized that Grimshaw didn't appear to be from the same genetic line as the captain. Jax didn't know how old the captain was, but certainly, he was much older than this fair-skinned, radiantly smiling, green-eyed, dimple-cheeked, oddly-dressed girl.

"The brief said they had served together, but she separated from the army before being promoted to captain herself," Hank said, his voice fading to a whisper as Hurley Grimshaw came closer.

"Jesus probably wouldn't tell you, but I think you've both impressed him," she said.

Jax again stifled a smile, this time at her Latin American pronunciation of Captain Hernandez's first name, which to Jax sounded more like, "Hey, Zeus."

"How old are you two?" She stopped in front of them and extended her hand. The four-o'clock sun scattered amongst the wild curls of her hair, turning the outer layer into a glowing firestorm of color.

"Seventeen, Miss Grimshaw," Hank said, taking her hand. Her bracelets jingled with the handshake. "Hank Schneps. This is your plane?" He pointed to the pearl-white plane behind her. The design was wide and flat with curves that were graceful and ornamental.

Grimshaw looked up at the plane and nodded. "She spoils us. I might have gone overboard with this one, but sometimes you just need to indulge."

"An Atticus Five. Resplendently sumptuous. I've read a

lot about them. I'm a big fan. Incredible to see one in person," Hank said.

"What about you?" Grimshaw asked, turning to Jax. She seemed like she was about to ask about the animal container he was carrying.

Jax started to lift the cage.

"Oh, what happened?" Grimshaw asked him. "Your lip, your ear. I'm certainly not a doctor, but I could at least help you get those bandages on properly."

She brought her hand up to adjust the bandage on his ear, but Jax recoiled and took a step back. He brought his own hand up to cover the ear.

"It's nothing," he said. "Little accident."

Her act of tenderness made Jax feel strange. When her hand had first reached toward him, he'd felt the warmth of her caring. It made him feel important to her, like he had always been her friend. But then his doubts had risen: *I don't even know her. Is she going to ask me for a favor? Expect me to care about her?* It was a responsibility to allow someone to care for you, and Jax had unconsciously refused that responsibility.

Her outreached hand turned gracefully into a handshake, and her smile never wavered. Jax took her hand, jingling her bracelets with a gentle shake.

"Jax Minette. Thank you for giving us a jump. It sounds like Captain Hernandez really admires you," Jax said.

She smiled modestly and furrowed her eyebrows for just a moment, making it hard for Jax to gauge her reaction.

"If he only knew," she said, then her gaze drifted to the trees gently swaying, autumn leaves shimmering with color.

Jax still couldn't reconcile the image of Grimshaw the captain had portrayed, and who she actually was. A relationship between the two of them was too disturbing to consider.

A chittering sound came from the cage in Jax's hand, and Grimshaw looked down at it again.

"What beautiful animals!" Grimshaw said, crouching to look at the creatures better. "These are the two Jesus told me about? Well, they aren't ferrets after all. Hello there. What are their names?"

Hank stepped closer and said, "These were rescued from an Animalis militant's plane. It's not certain, but I believe they are a new, and demonstrably dangerous, species that the Animalis have created."

"I'm sure they're very dangerous," Grimshaw said with a wink at Hank. "But who wouldn't want to protect themselves." She popped open the cage. "You don't like that cage, do you?"

Hank shook his head. "I'm telling you—"

But it was too late. Immediately, the white one leaped out. Jax set the cage down and reached to catch it before it could bolt, but it was too quick.

Grimshaw shook her wrists, jangling her army of bracelets. The animal stopped and sat up on its hind legs, watching and listening to the sound. After a moment, it went to her, sniffing her knee before batting at the bracelets. Grimshaw kept one hand jingling while she moved her other hand for the animal to smell. Instead of sniffing, the creature lashed out with a defensive bite.

"Watch it!" Hank said. "Are you alright? Did it bite you? We should sedate them. Jax, don't let the other one get out."

Jax quickly closed the door, pushing the little black nose of the second creature back into the cage.

"I'm fine," Grimshaw said. "He's just doing what he's learned to do: protect himself. Aren't you? It's okay. We're not going to hurt you."

She kept her hand in front of the creature. After a few sniffs, it started to lick her. "That's a good girl." Grimshaw looked up at Jax. "Do they have names?"

"Not that I know of," Jax said, looking at Hank.

Hank rolled his eyes.

The creature seemed to have warmed up to her considerably, pushing its snout against her fingertips, using her to scratch and groom itself.

"Well, then, what is your name?" she asked the animal. "You certainly have a lot of spunk. A lot of moxie. Oh, I like that—Moxie. What do you think, Moxie?"

"I don't think it's going to stick around," Jax said, watching the animal losing interest in the physical attention. If it got away, Jax was sure it would be him chasing after it, getting bitten, if he was able to catch up to it at all.

Although, this strange, happy girl did seem to have a way with the animals. She was perplexing, and intoxicating for Jax to be around, like stepping into a field of fragrant wildflowers.

"Shouldn't be too much to worry about," she said. "They were almost killed in a plane crash? The real tragedy would be to cage them up and dissect them now. If they want to leave, we won't stop them."

The animals were her responsibility now, and Jax didn't like it—from the red flush in Hank's cheeks, Jax could tell he *really* didn't like it—but if she let them go, it was her decision.

"Not considering the people it might bite," Hank scoffed. "I don't want to make you feel rushed, but you've had a chance to go over the information the captain sent?"

"Right, the violence is spreading to Australia," she said, and stroked Moxie's neck. Her smile was gone. "Then we should start taxiing for the launch."

Grimshaw sprang up and ran to the entrance of the plane, jingling her bracelets. Moxie stood for a moment, glanced at Jax, then followed after her.

"I just came up with the perfect name for the black one," Jax said, following Grimshaw. "Little Hank."

Hank stopped. "That's offensive."

Jax walked backward toward the plane, watching Hank's expression. Hank looked up at the plane, and a pleased smile broke across his face. Jax could feel it too: this assignment was important. Somehow they had impressed the captain, and now they were being entrusted with a delicate operation.

Then Hank looked back down and watched Moxie, chasing after Grimshaw. His smile soured. "Jax, they can't come. They'll spoil the Atticus! The smell. They'll poop on everything."

Jax took in a deep breath. Even with the bright sun overhead, tilting toward the western horizon, the air felt crisp. Excitement was spreading through him. No time to sit and worry, dread, or overplan—he was doing something to help humanity. Then, though, he remembered the rat plane—and the all too typical dread moved back in. Jax couldn't choke next time they ran into Animalis, and let another opportunity escape.

"Oh!" Grimshaw stopped with her hand on the door to the jumper. "I need to introduce you to my copilot, Hodge."

The door to Grimshaw's jumper swung out. Standing just inside the door was a fox Animalis.

5
Fox

The fox's ears perked up as it looked at the small group.

"Are these them? Boys? Oh, they stink, Hurley. Hi, hello. Where are you from?" it said to Jax. "Idaho?" It sniffed the air. "Oh, a rat! Who was the rat you were with?"

Jax glanced over the fox. Orange fur, small black eyes above a slender snout, two tall triangular ears standing high on top of its head, a patch of white that extended from its chin down into its shirt, and a two-foot-long puff of tail coming out from behind it. The corners of its mouth were pulled up, and its lips were slacked.

"The captain arranged this?" Jax asked Hank, waiting at the bottom of the staircase.

Hank shook his head. "This is a surprise."

Grimshaw walked back down the stairs and opened the animal cage. "Sorry if Hodge makes you nervous," she said. "Jax, Hank, this is Hodge. Hodge, Hank and Jax. And Moxie, and, oh what is your name?" Grimshaw jingled her wrist in front of Little Hank as it poked its nose out of the cage.

"An Animalis?" Jax said. "You mean, this is your copilot?"

"Can I get you anything?" Hodge started to wave their guests into the plane. "Water? Food? Lay down before the jump?"

"These two little guys could use a bite to eat," Grimshaw said as she walked back up the stairs. Little Hank crept out and followed her. "Let's get our departure request sent in as well," she said to Hodge.

Grimshaw walked inside with Moxie and Little Hank following her.

Jax started to follow them up the staircase. What made Jax uneasy about getting on the plane wasn't fear that the fox was a militant Animalis—for now Hodge was helping humanity's side— it was that Jax didn't know how to treat it. It had to be well trained to handle flight plans, but should Jax expect it to wait on him? Or, as Grimshaw's "friend," would it have the tenacity to invade Jax's personal space, sniff him, or whatever Animalis did in social situations?

It isn't any of that, Jax realized. *I just don't want it to upset Hank. I wonder if it will affect him.*

Hank was the last to enter, and from the look on his face, it seemed nothing could have spoiled his first time inside an Atticus more than sharing it with an Animalis.

Hodge bent down and sniffed Moxie. Moxie sniffed him back. Little Hank joined in, and the three of them circled for a moment.

"You're some strange fellows. Been around that same rat. Mm, healthy, aren't you?" Hodge said between sniffs. "Nice to meet you, yes, nice to meet you." With his snout close to Moxie, she stretched out and started licking his nose. Hodge straightened up and left down the hall to get them food. He kept talking to them as they followed him. "You'll like this. Oh, you'll like this. My favorite."

Grimshaw's hand softly rested on Jax's back. His muscles tensed, and he moved forward out of her reach.

"Just closing up the hatch. Thank you, Jax," she said.

Her slippers landed in a small hamper by the door, and she stepped on a lever that sent the stairway beeping, driving itself back to one of the airport's garages. Once she had pulled the door shut, she stepped past them and went to the right, where the hall opened into an open living space.

Grimshaw's jumper looked plush. The wall screens ran video of rolling hills of wheat, a gentle breeze sending waves across them. Currents of warm air flowed through the cabin to match the wind in the video. With only a short hall and an eleven-square-foot room in front of him, Jax felt like he was walking into an endless expanse of nature.

The floor was covered in a white, haptic surface that had a menu hovering above it in Jax's retina monitor. He had noticed that when Grimshaw stepped on the flooring, the surface pillowed up just under her step, and then looked like a marshmallow trail as she walked by. When Hodge stepped, a geometric, textured pattern bumped up under his feet.

"Well, he's fun," Hank said, hiding his sarcasm with what sounded like a sincere compliment toward Hodge. "Miss Grimshaw, would you mind if I used one of your cabins? There's another mystery to this mission that I'd like to start unraveling."

"He is fun. Sometimes more fun than I feel like I can handle. It's so nice to have some new company for a jump," Grimshaw said, smiling. She tapped on the wall screen next to her and manipulated a few menus. "Hank, this plane is at your disposal. Here, key in a password and you can lock up this cabin for as long as you need."

A password dialogue box popped up, and Hank typed in a quick password.

"Don't be too generous," he said. "If you offer for me to take this bucket off your hands, I might just accept."

Before Hank left, Grimshaw held his shoulder. "Now, Jesus asked me to transport the two of you as a favor, but I don't want to be involved with whatever you're doing once we land. I'm just making sure that's clear." She looked at Hank, then at Jax, and let go of Hank's shoulder. "A lot has changed since the last time I worked with the military, and I don't think Jesus has ever acknowledged that."

Hank nodded. "Absolutely. Thank you again for your help."

She tapped on the cabin door to open it. Jax noticed her smile revealed a dimple in her right cheek. "Beyond that, I want you to feel like you can ask me for anything. If you need us, we are at your disposal."

Hank thanked her again and closed himself up in the private cabin.

"He seems like a smart kid," Grimshaw said. Then she whispered to herself, "Why on Earth is he in the military?" She tapped another series of menus on the wall again. Two padded benches extended from the wall. "Might as well have a seat while you wait. Jax, have you been around many Animalis?" She sat down cross legged.

"I haven't, no."

Jax stood where he was and held his hands behind his back. Hank was gone, and Jax was left alone with this girl. Of course he wasn't uncomfortable, and it wasn't like he could be attracted to her, not with her being more than five years his senior. He wanted to just act normal, but somehow normal was a far off concept now. Even standing still at the entryway was unnatural.

He glanced at the floor and brought up the list of feedback options:

Carpet, Play Mat, Grass, Water Puddle, Stone, Wood, Therapeutic Insole, Memory Foam Pillow …

"I've always been fascinated with the idea that they might bridge the language gap between humans and animals. Wouldn't that be amazing to have clear communication with animals? I've seen it happen, and it's amazing. But that's a radical fantasy of my own, to welcome animals as equals into society, no one really wants to see that realized. The Animalis themselves are amazing, though, aren't they?" Grimshaw said. She pulled her hair tie out and let her mass of red curls fall loose around her head. The hair band was added to her army of bracelets. "Each one is so unique. Sometimes I wish I could get to know them all."

Jax gave a little nod, calculating how often to look up at her in a normal way. He didn't want to give the impression that he was just looking at her. And he still needed to figure out what flooring he wanted. The menu still floated above the floor, waiting for him to make a selection. He had usually used the Play Mat texture while growing up—he liked feeling he could roughhouse at any moment—but decided to try the Water Puddle.

He looked up again and saw her patiently sitting there. Her green eyes were watching him. Why was she staring at him? Was he doing something wrong? *Oh, she's waiting for me to respond,* he realized.

"They are—" he started to say. But what was he about to say, that the Animalis were amazing? "Well, what about the rabid ones?" he said instead. "The militants? They aren't pets." Jax glanced where Hodge had gone. "They aren't human."

"No," she said. She leaned forward and her voice became enthusiastic. "No, but that's it, isn't it? They really are completely alien. And that's where most people get it all wrong. You can't think of them like a human, and you can't assume that they're mindless, either. When they were first created people thought they would act like humans, they gave them human rights and everything, but they didn't take the time to understand. Almost no one takes the time to understand. Every species has unique ways they see the world. It's almost cultural, but the differences are more alien. If they had come from another planet, at least people wouldn't expect them to act human."

Jax pulled his boots off and dropped them into the shoe hamper. Her excitement for the Animalis was contagious and he found himself willing to delve into the conversation more. His mind's eye filled with planets populated by horse Animalis, and dog Animalis, all packed side by side. Hmm … He did feel better having them off in other galaxies, leaving the Earth clean and peaceful.

"You and the captain," Jax said after a moment. "You knew each other in the army?"

"Oh," Grimshaw said, looking surprised to be off the topic of the Animalis. "Yes. I wasn't expecting to see a message from him after all this time. We had some good times, and some bad times together. I honestly don't know why, but I don't look nearly as old as I should. And Jesus, I can only hope time has been as kind to him."

Jax asked before his conscience had time to stop him: "Well, how old are you?"

Grimshaw paused. She held her ankles, with her arms draped over her lap. "Old," she said. Jax heard, *"Too old for you."*

After a moment she continued. "About the Animalis, what do you think of them?"

"Well …" Jax walked back to the living room, the material of the floor tickling his toes with chilled ripples. "I guess I'm mad that we don't regulate them more. They shouldn't have human rights or freedoms. I'm mostly concerned about the militants. We don't know why they're attacking us, but it seems to me that we should've been able to stop them a long time ago." He hesitated before sitting down on the bench across from Grimshaw. He couldn't sit directly facing her, as if giving her all of his attention. But it would be rude to sit turned to the side and give the impression that he didn't want to talk at all. So he sat on the corner, halfway between Grimshaw and the cabin Hank had gone into. "I mean, they're more animal than human, right?"

Grimshaw rotated to face him. "They have reason," she said, her smile faded. "They don't just attack humans for the petty abuses. They could stand the threats and insults whenever they're seen working a job that a human could be doing. They could even get along in the slums they're forced to live in. But we've done more than that to hurt them. So much more." She turned and watched the waves of wheat flowing on the wall.

With her head turned away, her silhouette became pronounced. One of the thick curls of hair came down over the smooth curve of her forehead and thin, red eyebrows. The line of her face continued down to the round point of her nose. Her lips were slender and smoothly transitioned with a gentle slope down to her confident and modest chin.

"We tried to massacre them. Tens of thousands of them

killed, like we were the exterminators stopping an infestation. And I helped … Jesus, too. They have reason to hate us." She turned back to look at Jax. A bitter smile came back to her face. "The unknown terrifies a lot of people. Whether it's a new culture, or a new species. It takes a lot of effort to learn a new language, or new customs, but it's absolutely worth it. I think I might love Hodge more than I've loved any human. Once I put in the effort to understand him, that's when I could see him for what he was."

"Jump has been scheduled," Hodge's voice came through the speakers. "We will start taxiing in just a few moments. Arrival in Port Hedland will be in two hours, ten minutes. Local time will be 6:27 a.m."

Jax leaned against the wall and let his feet pat against the watery surface of the floor while he took in what Grimshaw had said. If it was true that humans had killed so many Animalis, it wasn't publicized. He vaguely remembered teachers mentioning the need for population control, but it didn't sound like the kind of slaughter Grimshaw was talking about. She sounded remorseful when she talked about it.

"You like the feeling of water?" Grimshaw asked, noticing the ripples.

Jax pulled his feet up. "No, not usually."

———

"You're not going to like the harness for launch, are you, Moxie? No, I wanted to tear it up my first time in it," Hodge said to Moxie. "But I learned, yes, much better to be safe in the harness than to be thrown around during takeoff."

Moxie, Hodge, and Little Hank had come back to the main cabin area once they had eaten. Grimshaw was stroking Little

Hank, who had curled up on her lap. She lifted her head a moment after hearing Hodge speak.

"I almost forgot about that!" Grimshaw said. "These two won't fit in any of our harnesses, Hodge. You're not going to like takeoff, are you?" She shook her bracelets at Little Hank, who batted at them with his little claws.

"That's right," Jax said. "I'll get them back in their cage, and strap the cage in where you keep other supplies?"

"Not the cage," Grimshaw said. She stroked Little Hank's fur.

"Or sedate them?" Jax tried again. Really, how else would they be able to get the two things to stay calm?

"We do have a compounding machine for emergencies, but I don't think this qualifies just yet. We have a 3-D printer, Jax. I'm sure there is something we can download that would be perfect, and perfectly comfortable." She winked at Jax.

Hodge pulled up a search on the wall screen near them. Harnesses came up, different designs, a globe or sphere of some kind, small plastic cages, leashes.

"I've seen that," Grimshaw said. She pulled over the window and expanded the globe. "This was in *Animalis and Friends Magazine* a couple of times. It's like a big hamster ball with wall screens inside to make it feel like it's even bigger. I think they might like this. Not as much as being scratched on my lap, though. Right, Moxie?"

Moxie bounded past, ignoring her.

"But the coolest part is that once we start to hit zero gravity, it has a powerful gyroscope that creates centrifugal gravity inside the ball for them." Grimshaw was already downloading the printer plans.

"Lots of assembly," Hodge said. He growled a little. "I'll put it together."

"Yes, you are so good at that, Hodge. Thank you so much." Grimshaw said, sounding reluctant.

It took about five minutes for the globe parts to be printed out. Jax stayed back, watching Hodge tinker with the parts. Grimshaw tried to lend a hand, but Hodge growled her away.

"I'll get it," he said.

Hodge started to spread the parts over the floor of the cabin. It didn't seem too complicated. Jax started to see where pieces fit together.

Grimshaw came to the wall beside Jax and whispered to him, "Hodge really loves to feel like he's helping out. I love to see him working. See? Look at how excited his eyes get! But he has a hard time focusing when he's like this. He'll start moving things around because he knows things are supposed to be organized. But then he'll move things around again. He can put it together—he always does—but he can't stop reorganizing things."

Jax nodded. He could see now how Hodge had moved apart the pieces intended to interlock. At this rate, Moxie and Little Hank wouldn't have anything to keep them from being slammed into the back of the cabin at launch.

"Here, Hodge." Jax moved toward him to point to some pieces.

Grimshaw held his arm and pulled him back gently.

Hodge snarled and snapped at Jax, teeth just inches from his hand. Jax pulled his arm away from Grimshaw, ready to defend himself.

"Hey, watch it!" Jax said. He cut his eyes at Hodge and felt a justified hatred boil up inside himself.

"Jax, move back please," Grimshaw said. She smiled. "Hodge, I'm sorry, but we need to get this together. Look at how organized it is. Thank you so much. Can you start getting together some supper for after the launch?"

Hodge smiled. "It looks good, doesn't it? I almost had it all together. What would you like, Hurley?"

"I think your stir fry would be great, and tonight definitely deserves a dessert. Don't you think?" Grimshaw said. "Does vegetable stir fry sound alright to you, Jax?"

Jax frowned a little. He still wanted to kick Hodge for snapping at him. How could Grimshaw live with him? One of these days, it could kill her in her sleep, and she never would have seen it coming.

"That sounds great, thank you," Jax said.

"Okay," Grimshaw said.

Hodge left down the hall.

"Can you give me a hand with this?" she asked Jax.

"I thought you said Hodge liked doing this stuff," Jax said. He started picking up the pieces of the gyroscope to put together. "What was that? He tried to bite me!"

Grimshaw knelt down with the parts that made up the shaft that would hold the ball in place on the cabin floor. "It's hard to explain. It's a duality of his personality, I guess." She handed Jax a piece from her pile. "I don't really know, but I do know when to expect it. There's this mental zone that's both intense, focused, and active, but at the same time, on edge. He might nip at you, but he would only bite you if he was really in a tight situation."

When she handed him another piece of the gyroscope, Jax noticed the warmth of her hand in his for just a moment. He pulled his hand away too quick, and the piece fell to the floor.

Both of their hands reached for it a second time and Jax started to pull his hand away to avoid touching her skin again.

With a gentle grip, Grimshaw caught his hand and turned his palm face up. She set the piece solidly in his hand while looking at him, said, "There," and pushed his fingers up around the object to hold it in place.

It made Jax feel silly for acting uncomfortable about the touch of her hand. He wasn't trying to hold her hand, and her actions showed that she knew that.

They put the rest of the ball together quickly and then attached it to the floor. It wasn't a moment too soon: they were next up for launch. Grimshaw and Hodge helped get Moxie and Little Hank into the ball, and then they all strapped into their harnesses.

A message appeared in Jax's retina monitor:

Jax, come to my cabin as soon as we launch.
~ Hank.

6

The Pyramid

The launch was smooth. After a minute of intense electromagnetic acceleration, the plane shot off the end of the launch shaft and into the air. Once they were climbing quickly to the upper atmosphere, they unbuckled their harnesses. Hodge went to the small kitchen, between the cockpit and the living room, to finish preparing dinner.

Jax excused himself and stopped at the cabin door, knocking lightly. The door folded open, and he saw Hank standing in front of three walls bulging with pictures and information.

"Hank, you're a much worse nerd than I ever imagined. Look at this, you could be an insane genius."

"Sorry I left you alone with that thing," Hank said when the door closed. He was still manipulating one of the blocks of information he had pulled up. "We're lucky the planes didn't put down in a private airport. The captain says the cargo of the first plane is gone. The first unit is already on site, and they found the plane empty. The one we were on has only been on the ground for four hours—almost six by the time we get there—so we'll be able to track it if it goes to a new location." He pointed to two images he had up of the planes. "But that's not what I have been focused on."

Hank expanded another image. It was an illustration of a machine. It looked massive, with several tanks full of liquid, and hoses creating a spiderweb tapestry among the tanks.

"What on Earth is that?" Jax asked. "It looks like something from the turn of the last century, maybe even the century before that. Did they even have computers back then?"

"This image is from a conspiracy theory about the origins of the Animalis."

Hank pulled over another image. This one was of a huge, black-eyed alien superimposed above the Earth, cradling a cylinder between its hands. There was a stencil on the cylinder depicting evolutionary steps from a monkey to a man to an Animalis.

"An even more ridiculous idea about the origins of the Animalis," Hank said. "But this," he said as he pointed to an image of a pyramid, "might be the real thing. The Ivanovich Machine that created the Animalis."

The image of the pyramid was from a CT scan. It was constructed as the outline of a pyramid, like it had been drawn with thick lines and breathed into life. Like a skeleton, strangely beautiful. Dimensions listed beside it said eight feet tall and nine feet across at the base. The surface of the beams was smooth and plain. Where the beams connected, at the corners, the surfaces joined in smooth curves. It appeared large enough to stand up in, and sturdy.

"Ivanovich Machine … You said that to the captain. I've never heard of it. Didn't Romanov create them?" Jax asked.

"No, Romanov funded it. Schools put all the emphasis on Romanov, and the blame. But the scientist Ivanovich actually created them. And no one ever knew how he did it. Perfect, seamless, self-sustaining genetics. Not sterile." Hank brought up more documents. "Not sterile—it's huge. For two centuries, that alone has stumped geneticists." Hank looked at Jax. "There has always been an unfulfilled promise by scientists, that they could start bringing back extinct species. But they can't. Every example—passenger pigeons, white rhinoceros, dinosaurs—everything they create that isn't a simple clone has all been sterile."

Jax just nodded, feeling like the material was getting beyond him.

"Even the theory of evolution is suspect," Hank said. "It postulates that through natural selection, where the mutations that improve an animal's chance of survival are passed on, whole new species can evolve. It's true for plants; you can modify, hybrid, and create whole new species all day, but its not true for animals. Whenever an animal's genes have been manipulated too far— say, breeding squirrels to have an opposable tail—instead of creating a new species, they go sterile. It's as if the species can bend a little, but always breaks before something new is created. Dog breeds are a great example, thousands of variations, one species. So when totally new species were suddenly walking around Russia, geneticists were actually shocked. They wanted to know what breakthrough Ivanovich had, what technology he used."

"I've never heard of the Animalis being a scientific mystery," Jax said. "How come you've never told me about this before?" He knew Hank wasn't making it up, but Jax felt like he should have heard at least some of this before.

Hank shrugged. "I wasn't sure I believed any of the specific theories before now. Of course, when the Animalis were created, it confirmed everything the scientists had been theorizing. Now they've spent the last century trying to reproduce the results. But they can't. It isn't that there's a moral obligation not to; plenty of scientists are trying. No evolutionist or geneticist is going to admit they can't reproduce what was supposed to be possible a hundred years ago. And everyone outside of that tight circle of scientists goes on thinking that there's no mystery.

"So people that know all of this genetic theory have made guesses at how Ivanovich could have done it. He knew something about genetics that we are still trying to understand today.

"There's a second mystery that the theorists try to explain. The Animalis had all been groomed for human society when they were discovered. And there were families of them with two-year-old pups. We know that most species of Animalis sexually mature at around age seven, which means that Ivanovich made most, if not all of the originals, at the very beginning of the ten years he was working for Romanov.

"The proponents of the theory claim that the Animalis DNA was altered remotely, all at once—as in, there had been no shots, no injections of viruses to mechanically change the DNA. Thousands of animal embryos were all altered within days of each other, something that would be impossible unless his machine worked remotely, and altered the DNA instantaneously."

"Okay, so he made them all impossibly fast," Jax said.

"Yes. Now, this is my own contribution to the theories: for every strand of DNA there is a unique peptide—which is a special type of protein—that can communicate with other DNA peptides in a remote exchange of quantum mechanical information. We already know about these peptides, it's how cells communicate, but I think the peptide could be like the radio operator. There is some scientific grounding to the concept of the DNA peptides being linked in a kind of wireless network. We know now that there's a connection between peptides in the cells of a living creature. Cells that are blocked from receiving messages from peptides in chemical reactions will still receive the information the host body is sending. Biologists think it's all handwritten messages being hand delivered from peptide to peptide inside the body, but this is evidence that they can, I don't know, call each other. I'm guessing the information is held as a kind of code in the spin of the atoms themselves; that's why I call it an exchange of quantum mechanical information."

"Mmmm," Jax said. "Now you're starting to lose me. So you think that DNA has its own sort of … internet? All of them are linked together in a network?"

Hank smiled. "Yes. That's a great analogy. And the Ivanovich Machine is a terminal to access that internet. Every form of life is like a personal computer, and DNA are the blocks of memory. They hold program codes that make organisms function. And like computers, they have security that blocks us from making changes. But the Ivanovich Machine would have a universal key that lets it through the security.

"When an animal is growing, the machine can change the instructions to create a new creature. But if the animal is too far along in development, changes in the DNA could be lethal. Say you wanted to give yourself wings instead of arms. Well, your heart is still pumping while your veins break apart to move into their new position, and you die from internal bleeding before taking your first test flight.

"I could still be wrong about it all, but it's a terrifying machine if it is real. All DNA would be in your control. You could try and force too great a change on a whole species, and have instant extinction, or change every human embryo to grow into deformed pig-men."

"So we destroy it … if it's real?" Jax asked.

"Not yet. And I believe it's real. So does the captain. I'm sending a proposal to him that we retrieve it, making it the top priority for this mission, so that the technology can be understood. We can't let it be destroyed, because we need to know how to defend ourselves against it if anyone ever builds another machine like it." Hank closed the programs running on the walls.

Jax folded his arms, thinking. Hank seemed to be convinced the pyramid was an advanced DNA machine. He had done the research. He knew more than Jax ever would about DNA, and genetics, and peptides—whatever they were—so it was hard to say he was wrong. But it wasn't what schools taught. He had taken it for granted that the origins of the Animalis were common knowledge. The idea of an Ivanovich Machine was almost too much; how could one machine make all life so vulnerable?

"When you're ready, dinner is waiting in the living room," Grimshaw's voice came in muffled through the door.

"Be right there." Hank stretched and gave a big yawn. He looked down and noticed Jax's bare feet, and the ripples around them. "Puddles? Aren't you more of a Play Mat, cushioned guy? Hmm. Puddles. That doesn't sound half bad." Hank knelt and methodically untied his shoes, staring absently at the floor.

"Are you feeling alright? Being around Hodge and all, and being dragged out here because of me?" Jax asked.

Hank stopped, but didn't look at Jax.

"I should have just moved, followed the orders," Jax said. "I'm sorry."

Hank nodded. "Yeah, that was pretty dumb not to follow

orders." He stood up with his shoes in hand. "But then we wouldn't have been able to do anything about this pyramid, hopefully stop some attacks."

Jax relaxed when Hank turned to face him. He wasn't upset.

"I'm at least glad they sent you," Hank said. "That's why you joined the army, to be the white knight, right?"

"If I can do it without screwing it all up."

"Don't worry about Hodge. He's like a big dog, and I can handle a big dumb dog. If it was a bull, though ..." He glared.

Hank went to the door and opened it. Grimshaw stood before the opening, wearing a vintage pinstriped dress and flowery apron, smiling as big as ever.

"It certainly smells good," Hank said.

The dinner was surprisingly normal, until orbital weightlessness set in. The little table that had risen from the floor stayed put, but the neatly set dinnerware and potted flower began floating around their heads. Hodge pulled out a net and scooped it all away, then floated out a plate of lemon tarts. Grimshaw announced it as a breakfast treat, now that they were entering Port Hedland's time zone.

Gravity returned once they were in decent. Hank and Jax excused themselves while eating their tarts, retreating back to the cabin to go over mission plans.

There was to be a lot of communication, with Hank as the spinal cord for the information coming from each of the units up to the captain. Hank had already given recommendations for where each of the units should land and traverse to, where they could most effectively respond to progressing situations. Two of the units were being sent to probable sites that the first plane's cargo could have been moved to. Jax and Hank were going to be landing by the rat plane they had been on, and were going to be backup for the transport unit.

The other units were all three-person groups. Gillian was heading a heavy-weapons unit, the tall staff sergeant was leading the transport unit, the third unit was infantry, and Hank was the information systems specialist. Jax almost laughed out loud when he saw that Felix and Maven had actually been assigned to the staff sergeant's unit.

He sent a message to Felix:

> The captain said you weren't going on this mission. He doesn't even know you exist. ~Jax

"I've arranged for kangaroo transportation when we arrive, Jax," Hank was saying.

Jax slid aside the message that Felix had sent back:

> He doesn't want the others to know I'm his favorite. ~Felix

Jax looked up. "Kangaroos?"

7

Port Hedland

As the Atticus descended toward the runway, Jax took in the view of the city. Nestled among the teal veins of the bay, Port Hedland was part cruise ship resort, part industrial wasteland. On the west half of the city, cranes and dull gray warehouses fought for water access. To the east, Jax's retina monitor lit up with luxury hotel names, amusement parks, and adventurous outback excursions, each with translucent icons extending up into the sky. To the south, where the plane was descending to, was the airport. The landing strip led to the corner of the massive half-circle complex of private and commercial boarding gates. Each line of planes radiated out from the center, where the four quarter-mile launch shafts extended into the air.

"What do you mean, kangaroos? Are you talking Animalis kangaroos?" Jax asked as he and Hank stepped down the staircase once they had landed.

Above them, the morning twilight was just breaking into a brilliant Australian dawn. Thousands of feathery clouds cut purple and pink slices into the deep blue sky. Jax could hear a constant, deep drone coming from somewhere in the airport, and it gave the atmosphere a palpable charge. Spring birds chirped and flitted past, dancing with and chasing each other. In the distance,

81

the blare of horns from ships coming into port signaled that the city was about to come alive.

"In case the transport team loses the Animalis cargo, we'll be more dynamic on foot and could continue to follow. These kangaroos are a world-famous attraction. Forty-five miles per hour. Can jump farther than their animal counterparts." Hank leaped from the last stair and landed with a dusty puff on the orange desert walkway.

The ground cover of the airport was impressive and brought Jax the instant satisfaction of visiting the Australian Outback. Trees and prickly shrubs broke up the winding paths. He became excited when he saw an exotic lizard sunbathing on the surface of one of the large, red rocks. As he watched, the lizard perked up, scurried to the edge of the rock, and disappeared, flattening back down into the surface of the rock. The wall screen surface of the rock had fooled him. *Clever.*

Just beyond the next section of desert, beside a large rock formation, were the two kangaroo Animalis. They stood talking while leaning back on their thick tan and white tails. Their khaki shorts and shirts were straight and starched, and matched the expedition hats they both wore. Straps from a harness looped over their shoulders and connected with a heavy buckle across the chest. One of them turned, noticing Jax and Hank approaching.

"G'day, mates! I'm Talon, and this here's Wes. Starting bright and early today, aren't we? So much to see."

As it stepped closer to them, stirrups bouncing at the hips, Jax could see the legs moving with distinctly inhuman muscle and tendon structures. The furry limbs had looked almost human while standing still.

Talon smiled as he stopped in front of them. "We can take you to all the best—"

"We're not sightseeing, and we're in a hurry," Hank said, cutting off Talon's prepared speech. He held his hand up to his ear, listening to a conversation in his earpiece. "Right. Captain, the transport team has pulled in behind the rat plane. Cargo is being unloaded, they could start to move at any moment. Jax and I are just about mobile, and will be on site within five minutes."

The kangaroo closest to Jax, the one named Wes, turned and squatted. "Hold the horn up here, mate." It pointed to a thick handhold at the top of the harness. "Once you get one foot in the stirrup here, you can climb on."

"Don't forget to buckle up," Talon said.

Jax stepped up to his ride, the long, horse-like head watching him from under the brim of the hat. He pressed his foot into the stirrup and grabbed the horn, just above waist height, while the kangaroo was bent over.

Once he had mounted it and buckled the belt around his waist, he felt the strength of the legs as the Animalis lifted him. He had expected it to feel like an awkward piggyback ride, but the Animalis was powerful and sturdy. With his weight spread between the seat and the stirrups, Jax felt like he was riding a force instead of an animal.

"Atta boy. Here we go." Wes started to bob, lifting and lowering Jax. The motion slowly built to a stationary hop. "First time in Australia, mate? Port Hedland is a beautiful city. For just two hundred more a day, I can be your tour guide and transportation. You can't get a better deal than that, not inside the city."

"Nope!" Talon called out. "Not in *this* city, mates."

"We need to go to Terminal G-2," Hank said, ignoring the offer.

"Our pleasure," they both said.

The hops turned seamlessly into bounding leaps, and they lurched forward. The walkway in front of them split, going around a grotesque tree and several large rocks. But the kangaroos weren't slowing or turning. Jax wanted to pull on the shirt to make it move. It was out of control; the stupid thing was going to crash.

"Hey, turn!" he yelled at the kangaroo.

"Everything's keen, mate. Enjoy the ride."

It didn't slow, but instead gave an extra powerful leap and shot over the gnarled tree. Beside them, Talon hopped on a rock beside the tree and launched high onto one of the towering rock formations and kept going. They both landed on the walkway again and started to leap side to side, like slalom skiers, down the path.

Jax forgot about his fear as it was quickly replaced with exhilaration. The hops were powerful, precise, and intelligent. And because the kangaroos were small, it felt like he was the one rocketing across the terrain. Jax held the horn tight and enjoyed the ride.

The kangaroos passed under an archway and Jax could see travelers starting to make their way down the rows of private planes.

There were more Animalis than Jax had expected to see. Kangaroo, koala, and dingo were scattered around, some carrying bags and luggage, while some seemed to be there as characters in a living amusement park. Jax was shocked to see an alligator Animalis, though it did have a restraining collar, and seemed to be in a controlled, exhibition environment. If it broke free, would it snap up one of the smaller Animalis, like in the arena videos?

They passed through a second pair of arches into the next courtyard, lined with more private planes. Like a small patch of junkyard, the rat's scrap-heap of a plane sat decomposing between two new, clean, normal-looking planes.

"Just arrived on site," Hank said to his earpiece. He waited for a moment, listening, gave an acknowledgment, then spoke to Jax: "We'll wait over here till they start moving."

The kangaroos stopped near a bench and a drinking fountain, crouching for an easy dismount. Hank's stirrup twisted, holding onto his foot as he tried to climb off. "You see anything from here?" he asked Jax. "Keep an eye out for that lion. We need to confirm if she is here," he said, struggling to remove his foot.

"Oh, there's a lioness alright," Talon said. "Smells like some other strange Animalis as well."

Jax tilted Hank's stirrup to release his foot. "You smell them?" He gazed up at the large ears. "Can you hear them saying anything?"

The ears began twitching. "No. Sorry, not over the moan of that turbine."

The droning sound of the huge turbine had disappeared when Jax had grown accustomed to it, but he realized it gave the air a thickness, like a kind of fog over his ears.

"We don't have visual confirmation, but our kangaroos smell the lioness," Hank said, holding his hand to his ear. He looked surprised. "Right. Yes, we've masked our scents." He removed his hand.

Once they had remounted, Hank put his hand to his ear

again. He listened for a moment and then turned to Jax. "They've started to move."

Jax saw a cargo truck with a big blue stripe pull away from behind the plane and start moving silently down the row of planes.

"We need to follow that truck," Jax ordered the kangaroos.

"Do whatever you have to not to lose it. But if you can, keep your distance," Hank added.

"Right, we like a good chase. Eh, Wes?"

The kangaroos began bounding after the truck. On the road behind the planes, a second truck floated along silently, following after the cargo truck.

"There's the staff sergeant's unit," Hank said, pointing to the truck.

As they approached the outer walls of the airport, the Outback areas started to shrink, and the building structures began to loom overhead. The truck turned, following the traffic that was leaving the airport.

"There!" Jax said. "Here, turn here, now."

The kangaroo kept going straight. "I dunno, mate. That area is cars only."

Talon started to pull to the left, where the truck had gone. "It's dangerous," he said. "But that there's the spirit of the Outback."

"Yes, we can't lose that transport," Hank said. "Turn now!"

"Hold on to that horn," Talon said.

It veered sharply and hopped onto the street filled with cars, trucks, and taxis. The flow of traffic in each of the three lanes was smooth and constant, and where Talon hopped, fast-moving vehicles swarmed and filled in around him.

Jax was next to enter the gauntlet. Wes took two bounds toward the road and leaped headlong into the mass. The car coming up in the lane buzzed with a static charge as the city's traffic computer readjusted the flow of traffic to avoid the new obstruction.

Wes turned to see the car coming at them and put his foot up to brace the impact. "You're far from the most dangerous thing out here in Australia."

There was a sharp smack from the impact. Wes struck down on the car, tipping the front bumper down to the surface of the road, and leaped backward. Lights flashed on the car and a warning sounded. "You are obstructing the public roadways," an officially dull voice said. "Please use designated crosswalks."

They landed back in a hop and dodged between the cars in front of them. Jax tightened his grip on the horn. It was all just for show, but it was a good show.

"Come on, Wes," Talon called. He and Hank floated past overhead, riding on one of the levitating trucks.

"Aw, riding a car. That's no fun," Wes said to Jax.

Ahead of them, the traffic was starting to pick up speed. The towering skyscrapers of the core of the city rose above the large gates of the airport. Gold shimmered up and down the walls of glass, reflecting the rising sun.

Hank put his hand to his ear. "Are you still tracking them, Felix? Jax and I are falling behind. Give me your location updates, and we'll try to catch up."

With another powerful leap, Wes hit the side of another smooth-surfaced car, using it to bounce higher and land on the roof of a truck. Talon and Hank were a few cars ahead, watching the cargo transport a block ahead of them. Warm air whipped around them. Wes reached up and held his hat from blowing away.

"Let's catch up," Wes said.

Now Jax was ready to put his trust in the kangaroo. Wes hopped in place, waiting for the truck to get into a better position in the traffic. When the car in the next lane began to overlap their truck, Wes bounced onto its roof. The car sank a few inches while the city traffic program adjusted for the new weight. When the electromagnetism increased, propelling the car farther away from the surface of the road, Wes leaped again, shooting into the air as if it were a trampoline.

After a few propelled jumps from roof to roof, Jax and Wes passed Hank. Talon joined in hopping from car to car, chasing after the transport. The two kangaroos hopped from the road into another plaza and headed toward the gates exiting the airport. They leaped through the gate and were suddenly surrounded on all sides by tall glass skyscrapers.

"Aw, there she is. Didn't lose her for a second. Not to worry," the kangaroo said. It bounded back down into the road, making some of the intelligently controlled cars hover to a stop.

"Is that it?" Jax asked. "How do you know it's the same truck?"

The transport was nearly two blocks ahead of them. Jax had seen several other trucks with big blue stripes as they had hopped through the airport; it could easily be a different cargo truck. As he watched, the staff sergeant's truck moved in behind it.

"Oh, yes, that's her alright," Wes said. "There's subtle differences, whether it's the age of the metal, the way sound comes off of it—little differences. I couldn't tell you exactly what's different, but I can always find it if it gets lost in a crowd. You two are in good hands."

"This building on our left," Talon said, pointing, "was used to house the first Animalis immigrants that were allowed to come into Australia."

"Can't you shut up and focus on keeping track of that transport?" Hank said. "Never mind, Felix, we're still following them."

Talon pulled his hand back to his chest and continued the chase in silence. The cargo truck pulled to the left as the street-light over it switched from yellow to red, leaving the staff sergeant's truck idling behind.

Talon and Wes quickly caught up to where the truck had turned. Since they were hopping along the sidewalk, they used the crosswalk and jumped in front of the staff sergeant. The smooth, curved surface of the truck was opaque, but Jax knew Felix and Maven would be in it, watching them pass, so he smiled.

Ahead, the cargo truck continued to move fluidly through the city. Behind, the staff sergeant's truck continued to hit streetlights. Jax and Hank always seemed to be a block behind the cargo truck, but always, just when Jax was sure that they had lost it, the kangaroos would hop around another corner and the cargo truck would be there.

They followed for an hour, making their way west, to the outer fringe of the port city. It was an older portion of the city that didn't expect to be visited by anyone but the daily work-ers, and the majority of the buildings were rusted and stained. Here in what seemed to be the slums of the city, Jax realized he couldn't see another human anywhere. They watched as a shipping door on a three-story factory opened, and the cargo truck pulled in.

"Here, let us off on this corner," Hank said. "Captain, they've stopped."

Hank gave the location of the Animalis transport and received an update on the location of the transport unit, which was now forty-five minutes away. Talon slowed to a stop, crouching to let Hank off, and Wes stopped a few feet away.

"What happened to the other unit?" Jax asked.

"The city's navigation computer sent them to the north harbors. Could be a glitch, but it's suspicious." Hank shook his head. "Every computer system is bound to have bugs." He turned to the kangaroos. "Hey, you two. Take a break. Just stay within five minutes of here to pick us up."

"Thank you, mates. You'll love Australia, so just send in a request for another ride whenever you'd like," Talon said and tipped his hat.

With a few bounds, they were gone, and suddenly, Jax felt slow and vulnerable. When they had been on their mounts, a city block seemed almost too close. But now, among the more feral Animalis, it felt like a death march.

"Let's make a casual pass in front of the building to see what sort of security they have." Hank said, holding up his ICT scanner. They started their walk to the building.

"The Vicarity Suit would have been perfect for this," Hank said. "We're undercover anyways."

"Next time. You might just have to outright ask the captain," Jax said. He could imagine the lines of the suit being highlighted with that ridiculous purple again, *Just like an octopus.*

Hank nodded. "Next time."

On the edge of the sidewalk they were on, a dingo Animalis paced back and forth. Its left eye had a gray film over it. Its upper lip had a long scar that extended up its face. He was muttering to himself.

While Jax was looking at him, the one good eye stared back at him. The hairs on the back of Jax's neck stood up. The thing lit up in a fury when it noticed Jax looking at it. It started yelling a string of words that Jax couldn't understand, a mix of several different languages.

Hank kept walking and grabbed Jax's shirt to pull him along. The dingo got right up in Jax's face, snarling. That close, the large canine teeth looked like daggers.

"You looking for something!" the dingo shouted, then something in another language, then, "I'm the boss of this sidewalk. I say when someone can look at me! Hey!"

It kept at it as Hank dragged Jax past him.

"Keep walking," Hank said to Jax. "He wants you to know he's tough, but he isn't going to do anything."

Jax felt Hank's hand tremble when he let his shirt go.

The dingo stopped at the next corner but continued to yell. After a moment, he turned around and went back to muttering. Several more Animalis walked along "his" sidewalk, but he didn't seem to notice.

The building that the transport had gone into was large, made with plastic alloy that had been a popular construction material twenty years ago. It had a lobby area in the front, and two big bays for receiving shipments.

Jax saw a badger scratching at the counter inside the lobby as they passed. It didn't move its head, but Jax saw its eyes flick up and watch them as they walked past.

"It looks like they aren't expecting any trouble," Jax said when they were past the building.

"They shouldn't," Hank said. "Hold on, this spot will do."

The building next to the warehouse had wall screens looping an animated fishing advertisement. They stepped into the alley between the two buildings, and Hank leaned against the wall trying to look casual. His eyes flitted back and forth.

"Here's the scan," Hank said.

A document blinked in Jax's retina monitor. He expanded it, sending a transparent re-creation of the inner rooms of the warehouse floating into the alley. The scan had only been able to penetrate fifteen feet into the warehouse, about five feet past the lobby area. As Jax looked over the image, Hank kept talking.

"This building is owned by Cybollo Corporation, which seems to be a middle man in the fish industry. It looks like they take shipments of fish from all over the world and sell them to hotels and restaurants. Could be that their latest shipment was not exactly fish."

Along the back wall of the lobby sat three office rooms. Then inside the garage bays was open space. Hank's program identified two hyena Animalis inside the offices, based off a foot and elbow caught in the scan. It was a strange breed to find in Australia, but other than that, the scan looked normal.

Jax felt anxious, he wanted to be doing something more than wait for the second unit to arrive, which was still twenty-five minutes away. The back of the building had to be checked for security, didn't it? He closed the scan.

"While you go through this information, I'm going to loop around the back of the building to see what's back there."

Hank nodded absently.

Jax jogged along the side of the buildings to the alley. Deadly scenarios started to creep into his imagination. There could be a group of guards ready to shoot trespassers, or a sniper on the adjacent building. The sniper's laser would create a clean hole through his head, every blood vessel cauterized. Probably wouldn't hurt, with all the nerves instantly numbed, either sending half his body into quiet paralysis or killing him. Hank wouldn't even hear the sound of his body crumpling to the ground when it happened.

He tried to prepare himself for each scenario. With a quick glance, he scanned the edges of the rooftops and pinpointed what seemed to be a position of optimal visibility, where he would be if he was a sniper.

Nothing was behind the building. The back alley was filled with boxes, trash and pigeons, but there weren't any Animalis. Jax stepped out into the alley to see if there was anything useful about this trip to the back.

There were two big glass windows on the back of the building. Jax crept up to the bottom of the nearest one and peeked in.

Boxes were stacked in the corner; there were a few chairs, a desk, but nothing that gave very much information. The glass could be cut into with Jax's laser tool. This would be the best way into the building. The door to the room was cracked open a little. He was about to check the other window when a message appeared in his retina monitor:

Someone's comin

The message ended abruptly. It wasn't like Hank to leave something so vague. He sent a message back:

93

What's the situation? Hostile?

He crept to the edge of the building and peeked around it. There wasn't anyone in the alley. Hank should have responded immediately, so Jax messaged the captain:

> Hank's gone silent. His last message was "Someone's coming." Can you get through to him?

As Jax crept back down the alley to where Hank had been, the captain's reply appeared:

> No response to me, either. If you can't find him, he was taken. He'll only have a few minutes before they kill him, if they haven't already. We need Hank. Can you get into the warehouse?

Jax sent back:

> Confirming that Hank is gone. There is a way in through the back. Checking the front before going in after him.

Jax came back out onto the sidewalk in front of the building, scanning left and right. He felt a panic rise up within. Hank must have felt in danger when he sent the message "Someone's coming." They had surprised him, came at him from behind.

If Hank couldn't use his retina monitor, he was either unconscious, or the internet connection was being blocked.

Jax's adrenaline was starting to tunnel his awareness. He had to go after Hank alone.

He messaged Hank:

> I'm coming for you. I'm going into the warehouse. If you aren't there, you'd better stop me now.

Then he messaged the captain:

> I'm headed in.

8
Warehouse

Jax sprinted back down the alley to the back of the building. At the window, he pulled out his laser tool and set the variable laser focus lens to one centimeter and lit the tip. He quickly cut a small circle in the glass.

A message from Hank popped up:

… h#rn … d … 0110 … dont@ …

Jax dropped below the window to read it. But it was gibberish, jumbled. A mind that was struggling with consciousness could send a message like that. Or a mind that was being tortured.

At least he knew Hank was still alive. He stood back up and wet his fingertips. Using the viscosity of his spit, he brought his fingers close to the glass and let the spit grab onto the glass. Very, very slowly, he pulled his hand back, and the minute suction from the spit tipped the glass out toward himself. He caught the little circle and lowered it down to the ground. Then, using the hole as a handhold, he hopped up onto the ledge of the window and cut another section of glass around the hole, large enough for him to fit through. When the glass came free, he stepped down into the room and set the glass against the wall.

He crept to the door. Through the opening he saw the large factory. Conveyor belts, racks of boxes, and several printers. Animalis in white coats and hair nets stood in a line, watching wrapped packages of fish on a conveyor belt.

Around the edge of the room was a maze of room sized refrigeration boxes, each marked with a fish logo.

Jax didn't see any guards, or Animalis walking around with weapons, as he had expected. It seemed so normal, like he was intruding on a legitimate business.

Jax crept out onto the factory floor. He noticed he was holding his breath and began to take in slow, controlled breaths. Jax stayed close to the refrigeration boxes, walking behind the group watching the conveyor belt as he moved through the warehouse. A transport sat parked near the front. He crouched down and moved over to the second conveyor belt, closer to the truck.

Two hyena Animalis came out of the back of the truck, pushing what Jax recognized as one of the large crates from the plane. They pushed it to the far wall, near Jax, and went back to the transport.

Once the two hyenas were back inside the cargo truck, Jax silently moved to the first crate.

There was a menu to interact with the crate in Jax's monitor, but he knew that might set off an alert somewhere. He'd have to make an incision small enough that it wouldn't disrupt any electrical equipment in the plastic.

Jax reset his laser to an inch and cut it open on the back. The click of footsteps on hollow metal echoed through the factory. Jax abandoned the crate and ran in a low crouch to the nearest refrigerator.

The two Animalis pulled the next crate over to the wall and

went back to the transport for another. Jax ran back and finished his cut. The piece of plastic fell away to reveal weapons—pistols and rifles. A rush of panic hit Jax—he had found them! And the Animalis had Hank.

Jax reached in and tried to pull out a rifle from his impromptu opening. It clicked against the plastic and got caught against something. He could hear the hyenas moving out of the transport. Trying again, he pushed the tip in, twisted it, and pulled the rifle out by the butt. Their footsteps had left the walkway, and they were making their way across the glossy warehouse floor. Jax dashed back to the refrigerator and held his breath, listening. The hyenas were talking in another language—possibly Russian. They put the crate against the wall and went to another room.

Breathing a sigh of relief, he looked at his new weapon. It was an advanced laser rifle. Jax checked for a cartridge and found it loaded with three power cells. Laser guns had been a fantasy until the introduction of power cell batteries. The super-saturated electron carbon mixture of one power cell could supply enough electricity to take thirty shots. You could set the penetration level and the distance for what you wanted the beam to stop. The lens tried to mimic what a traditional firearm would do by adapting the focus of the laser in a fraction of a second, creating a deadly tip of laser that moved away from the nozzle of the rifle.

Jax came out from behind the refrigerator, ready to search the offices for Hank. A staircase in the corner would provide some cover.

A door opened and Jax's blood froze. Jax stopped at the foot of the stairs and glanced around. The opening door was down the line of rooms to his left. He raised the rifle to his shoulder.

Through the sight of the weapon, Jax watched a leg step out

of the door. The foot looked human, but with the distance, Jax could be wrong. He pulled the sight up and waited for the head to appear. If the head looked at Jax, crouched at the foot of the stairs with a laser rifle pointing at it, he would have to act fast. The face came into view but it wasn't a face.

A black fabric had been pulled over the head and snugged tight around the neck. Behind the mysterious figure, the tip of a gun pushed him farther past the door. The masked figure cowered, tucking his head down. His hands were behind his back.

The height, the build, the unique retro fashion—it was Hank. Jax tightened his finger against the trigger of the laser, watching the weapon bob up and down.

A hairy hand came out and pushed Hank forward, then came the rest of the badger—the same one that had watched them from the lobby of the warehouse. It sniffed the air, scowled, and tilted its head left and right. Jax could hear something muffled being said to the badger from the room. It said something in return. Then it turned back to Hank and started to raise the pistol up to Hank's head.

The middle of the badger's head was in Jax's sight. He slowly exhaled, steadying his aim, and fired. Silently, and instantly, a small red-rimmed circle glowed in the middle of its head. It was a perfect shot, just like the thousands of targets Jax had practiced on in training. The badger dropped to the floor.

No one working at the conveyor belt noticed. The sound of the body falling was as subtle as fabric piling up on the ground.

Whoever had ordered the badger to kill Hank would need a moment to realize what was happening, and that moment was Jax's chance to get Hank.

Jax sprinted down the line of rooms to Hank. Jax slammed

into Hank, pushing him away from the open door. "Hank, run. This is Jax. Just keep running!" Jax tried to whisper. He held onto him and forced him into a run.

It was useless to worry about a shot from behind: either the other Animalis in the room would respond quickly and shoot them in the back in the next moment, or they would reach the first refrigeration box safely.

Jax's eyes were on the box in front of them. A red dot appeared on it. Someone had fired a laser and burned a hole in the box. *Just get Hank out of sight,* he told himself.

With a hop, Jax leaped horizontally into the air and kicked his legs into Hank's side while turning around to fire at their attacker. Hank shot to the right, hitting the slick floor and sliding to the wall behind a rack of printers. Jax fell toward the ground with the hyena's hideous face passing through Jax's sight. Fire.

There was no blood and no sound. The hyena kept moving, unfazed by the hole. Jax fired again from the ground—another hole. The Animalis kept moving, now with a mindlessness that awakened a fear in Jax's subconscious mind and manifested as a weight sinking in his stomach. He fired again. Three holes, and the hyena finally dropped to the floor.

Someone was yelling from the room Hank had been in. Jax couldn't understand what was being said, but he was sure a dozen Animalis were about to pour from every room. Lying in the middle of the open floor, Jax could be shot from any angle. He had to find a spot to shoot from.

He couldn't draw fire to Hank, helpless on the floor, with his head covered and hands tied, a desperate attempt to grab him and flee would get them both killed. He'd have to get to a place where he could defend himself.

A section of shelving looked promising, just beyond the maze of refrigerators, to the side of the now confused conveyor belt workers. Jax would be surrounded by clutter, and it would be hard to see him. The Animalis would be coming out into the open, perfect targets for him to pick off.

Jax was on his feet and running a second after the three-holed hyena hit the ground.

Another Animalis was coming out of the room; Jax could hear the squeak of its shoes coming to a stop. Jax dove to his back, using the momentum he had built to slide behind the metal rack while bringing the rifle up to fire again. He slid past one of the workers dressed in white. It watched him, a confused look on its face.

A hyena dashed out of the second room, swinging its rifle around, looking for a target. Jax fired and missed. Apparently the hyena still didn't know where the shooting was coming from. It ran, wildly pointing its weapon in every direction.

Jax slid to a stop, flipped onto his stomach, and scurried to the small space below the rack. He aimed, catching the hyena as it spun to face him, and fired. The laser hit at an angle across the side of its face, cutting a slice instead of a clean little hole. Jax's stomach churned. The hyena fell, splashing in its own gore.

The sight of the blood was shocking. They weren't just targets, like in training. Jax could see the creature still struggling on the floor, tremors starting to shake its limbs. It was just supposed to fall down and be still, like the other targets. Jax could hear the conveyor workers stepping back, away from the blood, speaking in frightened voices.

A gun barrel extended through the door frame where the hyena had just come from. Jax tried to ignore the dying Animalis, keeping his crosshairs locked on the gun sticking out of the doorway. It moved. Jax fired. The weapon dropped and the victim fell forward, hitting the ground with a dull thud. A man. Jax had shot a human.

There was no time to think about it. Another movement from above, and Jax shot. Then came return fire, burning perfect holes in the boxes and shelving around him. One of the workers behind Jax dropped to the floor, hit by one of the lasers searching for Jax. He heard loud gasps and cries from the other workers.

Jax found where the shooting was coming from and shot. Death. Another movement, shoot. Shoot, death. More death.

Finally, there was stillness. Nothing moved. Even the flailing Animalis had stopped. The conveyor workers had moved farther back into the warehouse.

Jax's muscles started to tremble. He chanced a glance at the clock in his display. Fifteen minutes had gone by. Jax couldn't even tell how the time had been spread out. It had all happened so fast, no more than two minutes.

A realization hit him: Hank hadn't moved for the last fifteen minutes. A cold chill started to spread from Jax's sternum.

He ran, dodging behind a refrigerator and coming up behind Hank, who was sprawled on the floor. He crouched, about to lift Hank's shoulder, when he saw two holes in the black head covering. They were close together, along one side of the covering.

Jax didn't want to move him, didn't want to pull the fabric away.

"Hank?" Jax whispered.

"Are they all dead?" a muffled voice came out of the bag.

It took a moment to realize it was Hank's voice. Now Jax

could see the eye looking up out of one of the holes in the bag. He would have felt relief, but the trauma of the firefight was still consuming his mind.

"I don't know. There haven't been any for a few minutes." Jax kept watching the doors. "We've got to get out of here," he said, lifting Hank to his feet.

Jax loosened the bag covering Hank's head and pulled it off. Just above Hank's left ear, Jax could see a line of singed hair.

A sharp plastic click echoed through the warehouse behind Jax. Before any mental command was given, with his adrenal gland squeezing out every last ounce it could produce, he turned and raised his rifle.

It was a blurry movement, down the line of conveyor belts. Jax pulled the trigger and the figure dropped to the floor. A loud shriek echoed around the large open room. Another Animalis, dressed in white, moved. It was raising its arms. Jax fired, and fired again till it dropped to the ground.

There was another Animalis in white, backing away. There were two more farther back in the warehouse. They were all trying to get away. Another shriek cut through the silence and through Jax. These were the workers. Just the workers. Two of them lay dead on the glossy floor.

One of the workers had fallen face-first onto a conveyor belt and was being slowly dragged back toward its coworkers.

"I didn't mean to," Jax said, turning back to Hank. "I thought … I … I …"

Hank nodded. "You're fast, Jax."

Jax felt a numbness wash over him. His hands were shaking. But he kept moving, not stopping long enough to let his mind come back. He turned to fire at the crates of weapons.

From the wall of offices, he saw a blur of movement. The Animalis bounded on all fours and dove into the open cab of the transport. There was a hiss, and light from the street streaked across the floor as the garage started to open. A gun stuck out of the window of the cab.

"Move!" Jax yelled at Hank.

Jax dove to the side. The glossy floor made him skid, and he flew into the side of the refrigeration box. He brought his gun up again and fired. The Animalis pulled back into the transport. Red circles appeared on the glass as Jax fired over and over again. Behind the glass, he could finally see the Animalis: it was the lioness.

The garage door finished opening and the transport began to move. Two more Animalis dashed out of the rooms and ran for the transport. Jax shot one, and it crumpled and slid across the floor. Jax took aim for the second. It ran, his crosshairs trailing its movement. It looked over its shoulder, terrified that death would find it at any moment like it had its friends. Its short mane whipped with the bounce of its run. Tusks extended from the corners of its mouth—a warthog. Like the conveyor workers, the Animalis had no weapon in its hand.

This one, too?

Jax fired and missed. Fired again, missed. The warthog Animalis dove into the open door of the transport, and the vehicle pulled out onto the street and was gone.

Jax held his rifle up, waiting for more Animalis to come from the rooms. The scent of burnt hair filled the warehouse, mixed with the smell of seared meat and defecation. Eight figures lay on the ground, seven Animalis and one human, their limbs twisted under their heavy, lifeless bodies.

The shaking started to return. Jax didn't want to look at Hank. The barrel of his gun trembled in his hands.

"Jax, can you get my hands free?" Hank asked, pushing himself off the ground.

Jax pulled out his laser tool and cut the handcuffs off.

"You were incredible." Hank said. "You saved my life. You should have seen yourself when that koala one made that noise. I've never seen someone move so fast, Jax. You blew them away. Oh man, I was this close to dying." He held the bag up and put his finger through the two holes in its side. "But when I was lying there, I could see you just slaughtering them! Wait till Gillian sees this." He waved his hand out toward the bodies.

"Shut up," Jax said.

"I'm serious. You were amazing!"

"I mean it, Hank! Don't say another word."

Hank should have been yelling at Jax: "What have you done? You killed them! Nobody was supposed to die, and you killed them! You made them run, in tears, for their lives!" But instead, he had said "slaughtering them" as if it were the highest praise.

"Alright." Hank threw the mask at one of the bodies. "I can't believe you came after me alone."

"Let's destroy the weapons and get out of here," Jax said. He turned his laser gun to a wide beam and fired into the first crate till it caught fire. The second crate drained the rest of his power cells. He took another gun and finished off the others. The fire blazed and popped.

The emergency sprinklers would start soon. Jax fired another beam at the crates and threw the weapon into the fire. As he ran back toward the open door, his foot slipped on something and his leg shot out from under him. Blood splashed under his hands when he caught himself. Next to him was the face of the horrible hyena. Its furry skin wrinkled where its weight pressed against the floor.

Jax moved to get away. His hand slipped and his side hit the floor. Blood soaked into his shirt. He couldn't get away from the face. The eyes were open, one angled at the puddle of blood, the other looking right back at Jax.

It shouldn't have bothered him. He had seen hundreds of images and videos of worse gore, and it was just an Animalis, but he hadn't been the cause of any of the bloodshed before. This, these bodies all around him, silent and still—he had done it to them. He had killed them.

Finally, his hands stayed under him, and he crawled to his feet.

Jax ran. He passed Hank and kept running,

"Where are you going?" Hank called. "We've got to find out where that truck is going. Jax, I need you!"

Jax didn't answer. He had thought the world needed him to save it. Killing the Animalis was exactly what he thought he wanted to do. But now that he had done it his stomach had a shooting pain. Nobody needed him.

He kept running, not turning around to see if Hank was behind him. A message from Hank came, but he ignored it.

The face of the hyena didn't leave.

"Eh, mate." It was Wes, the kangaroo. It hopped alongside him. "Heading out? Climb on. I'll take you, anywhere you need to go."

"Get away from me, Wes—now!" Jax said.

The kangaroo continued to bounce along with him.

Finally, Jax stopped. Wes came to an idle hop beside him. "Ready to go? Climb on."

"I can't ride you!" Jax yelled. He held his arms wide to show the blood covering his chest.

Wes barely glanced at it. "Sure you can. No worries, mate. Climb on. I'll take you where you need to go. Back to the airport?"

Jax closed his eyes. *Back to the airport …*

He took hold of the horn of the saddle. "Alright." He climbed onto the kangaroo's back and hunched forward.

Take me to the plane. Take me to Grimshaw.

He shook with the leaps of the Kangaroo. With his eyes closed, the face of the hyena was still there. *Why did they have to attack us? Why couldn't they just leave us alone?* He opened his eyes, but the hyena was still there.

9

Grimshaw

When they entered the airport, Jax hugged tight to the saddle, hiding the blackening blood that had soaked into his clothes. The ICT scanners in the security hall would find the laser tool in his pocket, see who it belonged to, and check his ID to see if it matched. It wouldn't check for Animalis blood on him. It wouldn't know that he was a killer.

The door to Grimshaw's plane opened, and he stopped at the top of the stairs. Everything in the plane was white—pure. What was he thinking? Grimshaw was going to be furious. Had he imagined that she would hold him in her arms and tell him that he was safe, that the war didn't exist inside of her fields of golden wheat?

He turned to walk back down the stairs.

"Jax?" Grimshaw's soft voice said. She came to the hatch. "Where are you going? You can come in. Hank said you left him—"

He turned to face her and her eyes went wide as she glanced over him—and saw the dried blood on his hands.

"Are you hurt?"

He shook his head and turned back around. Metal clicked under his boots as he descended the stairs. Now that he had seen her face again, how could he be around her? She couldn't know what he had done. She didn't know him, and wasn't supposed to. She was just giving them a ride. What had made him think he could come to her like this?

But then he heard a light patter from her bare feet following him. She caught him on the last step with one hand on his shoulder.

"Jax, you should come inside. Come on. It's alright. You don't need to tell me anything. I'll get you cleaned up."

Her hand felt light on his shoulder; he could have pulled away easily. But the lightness—no, the tenderness was stronger than if she had wrapped her arms around him. Tears started to stream down his cheeks.

Grimshaw took his hand and lead him back into the Atticus and into one of the cabins. They passed Hodge standing in the living room.

He perked up when he saw Jax with Grimshaw. "Jax, I'm glad to see you! How was your day?" He sniffed, but Grimshaw raised a hand before he could continue.

"Hodge, close the hatch, please. Make sure Moxie and Little Hank are taken care of for a moment, alright? Please, don't worry—don't ask questions. Jax needs us right now."

Hodge nodded and went to close the door to the plane.

Grimshaw went to the small sink in the cabin and started to soak a rag. "Are you hurt anywhere?"

He stared at her for a moment, then blinked and shook his head. "No. No, I don't think so. I … I can't tell."

"Hank was worried you were hurt, the way you left."

Jax looked down at the floor. "No, I didn't get hurt at all. It's … It's all … Animalis blood." He stayed where he was, just inside the doorway of the cabin, hesitant to move.

Grimshaw brought the rag over to him. "Jax, don't worry about anything in this cabin, we can clean it later. Right now, I just want you to feel like yourself again. Do you mind?" She reached for his hand.

Jax didn't say anything. She crouched beside him and began to gently wash his hand.

"Sometimes," she said, "the world crumbles in ways we never thought it could. I have no idea what happened, Jax, but I know that the person I met this morning was good. And it's the same person I'm with right now." She stood up and looked into his eyes. "Just do whatever you need to do to survive, Jax. It's never immoral to stay alive."

Jax closed his eyes; her words pricked at the fear building within him. He pulled his hand away. "How could you know what you're talking about? You've never hurt a thing in your life. You don't protect yourself, and you love everything you meet. It's worse than being ignorant."

"I'm sorry," she said. "You're right. I don't know what you're feeling. I don't know what you've done."

A tousle of red curls hung down over her nose while she knelt waiting for him to let her continue washing his hand. She looked up, and he could see into her golden-brown eyes. He realized he was vulnerable, letting her eyes stare into him. He looked away.

He lifted his hand and she began cleaning it again. The rag pressed against his hand. The dried blood softened from the moisture and soon absorbed into the warm fabric.

Then Jax heard a soft scratching at the door. Something chittered. Grimshaw went to the door, opened it enough to let Little Hank in, and closed it behind him. The little black creature scampered over the floor to Jax.

"He loves you, Jax," Grimshaw said.

Little Hank stood on his hind legs and began to lick Jax's hand.

"No!" he said, jerking his hand away.

Don't lick that, Little Hank! That's someone's blood.

He looked at Grimshaw. "How? How could it love me? It doesn't even know me," Jax said. "He doesn't even care whose blood it is—just loves the taste of it."

"He doesn't care if it's blood," Grimshaw said as she continued to wash his hand. "All he wants is for you to be clean—and safe. It's a friend's instinct."

"I … killed a man," Jax said without thinking. But part of him wanted her to despise him for it. "Animalis, too."

Slap me, Grimshaw. Throw me out of your beautiful white plane.

He looked down at her to see her reaction. The rag continued to scrub back and forth on his hand. She didn't look up at him. Little Hank moved around his legs, licking his boots and pants.

"I don't know how many," Jax kept talking. "A dozen."

She stood up.

"They kept coming … and I kept killing."

She was almost as tall as he was.

"Some of them were just working there. They had no idea what was going on, and I—"

Without speaking, she wrapped her arms around him. Her chest trembled, and tears dripped down onto his shoulder.

Jax wanted to push her away before the blood on his shirt soaked into her blouse, but it was too late. His stomach twisted into confused knots.

"I'm sorry, Jax," she said quietly. "I'm so sorry. No one should ever have to kill. You can't take it back. You can never take it back. And they will never leave you alone. I'm so sorry, Jax." Her hug tightened. "But you can't trade places with them. No matter how much you want to. Your blood will never be able to pay the price for theirs."

Jax furrowed his brow. Had he been wrong about Grimshaw? Had she gone through something like this? It sounded like it, and now it felt like her pain was resonating through him—and it seemed to wash him cleaner than the rag could ever have done. He brought his own arms up to hold Grimshaw's trembling body.

"I'm sorry," he whispered. "I didn't … I didn't think you would understand."

As he held her, and she held him, he could feel the knots loosening inside him. Somehow, Grimshaw mourning with him had given him the forgiveness he needed. Knowing that the person he had unconsciously elected as the symbol of purity could still accept him, he could choose again what he would become and what mark he would leave on the world.

With the hatred washing out of him, Jax could feel the marks that were left. He had saved Hank, and was proud of that. He had survived the only way possible—by killing—but he didn't want to be put in a situation like that again.

The outer hatch clicked open, and Jax heard voices. One had to be Hank's voice, it was sharp and precise, and the other was someone mumbling.

Jax wanted to stay there in Grimshaw's arms. Letting go would mean acknowledging the world and its responsibilities again. Little Hank ran to the door and sniffed. Grimshaw let go, pulling back to look at Jax. All Jax could see was the smear of blood staining her white clothes.

Then Jax heard a growl in the main cabin. Hank yelled something in return.

"Hodge?" Grimshaw called, looking worried. She moved to the door, throwing the rag into a basket attached to the wall. "Hodge?"

The growl was interrupted with barked words.

Jax followed Grimshaw out into the main cabin. He had to push the firefight out of his mind. Hank had come back. *Is he coming for me?* Jax couldn't think of any other reason he would be here.

"It's Hank—I didn't want him to come in, not with that thing!" Hodge said. His ears were flattened out to the sides, and his lips were pulled high, exposing wrinkled, pink gums and his big canines. "Hurley, don't go near him. I'll chase him off this plane if he comes back out."

"Did he go into this cabin?" Grimshaw knocked on the second cabin. "Hank? It's Grimshaw. Can I come in?" She paused for an answer, then turned back to Hodge. "What do you mean he brought something with him?"

"An Animalis. I don't know, a dog, cat thing. I don't like it. It was covered in all sorts of horrible smells. Jax, don't go in there," Hodge warned.

Grimshaw tried the manual handle, but it was locked. "Hank? Do you need us?"

A hyena, Jax realized. So he wasn't after Jax?

"It was alive, muttering some other language. I couldn't understand it," Hodge said.

Jax turned to Hodge. "He was carrying a hyena on board?"

Hodge growled again. "He's doing something in there." His hair started to stand up. "I don't know who is more wild: Hank or that thing."

Jax sent a message to Hank:

> Are you alright? What are you doing with that hyena? Where are the other units?

Hank replied:

> I'm sorry, you should take Grimshaw and Hodge away for a bit. Stupid, I just need her compounding machine. We'll lose the pyramid, Jax. It was the only thing I could think of. We have to find it. This thing is going to die anyway, but I think I can get the location. I just need this room to myself. Help keep Grimshaw away.

"Is he printing something?" Grimshaw asked above a subtle hum emanating from the room. She pulled up a menu on the wall next to the door. Jax saw a printer menu, with downloads for Room 2, but Grimshaw was blocked for going further when a passcode box came up.

"He used his password," she said.

Another menu came up. She navigated to the door locks— blocked.

"Hank?" she called, "Don't do anything you're going to regret."

Jax stood struggling with what to do. Hank wanted him to keep Grimshaw away. He needed Jax to be the muscle again, clear the way so that Hank could get the information. He was in command. Jax could just hold his arms in front of the door and ask her to step outside.

But something was wrong. Everything inside Jax was saying to stop Hank, help Grimshaw. Hank was going to extract the information from the Hyena, painfully. That was enough for Jax to disobey orders. He had to prove it to the captain, then he would be ordered to stop him.

No. He couldn't report it to the captain. He couldn't go against Hank, his one true friend.

"Hank," Jax muttered. "Do you have an ICT scanner?" he asked Grimshaw.

"Hodge, could you bring an ICT scanner?" she asked.

Hodge was still in a furred-up state, ready to go into attack mode.

"Hodge?"

He snapped his head toward her, then blinked and finally said, "Oh … Yes, Hurley?"

"Bring an ICT scanner."

"Yes, Hurley," he said.

Hodge left the room, sending Little Hank skittering away from where he had curled up underneath one of the retractable seats. Moxie, though, was nowhere to be seen.

A moment later, Hodge returned with an ICT scanner. Little Hank had curled around his shoulders.

"Thank you," Grimshaw said, taking the scanner.

She pulled up a program on the wall screen and moved the scanner over the door to the cabin. The program quickly compiled the information in a simulated three-dimensional image, only lacking color, and frozen in time. Hank had his back turned to the door. On the floor beside him was the hyena. A hole could be seen just under the hyena's left clavicle. Jax noted straps holding its arms and legs tightly, and a blindfold covered most of its face. Hank was holding a syringe. The computer quickly interpreted the chemical formula held within it and displayed the product. Jax recognized it: Recoil. It was used for interrogations—banned from use on humans—that left some of its victims in a crippled mental state, or dead.

Jax's retina monitor downloaded the image. It would be enough to justify Jax's actions, going against orders and trying to stop his commanding officer. But it would never come to that. Hank just had to be reasoned with.

"Oh, no. Hank, please no," Grimshaw said. She slammed a fist on the door. "Hank! Don't you dare touch him! Don't you dare hurt him!"

She pulled on the manual handle and shook the door. Her hand slapped the wall screen beside the door, bringing up another menu, navigating to security settings. The authorization to reset passwords had been blocked as well. The door would be impossible to open without Hank's permission, as long as it had bolts to hold it shut.

Jax pulled out his laser tool and set the focus to one inch. "Here, is it alright to cut into your door?"

Grimshaw stepped back and gave a quick nod. "Yes, hurry! Thank you, Jax." She pointed to spots around the frame before stepping back farther. "The locking bolts are here."

Jax pressed the laser to the frame at the first bolt and lit the tip. He heard a sharp pop from tiny bubbles of air expanding rapidly under the heat of the laser. The plastic frame of the door melted and oozed beside the cut. He moved to the next and began to slice through again. Halfway through it, the tool beeped. Jax kept going, moving to the next bolt. The alert began again, and a moment later, the laser gave out. The power cell had dried up.

"Do you have any power cells this size?" Jax asked, pulling out the cell. "I'm empty."

"Hodge?" Grimshaw said.

A piercing shriek came from within the cabin. Hodge growled.

"Hodge!" Grimshaw said louder. "Power cells! We need one this size."

She tossed the cell and woke Hodge from his focus. He caught it and left.

"What's going on, Jax? Why is he doing this?" Grimshaw said. "It isn't right! I can't let him do this!" Grimshaw struck the door again and her bracelets shook with the sound of shackles. "Hank! Stop it! Stop, please, stop! There's another way! Please, let us find another way. There's no information he can give you that's worth putting yourself through this!"

Jax remained silent. knew what Hank was doing: he was trying to find where the pyramid had been taken. But why come here? The other units would be at the warehouse by now, and they could have devised a way to find it. Instead, he had invaded Grimshaw's serenity, like Jax had done.

"Can we get another ICT scan?" Jax asked.

Grimshaw stopped pounding and let her fists rest against the door. Her chest rose and fell, her eyes staring far beyond the barrier in front of her.

"Yes. Alright," she finally said.

The scanner ran across the door again. The material of the

wall extruded and shifted, forming the 3-D scene scanned from behind the door again. Grimshaw leaned her head against the door, not looking at the image appearing.

"Please, Hank," she whispered.

With a slight turn of her head, she looked at the wall screen. Immediately, she turned her head back against the door and groaned.

Jax took in the image that had formed on the wall. Hank was frozen in time, kneeling over the hyena with an empty syringe in his hand. Below him, twisted in a grotesque combination of angles, lay the hyena. Its spine arched to the side with a sharp bend that would have broken a human's back. Held together with restraints, the hyena's hands had clenched into tight fists, the nails digging into its own palms from the strain. The face was …

Jax couldn't look at its face. He wiped the image away from the wall. Jax couldn't let this happen.

"Here, I found these." Hodge thrust a handful of various-sized power cells toward Jax.

Another shriek penetrated the door, followed by a string of incomprehensible sounds coming from the hyena.

Jax held Hodge's hands steady as he fingered through the pile. A matching battery slid into the tool easily and he lit up the laser to finish cutting through the last bolt.

"I'm sorry, Grimshaw. He's a good person, really. I didn't know he could do something like this. He's …"

The tortured Animalis continued to babble in the room. Grimshaw went to Hodge, stroking his ruffled fur, looking into his eyes and trying to soothe him.

Sparks shot from the bolt when Jax cut through the last bit.

With a kick, Jax hit the door hard and it folded open. Hank

leaped away from the door, tossing the syringe and backing toward the wall. His foot hit against a laser gun he must have taken from the warehouse, and it clattered onto its side.

The hyena writhed slowly on the floor, words slurring out of its mouth. Fresh blood seeped from the hole in its chest covering it's shirt and the floor around it.

"Jax, I got it! It was all—Hey!"

Jax shoved Hank into the wall. The image on the screen rippled from the impact.

"Jax," Hank wheezed, catching his breath, "the pyramid." His face showed confusion, apparently surprised that Jax would come at him like this.

"Hank! What are you thinking? You tortured it!" Jax held him to the wall, but it was his own face he saw on Hank. Jax pressed the face into the wall screen in rage.

Grimshaw ran to the hyena, leaving Hodge at the doorway. Kneeling over the hyena, Grimshaw pulled off the blindfold and checked its eyes.

"You didn't even know what you were doing!" Grimshaw said. "You might have killed him, Hank! You can't tell what their reaction to the serum is unless you watch their eyes!" She grabbed its wrist and laid two fingers on the skin, checking its pulse. "Jax, I need your help with him."

Jax pressed Hank for a moment longer. Hank knew what he was doing, he always did. Maybe he wanted to get the information without worrying what it would do to the Hyena, or maybe he just wanted to kill it in the process and not leave a loose end. Whatever the reason, Hank was his friend. He had stood by his side for the past six years, before they joined the military, and he would be his friend after the military. Jax knew that.

Let him go, Jax told himself.

"He was dead anyway, Jax. You left him there to die," Hank wheezed. "He knew where the other transport was taken. We might be able—"

Jax dropped his hands away, releasing him from the wall. "I'm sorry, Hank." Jax didn't want to look him in the eyes. Hank had said it was the fate of humanity at stake.

He looked into Hank's eyes and felt a cold chill on the back of his neck when he saw Hank glaring at him. Jax backed away, feeling the distance between them manifest. He turned and went to Grimshaw.

"Take the medical kit," she said. "We need to stop the bleeding in his chest. His blood isn't coagulating like it should. He needs an IV, and I should put in a call for an emergency car."

"No," Jax said, stopping her.

What would happen if it was taken to a hospital? What would they do if they were able to revive the hyena? Let it return to the Animalis militants?

"We have to!" she said. "You saw the ICT scan. That lung is completely separated in its chest. It's floating around in there, and now it's bleeding again. I have to. I'm not going to let this life die, Jax. Help me, please."

She got up and headed toward the wall. Hank moved away from her as she came to it. It looked like he expected her to attack him. When she ignored him and pulled up a request for an emergency car, Hank's eyes started shifting around, navigating his retina monitor.

Jax shut out what had happened between him and Hank, and instead focused on the bleeding hole in the hyena. He took out an expandable splint from the medical supplies Grimshaw had revealed on the wall and rolled it into a cylinder. The hyena trembled and winced as Jax slid the splint into the laser hole, hoping it would stop some of the bleeding. He pulled open the kit and searched for a stimulant. After the energy it had exerted during the torture, the hyena would need a boost to keep its heart going.

Grimshaw came back and pulled out an ice pack. She cracked it and held it to the hyena's forehead.

"Jax, we have to go after the pyramid," Hank said. "You want to let the Animalis win? Let that stupid hyena die! You want the whole human race to disappear when they start using the pyramid? Better them then us. I did what needed to be done! He knew where it was going, Jax—and it's leaving tonight."

"Hank, how dare you say that." Grimshaw pierced him with her stare. She used Jax's shoulder to help her stand. Hank shrank against the wall as she approached. "You would have murdered this creature in cold blood!" She stopped inches from his face. He tried to squirm away, but she followed him with her glare. "And you will be a maggot beneath the burning heat of your own guilt for the rest of your life."

She held Hank with her eyes. Her expression softened, and after a moment, she spoke to herself, "Pyramid?" She moved away from Hank and he relaxed a little. "A pyramid." She pressed her fingers to her temple with a bewildered look. "And you're saying it's some kind of weapon?"

Hank moved out of her range. "They already used it once. Those adorable little creatures you let run loose in here could be genetic weapons. It's a machine that can alter DNA. All DNA. It created the Animalis, and it could destroy them. Or us ..."

Grimshaw closed her eyes, and a pain passed over her face

that Jax didn't think was possible on her. "Hank, nothing's going to change what you did to this hyena." Her eyes opened and she looked at him with pity. "You might not acknowledge its pain, or its value, but it's there. I can't give you any more justice than the guilt you will feel as you live with this, so I won't try."

She stepped back and looked from Hank to Jax. "The pyramid. It was—I don't know. I saw something, just before you came back." She shook her head and scowled.

Jax felt a tingle run up his spine. She was struggling to find the words to describe what she had seen.

"Like a dream, just out of reach." She blinked, and her scowl went away. "And it makes me afraid for what you're getting yourselves into. You don't think you know me, or I you, but I don't want anything to happen to you. I have an idea of what's going to happen when your teams try to enter that building. It might not help, but I have some equipment you could use."

Hank didn't react, and Jax was still catching up with her change in tone, wondering if she had heard the same etherial voice he had.

"Hodge?" Grimshaw called out. "Give me a hand here, will you? The emergency car is going to be here any moment, and we need to get this hyena out to it."

Hodge ducked his head through the door opening, his expression moving in and out of a snarl. "Yes, Hurley," he said, staying at the door.

"You're not coming," Jax said to Grimshaw, "if that's what you're thinking. We barely made it back alive. The Animalis militants are trying to start something here, and we are right in the middle of it."

"I know, Jax. I know," she said with a frown. "Something

big is coming or Jesus wouldn't have sent you here, but that isn't what you're worried about. Hank, you're saying the conflict is going to be over soon?"

Hank looked thoughtful, and Jax knew that a plan was already forming in his mind.

"They're going to be scattering," Hank said. "What is it that you have?" His eyes flitted to menus in his retina monitor, but he continued speaking: "We have to surround the new warehouse so nothing can get away. I'm sending the location to the other teams now."

"Can you tell me more about this pyramid?" Grimshaw went to the wall and revealed a closet full of clothes. She pulled out something black, with arm and leg straps, and brought it to Hank.

"A flight suit?" Hank took it from her hands.

Jax could see Hank hesitating, fiddling with the flight suit. His eyes were watching Hodge and the hyena. *Right ... He doesn't want them to hear more about our plans.*

"Hodge, come here," Jax said. "He's unconscious. Grab his knees and let's get him out of here."

That would give Hank the privacy to share more information. Hank and Grimshaw moved to the corner so they were out of the way. Little Hank leaped from Hodge's shoulders and scurried away as Hodge came to the hyena. Hodge and Jax then carried the hyena out of the Atticus and through the midday heat of the courtyard. The bright sun was shocking to Jax. His emotional exhaustion and the events of the morning had tricked his mind into believing it was night. Some travelers stopped to watch them carry the bloody, limp body to the emergency car that waited with flashing lights. They slid the body onto the padded cot and strapped it in. Jax pulled up a menu on the wall screen and put in the injury information, then he sent it off to the hospital.

"Hodge," Jax said as they started back to the plane. "Can you stay out here? Watch for anyone that might seem suspicious?"

"Yeah." Hodge nodded with a big, slow blink.

"Hurley's alright," Jax said. "Everything's alright." He stroked the hair sticking up on top of Hodge's head.

Jax left Hodge and walked up the staircase. Before he reached the top, an icon of the captain appeared in his retina monitor—a video call. Jax felt a wave of dread, his body reacting to the recent memory of killing. The dread turned into a cold sweat as he stepped into the plane and closed the hatch. Hank and Grimshaw were still talking in the second cabin with the door open; their words passed over Jax without registering. He opened the first cabin and went in, closing the door behind him.

Hernandez's icon continued to flash, waiting to be answered.

I have to answer, Jax told himself. The thought of explaining his panicked flight from the warehouse to the captain made his throat swell.

Jax accepted the call and sent the face of the captain onto the wall screen. He held his arms behind his back and stepped away from the wall.

Hernandez was in his own cabin, sitting in a black, thickly padded armchair. He was bent forward, resting his forehead against hands that were laced together. Hernandez hadn't noticed the call had been answered.

"Captain," Jax said after a moment of silence.

The captain raised his head and unlaced his fingers. "Jax," he said. His words came out cautiously. "You left Hank and the other units." He paused, but clearly didn't expect a reply. "That was a hard thing I asked you to do, going in alone." The chair groaned as he leaned his weight against the backrest.

Jax stood straight and still.

Hernandez nodded. "It was the right thing. Hank is hard to deal with, but his ability to solve problems is remarkable. The two of you are both at the top of your class. He was your friend even before joining the army, is that correct?"

Jax nodded. "Yes, sir. We're very close."

He watched as the captain leaned to his right and reached to his desk beside him. When he pulled his hand back, he held a small marble figurine. It looked like a Greek maiden, raising her arms and face to the heavens, draped in a flowing, loose gown. The captain's thick thumb passed over her face absentmindedly.

"Most people will never understand until they have killed an enemy before they had a chance to kill them—until you have had to watch friends die for your mistakes." He turned the maiden over in his hand and gripped it tight. "When you have had to live for years with their faces appearing just when you think you have forgotten them. War can't be won by idealistic boys that think it's a good, clean fight." He loosened his grip and turned the maiden over and over in his hands. "This is not a playground game where you can say 'Stop' and run to a teacher if someone isn't playing by the rules. These things are not people; they don't have the moral conscience of people. They will kill and kill and kill until there are no more humans left to kill, and then they will kill each other."

Hernandez glanced at Jax. "I was worried," he said. "The way you left, made me think it had been too much. It is for some people. They reach the edge of their ability to serve, and they turn back on themselves."

Jax stopped tapping his finger and changed the position of his hands.

"Isn't that what happened to your father?" The captain looked up at Jax.

Jax swallowed and cleared his throat. "My ... father? He— Yes, he came back home."

"But he had lost his arm. Was that enough? You grew up with the other military families. If that was all he had left in him, that was enough, right?"

Jax shook his head, remembering the shame he had held for his father when he had come home. That was when he had started getting into fights at school, with the boys who thought Jax would run away like his father.

All the adults had said that it was alright, though. His mother's friends were always coming over. They'd pat him on the head and tell him his father had done a good job. It was better to have him home, they said—that he should be so proud of his dad. But they had all just been polite reassurances.

Everyone that gave up and weaseled their way home early lost their honor. His dad had been given the option to continue serving with an artificial limb, but he chose to come home instead. He still got a new arm once he'd returned, and it didn't hold him back.

"Don't you want to be just like your daddy when you get older?" the ladies would ask Jax. "Oh, you look just like him."

Jax had said "No!" once, but the ladies just laughed. "You've got your hands full, Kelly. He's just like his daddy."

So Jax had just ignored them and moved to another room to play.

"You're a good soldier, Jax," Hernandez said when Jax didn't reply. "You've got instincts like your father. You can be proud of that. He deserved the honors he received." He set the maiden back on his desk. "I want to hear that you aren't going to run away again."

Jax opened his mouth, then closed it and nodded.

"Say it with me," Hernandez said. "I'm not going to run away again."

Jax took a deep breath. It was what Jax had already committed to; he shouldn't need to say it. The ache in Jax's chest came back—the point of his mother's finger against his sternum reminding him to always tell the truth.

"I'm not going to run away," he said, ignoring the ache.

"I'm not going to leave my unit," the captain said.

"I'm not going to leave my unit."

"I'm not going to quit."

"I'm not going to quit."

"I'm going to follow orders," Hernandez said with finality.

Jax stopped. He didn't want to say it. Now was the time to tell the captain he had killed civilians. *I can't … I can't do that again. They didn't deserve to die*—their faces, the bodies falling to the floor, because he had chosen to pull the trigger. He wouldn't be able to ask Grimshaw to wash him clean again, even though he knew she would do it for him, as many times as he needed.

But he couldn't back down from what he had committed to. He wouldn't quit. To keep moving, he would shut out the protests in his mind.

"I'm going to follow orders," he said.

The captain nodded. He stood from the chair. "Not everything in the army is as difficult as what you are facing right now, Jax. You're doing a good job."

Jax nodded and then saluted. Hernandez returned the salute, then the colors on the wall faded, and the face of the captain flattened out and disappeared.

When Jax stepped out of the hall and into the second cabin, Hank apparently had finished telling Grimshaw about the pyramid. Now Hank stood there, turning the flight suit around in his hand, checking the five-point harness, while Grimshaw watched him, shaking her head. Four heavy cylinders weighted down the edges of the flight suit, and Jax noticed a large section of power cells on the back. Hank looked up and glanced at Jax, but his expression appeared stony.

Grimshaw kept shaking her head and finally said, "Please, try not to kill anything. Human or Animalis. You just need to destroy the pyramid and get out."

Hank turned to her. "What? Weren't you listening? We're not going to destroy the pyramid. We have to save it to understand it. It's where the next battlefield is going to be, and we'll be defenseless without it."

Grimshaw snorted a laugh. "Seriously? You think that the military is going to just hand it over to science? They'll use it, Hank! And not just to stop the war. They'll use it on anyone that threatens them—human or Animalis." Grimshaw's eyes showed an intensity that Jax hadn't seen before. Then her focus seemed to drift from the moment, and she stared through Hank at something in her own mind. "They tried before, to kill them, in the forties. There were great big colonies of Animalis across Russia. When the first militant attacks started happening, the military wiped them out, whole cities at a time."

"We're going in to get it, not destroy it," Hank said, coming to stand beside Jax.

Hank looked at him while he spoke, and Jax felt the cold sting within his heart again.

Grimshaw looked at Jax with a solemn expression. Her eyes held his for a moment, until Jax looked away. "Alright. You're right. It's not my place to decide." She turned back to Hank. "But, please, if it is what you think it is, it needs to be destroyed. Before anyone else finds out. It would be the worst weapon the world has ever seen."

Hank stepped away from Grimshaw and held up the flight suit for Jax to see. "While the other units come in from the street, we'll land on the roof and enter from there. Hernandez doesn't want you put into any danger, Miss Grimshaw, so I'll ask you to stay out of it."

She nodded.

"Jax," Hank said, "you and I are going to arrive first and try to disable any cargo transports before they can leave." He picked up the laser rifle he had brought back and held it out for Jax to take. "Rounding up anyone who flees will be second priority. All that matters is getting that pyramid." He pushed the gun closer to Jax. "Are you ready to go?"

Jax wanted to protest. Maybe long enough for the other units to finish the job without them. If he went out there again, he wouldn't be able to escape again, run away like he did the first time.

"I'm ready," Jax said, taking the weapon.

10
Narasimha

The afternoon air should have felt like freedom. Jax's short brown hair tossed and bounced, flattening against his scalp. The wind drowned out all other noise, creating a steady, powerful hiss in his ears. His stomach had reached an equilibrium between fright and exhilaration from the high altitude, sending a constant tingle through his body. With the four powerful superconducting fans propelling him from his back, he could imagine what it might feel like to be a bird. It would be wonderful.

Hank was holstered securely to Jax's chest, grabbing onto the harness straps like his life depended on it.

The city curved and spread along the edge of the bay, where the red earth melted into the green-blue ocean. Hank had fed the location to Jax's retina monitor, and the icon hovered above a building near the edge of the port city. Along the short flight, Jax had resisted talking about the shootout, or what the captain had said to him. He still wasn't comfortable admitting all that had happened. But something still disturbed him about it.

Jax messaged Hank:

One thing that has been bothering me is why

there was a human working with the Animalis
in that factory. Did you see him?

Hank's reply came quickly:

Yes, I saw him. It's not too surprising. I think he
was one of the people profiting from the Animalis conflict. Those were probably his shipments
of weapons that the Animalis had. I've heard of
humans being tried for crimes against humanity
for helping them.

The building was almost underneath them. Jax pushed the thoughts of the Animalis out of his mind. Feelings that he had felt earlier that day started to come back to him. The painful, vulnerable dread that he could be shot at any moment. Over-looking a simple detail, moving when he should have been holding still, or not reacting fast enough. His body was starting to ache from the tension the fear created. It was the military training he had been through all over again. A sergeant's con-stant degrading screams were unnerving and infuriating, and having his fragile life exposed and naked before his enemy was no different.

The hiss of the wind diminished as they began to descend. Jax would have to execute the landing perfectly to not send sound waves through the warehouse that would give away their landing spot. Their legs would be useless after having a hot shaft of laser bore up through their heels.

The controls for the flight suit were linked to a small pad pressing into the base of his skull, which listened to signals from his brain. Jax pushed his mind up, an urge to resist falling, and the fans slowed their descent.

He set down, with the subtlest tap, near the south wall of the building. Below them sat the garage bays and, if it was the same layout as the last building, a line of second-story offices they could drop down on top of.

Hank released himself from the harness and stumbled forward. Jax caught him before he fell, but it sent an uncomfortably loud squeak reverberating into the air from his shoes sliding against the surface of the roof.

Jax motioned for Hank to move with a wave of his hand. The two of them lightly crept away from the spot the squeak had emanated from.

Jax messaged Hank:

Run your ICT scan.

Hank's face was growing pale. He nodded and pulled the tool from his pocket. Holding it close to the rooftop, he swung the scanner from right to left.

While Hank did the scan, Jax removed the flight suit. He set it down lightly and pulled the laser rifle from around his chest.

Hank sent the scan, and the image came into Jax's monitor. The building was well shielded, blocking out the scanner's gamma rays after three meters. It was just enough to see that there was a platform they could drop down to when they needed to enter the building.

First, Jax would cut a hole, and then disable any cargo transports. Once that was done, Gillian's unit on the ground would send in gas grenades to knock out any Animalis that were too slow to escape in time. The ones that fled would be stopped by the three units surrounding the building.

Hank gave a thumbs-up, and Jax cut a large hole, then pulled it away to reveal the layer of insulation beneath it. After he'd cut through that, he removed the material. The last cut was small, just big enough for Jax to aim through.

Jax put away his laser tool and peeked in. The building looked similar to the fish warehouse. He saw rows of large refrigeration boxes, and conveyor belts with Animalis watching for product defects. Their heads turned from side to side, looking at each other, the fish on the belt, the front of the building, back to the fish. The offices were lined up beside the garage doors, and one cargo transport sat parked in front of the doors.

It wouldn't take much damage to disable the transport, but getting through the protective outer layer would take several precise shots to the same location. Then, when the computer detected damage, it wouldn't risk allowing it to travel on the roads.

Jax aimed the rifle at the edge of the transport and fired. The material glowed red, then the color spread out and diminished. Before the color disappeared, he fired again. Again and again, till the material stopped sending the heat away and grew black. He kept firing until the first power cell in the gun was drained. The last mark glowed with a bright ring, showing the laser had penetrated the armor. Before signaling Hank, Jax scanned the warehouse a second time. He saw no other transports.

Jax gave Hank the signal. A moment later, Jax heard the sound of glass breaking in the warehouse. Then came frightened cries from the workers. Jax looked through his peephole and saw that the gas grenades were doing their job, filling the room with smoke. Doors below them opened with a flurry of running and shouting. Out on the street, they could hear shouts of commands from their units. It sounded like some of the fleeing Animalis had made it past their barricade.

Jax cut a larger hole, preparing to drop in and search the building once the commotion stopped. When he pulled the section of roof away, the chemical fog in the warehouse was already beginning to dissipate. The machines were still going, humming and sending packaged fish along the conveyor belts, but the remaining workers had all fallen unconscious a few yards from their stations.

Hank held Jax's arms and lowered him down. He could feel the office roof with the tip of his shoe. He messaged Hank:

Drop me.

Hank's grip loosened and Jax slid down, crouching to cushion his impact. Before reaching up to help Hank down, he peered over the edge of the roof he had landed on, checking the warehouse floor below. The fog had cleared to a gentle haze. Jax's eyes detected a swirl in the vapor, still curling from some recent movement.

Jax lifted his rifle, following the movement. It led behind a refrigerator. More movement—dashing across a section of floor and into the back of the cargo transport. It was white and ghost-like in the fog.

He messaged Hank:

Someone's still moving in here.

"Jax."

Hank's voice sounded like a whispered hiss from the hole above—and there was a strange tone to his voice. Jax stepped back to listen.

"I can't … I can't come down," Hank whispered. "You have instincts I just don't have. If I go down there, I'll … I'll die, Jax. I know it."

Jax shook his head. Hank actually sounded frightened.

"That … That badger didn't even have a gun," Hank said, "and I panicked when it found me. But you … oh man, you tore the place apart like it was nothing. I thought I could make it up by bringing that hyena back, and finding where they went. And I couldn't—I couldn't even think clearly doing that."

Jax didn't want to risk speaking aloud, so he messaged:

> You got us here! We would have lost it without you. But there's no time to argue. I'll message you when I find where it's going.

Jax sent the message, and a moment later, Hank's head moved away from the hole, then Jax saw the missing piece of roof slide back into place. Jax grimaced. This wasn't going even close to plan.

Focus. Just focus!

He looked around. He had one more task before they could secure the premises. The exhaustion from more than a full day of intense stress was taking its toll on him. Jax could feel his body tingling and his skin going numb. It felt almost like he was getting sick.

Jax climbed down from the office and landed on the floor, crumpling in a useless heap. He pulled himself up and took a deep breath. *You'll make it,* he thought. He took another breath and held it. With a quick jerk, he shook his arms and head. The feeling of movement was refreshing. As he let the breath out, he felt his focus returning.

On the floor below, the gas had dissipated enough that it wouldn't knock him out. He crept down the stairs and walked through the warehouse, following after the movement he had seen from above. He stepped past the bodies and came around to the back of the cargo transport.

The rear hatch of the transport was open, creating a wide ramp down to the floor. Jax continued to breath slowly, not letting his imagination take over with the deadly scenarios that lay waiting for him around the corner. Rifle raised, he crept forward to look in, but didn't step onto the ramp yet.

His retina monitor showed the interior to be ten feet wide and forty feet deep, and it looked like the transport held an enormous load. In the cargo hold, Jax saw some of the same white crates, and others that bulged with strange angles. Near the back of the space, a smooth, metal, triangular point reached nearly to the ceiling.

The pyramid, Jax guessed.

Something shifted inside, moving behind the first row of the crates. His ears picked up a sniffing sound. A second later, yellow eyes popped up and looked at Jax.

"Don't move," Jax ordered. He stepped onto the ramp, walking slowly toward the eyes.

"You found me." It was a smooth, low, feminine voice. The individual sniffed the air. "You were at my warehouse, human."

To Jax, the voice had a vibrational quality to it—a mix between a growl and a purr. As he came closer, his eyes adjusted to the low-light interior and he could see the lioness.

"Stay where you are. Slowly show me your hands," Jax said.

The face followed him as he moved closer. Jax started to make out the details he had seem from the arena video, and they were far more terrifying in person. What commanded Jax's attention weren't the muscles, which were thick, defined, and more powerful than any on Jax's body—but the movements. They were small, and controlled, hinting at a tidal wave of strength being held back.

"I'll show you my hands," she said, "but what you should really be looking for is my claws."

As her hands lifted, her appearance transformed, increasing in intimidation. She could have been a gladiator preparing to defend herself while her hands were at her sides, a queen encircling her dominion while her arms rose wide, and a goddess ready to cast down lightning as her hands towered above Jax.

He had wanted to see her hands to verify that she had no weapon. The hands were indeed empty—but he now realized that *she* was a weapon: powerful, intimidating, lethal. Standing in front of her, Jax could see himself as the disheveled human from the video, hopelessly doomed to be devoured in her arena. The distance between them, he knew, was inadequate in terms of a safe zone for him.

An alert began beeping, and the hatch Jax stood on started to lift. They were closing the door. Jax had to move before he lost his footing on the rising angle of the door.

He figured he'd be safe on the outside, protected from an attack from the lioness. But then she would have the pyramid, protected by the armor of the cargo transport. Hank needed a situation report:

> The Lioness is here. I'm holding her inside the
> transport. The pyramid is here.

He sent the message as he walked down the slope of the rising door—right into the lair of the lioness. He didn't have time to wait for an answer from Hank; he had to trust his instincts.

Jax's eyes stayed on the lioness as he moved, watching her head turn to the side and her arms lower back down. He had to stay focused on her to make sure she didn't move. Even the slightest movement from her position—

She's moving! Jax felt his insides twist with the realization. He tightened his finger on the trigger, ready to shoot. His mind, though, felt slow, crippled from the effects of adrenaline from the day.

Wait ... She wasn't moving toward him. Her body turned away, and she walked farther into the cargo hold.

"You're slow, human. I could have killed you. Maybe I still will. I don't think you will shoot me, like you did my people. You reek of fear." She purred. "Hmm ... Yes. It was your first time, I think? Ahh, Your heart is racing. But that gets me excited."

Jax's heart *was* racing.

"Stop," Jax ordered. "I will shoot you."

The door sealed shut behind him. He stepped forward, following her from a distance.

"No." Her voice was regal, as if she were declining a petit-four. She kept moving, walking slowly between the crates. "Malick, let's get moving."

Jax kept his sight on the back of her head. *Malick ... So there's someone else in here. Maybe the white ghostly figure I saw before ...*

"What is your name, human?" the lioness asked.

The floor started to shift under Jax, throwing him off balance. The cargo transport was moving. He adjusted his feet to keep from falling over.

From outside the bulkheads of the cargo hold came the sounds of a violent crash. The transport shook, but the momentum kept going, increasing in speed. It was accelerating recklessly fast. The city's traffic computer would never allow a car to travel at such high speeds, which meant they had moved the transport to its own driving software, also making the damage Jax had done to it useless.

Hank

Jax began a message, but he stopped when he saw his connection to the internet had been blocked. The walls of the cargo hold were blocking his signal.

The lioness turned to the right and was gone from sight, blocked by a large crate. Jax continued to move and heard her begin speaking again:

"I want you to know my name, before you die, human." Her voice lowered, and became even more textured and powerful. "I am Narasimha," she said. The words reverberated through the cargo hold. "I don't think I'll let you live, not after you slaughtered my people today."

White crates passed by on either side of Jax. As he moved down the rows, he glanced left and right, around, behind the aisles of cargo.

"What are you looking for?" she asked. "My weapons? The explosives? Or … something else?"

She was talking too much. *Holding my attention … But why?* He stepped farther into the cargo hold. Now his nostrils picked up a rotten smell—a musky, decayed smell.

He took a step back and turned to recheck the crates he had already passed.

A blur of dark-brown fur, tusks, and a sharp head-butt, Jax flew backward. He hit the ground headfirst with a hard bang and slid down the aisle of crates, the world swirling around him.

"Nara, I got it!" a snorting voice squealed.

Something moved out of the darkness of the transport and stood over Jax. He tried to lift his head, but his neck muscles tingled and then seemed to fall away from his awareness. Colors, shapes, and the face of the warthog swirled in his vision.

Made … big mistake … His thoughts joined the stream of images tunneling away from him. *Thought it would have white fur. Where … Where's the white one?*

"Today is not the day I die," Narasimha whispered into the dark void where Jax's consciousness was heading. "Send him to the arena, Malick. I want to see him fight before he dies."

Moxie … She has white fur and—Wait. No. Not the arena, please. Don't …

His body pulsed and tingled, then there was nothing but darkness.

11
Missing

Official transcript: *Communication between Warrant Officer Hank Schneps and Captain Jesus Hernandez. September 21, 2097.*

Schneps: We lost contact with Jax at 1900 hours. His last message indicated that he was inside the cargo transport the lioness escaped in. We captured twelve Animalis, but the contents of the second plane were taken in the transport.

Hernandez: In Gillian's report, he indicated that you used one of the Animalis to find the location of the second warehouse. How?

Schneps: … Yes, sir. I … determined that the priority of finding the Ivanovich Machine was justification to use a pain-inducing drug on one of the Animalis found alive at the first warehouse.

Hernandez: What compound?

Schneps: … The Recoil compound.

Hernandez: Recoil? Did it kill the Animalis?

Schneps: No. The hyena Animalis was taken to a hospital.

Hernandez: APE would burn me alive if they found out about this. Do you understand that?

141

Schneps: But it's only banned from use on humans.

Hernandez: Don't play stupid, Hank; it makes me feel like I'm the fool when you do it. The political atmosphere around Animalis has always been volatile as hell. I can't have my men torturing the things and leaving them for the world to see in hospital beds.

Schneps: I'm requesting that the company be deployed in full force to take the Ivanovich Machine.

Hernandez: I'm growing impatient with your behavior. Your actions have consequences, Warrant Officer. At first, I was willing to listen to you about this idea of a weapon, but now I'm starting to think that it has only ever been a sculpture. I've had the information from the rat's computer analyzed, but each facility has confirmed that there is no such DNA device.

Schneps: I know it seems crazy, but if it is real, it's the most dangerous weapon in existence!

Hernandez: I'm aware of your convictions.

Schneps: We have to go after it! Someone has to!

Hernandez: I have a responsibility to protect the United States—

Schneps: By—

Hernandez: At this time, by keeping the border secure. I have limited resources, Schneps.

Schneps: …

Hernandez: …

Schneps: Grimshaw wants to aid in a rescue for Jax.

Hernandez: What? You told her details of an active operation?

Schneps: She wants to leave right away to follow the cargo transport, and I can go with her.

Hernandez: You're crazy if you think I'm going to let her—

Grimshaw: Hello, Captain.

Hernandez: H-Hurley? Is that you? Why, you haven't changed a single bit. You're so beautiful.

Grimshaw: I'm going to try and find Jax. Hank says he can find where they went.

Hernandez: But, Hurley, you're a civilian now. That's a job for the army.

Grimshaw: Are you going to stop me, Jesus?

Hernandez: Wait, we have to talk about it first.

Schneps: Please, sir. If needed, I will find the machine on my own.

Hernandez: Hurley, it's too late. The Animalis don't keep hostages for long, unless they are sent—

Grimshaw: To the arena. I know.

Hernandez: And you know we can't get in their way to—

Grimshaw: Are you going to let Hank join me, Jesus?

Hernandez: I ...

Grimshaw: We have to leave.

Hernandez: Warrant Officer Schneps, join Miss Grimshaw. Help her with anything she needs in the search for Officer Minette.

Schneps: And the machine?

Hernandez: If you are able to give me proof somehow that it is what you claim it to be, then we can talk about it some more.

Schneps: Understood.

Hernandez: It's so good to see you again, Hurley. It's been to long.

143

Grimshaw: Likewise, Captain. We'll have to catch up another time. I've got to go.
End Communication.

————

In a private hangar at the Moscow airport, Hank sat in the cockpit of the Atticus, leaning forward in the captain's chair, scanning
a wall of information in front of him. It had been two days since
the captain had allowed him to chase after Jax with Grimshaw.
The first day had been spent going through shipping records until they were able to find where the cargo transport had been
sent. It was taken to an airport and then jumped to Moscow.
But the cargo transport had vanished once the plane had landed.
Grimshaw and Hodge were somewhere in the city, checking in
from wall screens with updates to their search.

Without her near him, Hank could finally breath comfort-
ably again. She had accused him, after he had been the only one
willing to do what was necessary to track down the Ivanovich
Machine, staring him down with blazing fire in her eyes like he
was guilty.

He shook his head. It didn't matter what she thought. The
day would come when they would all see what kind of devasta-
tion the machine was capable of—unless Hank got his hands on
the machine first.

The information floating in the air sat motionless while
Hank's eyes danced around, devouring it. Some people would
have relied on their retina monitors to capture and store the information, as if it were a way to have a photographic memory, thinking that it could give them a superhuman mind—like
Hank's—without any effort. But as they relinquished their mind's
responsibility to hold onto memories, they lost the ability, and

with the loss of that ability, they lost their reasoning mind. With no memories to form stories with, they couldn't link cause-and-effect relationships, they couldn't predict the future, and they became robotic and computer-like, acting out whatever programming was passed into them from the media they drenched themselves in. A truly genius mind required effort, and Hank had put in that effort.

What Hank was currently doing with the information had become easy, but only after years of practice and mental training. A page of information was taken in as a whole block of data. It was different from reading the words; there was no voice in his head phonetically sounding out each word for his mind to listen to. Instead, the page of information was held in an almost subconscious state. He was able to draw on the individual words when needed, since the whole page was stored in his mind. The pages, or blocks of data, were placed into a mental picture that represented the context that the information was coming from. At the end of the day, lying on his bed with his eyes closed, before falling asleep, he would take the catalogue of mental pictures and sort them into permanent memory files in his mind. If the information was about an apple, he would make a link, or tag, from memories of pears, oranges, lunches, pie, and the specific information he had learned: deliveries from an apple supplier in Moscow that produces fifty thousand pounds of apples a year, but somehow delivered fifty-eight thousand pounds of product—a company that Hank suspected sold laser rifles to the Animalis militants.

His mental process had been developed over the last seven years, after he had heard it was possible to gain a photographic memory. His mother had died a year before, and his father was struggling to teach Hank the religious foundation he wanted him to have. So the missionaries from their church had been visiting the family to teach the fundamentals of the doctrine. One evening, they captured Hank's imagination by making a promise that if he were to memorize one scripture a day for a year, he would gain a photographic memory.

He was so excited that he made a public announcement to his friends and relatives in his social network. His uncle warned him that if he didn't investigate memorizing techniques, he would quickly be overwhelmed and quit. One of his friends, who attended the same church, decided to try the same thing. And nearly everyone else told him it would be pointless because all information was just a brainwave away with a retina monitor.

The uncle was right. After the first week, Hank felt like all of the memorized scriptures were being crammed into the same tiny space in his brain. He did an internet search and found the idea of "filing" memories in a familiar childhood building. Through the second week, he discovered what that actually meant with trial and error.

During the third week, he found out his friend had quit. He was starting to have second thoughts as well. The retina monitor worked as fast as thought, so why should he waste his time on something most people didn't believe was possible? But he wanted to prove them wrong.

After the first month, he had developed a reliable process. As time went on, his mind began to feel lighter, like it had been filled with tar and clutter before, but was now washed and organized. Instead of spending hours a day, painstakingly visualizing rooms with trinkets representing each scripture, and fearfully reciting memorized scriptures to make sure they were still in his mind, he found he only had to read through the new scripture once in the morning, and then again at night.

His social network wasn't interested the closer he came to having a photographic memory, so he stopped talking about it. After the first year, he couldn't be sure that what he had developed in himself was truly a photographic memory, but whatever it was had to be close.

Grimshaw's icon appeared in front of him. Hank quickly set aside the mental tapestry he had been weaving with the information and answered the call.

"Arbat District seemed promising," she said. "I'll come back and visit it again tonight. Hodge didn't find anything in the streets below Arbat. Do you have any leads for us?"

Hank eyed her. Her cheeks and nose were bright pink, flushed with blood trying to keep her skin warm. She was wrapped up in a big Russian coat, looking like a young, weary tourist. Behind her stood rows of cold gray buildings, each with a section of wall screen advertising sex, drugs, or gambling. With a quick mental command through Hank's retina monitor, the image before him reduced to show only Grimshaw.

Hank folded his arms. "He hasn't shown up in any new arena videos—yet."

"That's good," she said, smiling grimly. "He's a good, healthy kid. It'll take some time for them to starve him a little."

"It only takes a week to lose five pounds of muscle," Hank said.

"You didn't answer me about having leads."

Hank pulled his hand up to his forehead and pinched his eyebrows while he spoke. "Nothing concrete," he lied. "It's no wonder the place hasn't been found after ten years." He shifted his weight in the seat.

"Well, don't give up," she said. "I'll let you know what we find tonight."

The call ended with a melodic chime, and Hank's program windows and documents appeared back in view. In the top left corner of the array was the last message from the captain. Hank looked away from it quickly, but his mind knew the message, and the words floated involuntarily to the surface of his awareness:

> The arena is off limits. Jax is an excellent soldier, but he is beyond our saving if he has been taken there. There's a classified operation, or protection being dictated, that is likely tied to something political. I'm giving you three months to give me something substantial on this Ivanovich Machine, then I'm pulling you back.

Hank's heart ached with the thought of giving up. Jax had always been such a fighter. In boot camp, putting in extra time to prove he would be ready for active duty by the time Hank was promoted to warrant officer, and fighting Gillian when the whole thing was unfair, and now, taken by the Animalis. He would fight; he always fought.

12
Cold Storage

The animals were all sitting upright on their haunches. A gathering of the strangest group of animals: elephants, horses, dogs, cats, snakes, pigs, worms, and insects. It was an audience, watching something.

Jax awoke in darkness. The sounds of the animals in his dream transformed into a drone of incomprehensible noise around him. He should probably get out of bed soon and take a shower before the rest of the men in his company woke up. He tried to move his head, but couldn't.

He tried to move again and felt a wave of dizziness. *What happened to me?* The dizziness turned into a throbbing pain in his head. He finally opened his eyes and felt his head ache double. The dim light of the room was enough to send a stinging pain through his eyes and into his skull, so he dropped his eyelids shut.

It hurt too much to move, so Jax stopped and listened to the sounds around him instead. He heard maybe a dozen voices, moaning, grumbling, talking in another language. A hollow clank from metal hitting a hard, stone surface. The acoustics of the room sounded different than the barracks he normally awoke in. Instead of the warm reverberation of the walls of the barracks, the walls around him deadened the sound to a cold flatness.

Something was wrong—he could be in danger. He had to remember what had happened before. Images of a recent memory came to him. A fight. *Yes, I fought Gillian.* What happened after that? *A rat.* He and Hank had been sent to a rat plane.

The memories finally started to fall into place. Someone with bright red curls of hair—*Hurley ... Hurley Grimshaw.* He remembered pieces of a car chase, riding on a kangaroo Animalis. *Who was crying?* Grimshaw, on his shoulder. The door, pounding on it, screaming at Hank. *No, he had been with Hank in the warehouse. Going to get the pyramid ...*

He could see Hank in his mind, staring with cold indifference at Jax. Seeing the face cut into Jax's heart. *That was just a bad dream,* Jax thought. *Hank is my best friend.* And he pushed the image out of his mind.

So much had happened in the last twenty-four hours: the guns, the slaughter, the face of the hyena, holding Grimshaw, and facing a fierce lioness Animalis. The memory of her voice came back—"Narasimha."

He felt his spirit deflate: he had utterly failed; the Animalis had gotten away with the pyramid. Had Hank and the others gone back to join Hernandez's company? Where had he been taken?

He tried to move his head again and something creaked. He felt no pain, though; the noise didn't seem to have come from him. He was lying sideways, the weight of his body held his right arm pinned and numb.

"I see you moving in there," said a deep male voice. It was closer, and louder, than the other voices Jax had heard.

He tried to open his eyes again, holding them nearly shut. The pain wasn't as bad as before. Now he could see a dull gray wall across from him.

"Who … Who are you?" Jax's words barely made it to his own ears. His throat was dry and his lips had cracked. He tried to swallow, but the tiny amount of spit that had been in his mouth got caught in the wrong tube in his throat, and he began to cough. His chest tensed convulsively, sending waves of intense pain through him.

"Careful, that looks painful," the voice said. "I'm sure a big glass of water would help. Would you like a glass of water?"

Jax held his breath, forcing the cough to stop. He could feel most of his body now, tingling and stinging, as sensations returned after the coughing. To sit up, he dropped his legs over the side of the bed he was lying on and pushed past the pain of his headache.

"Yes, please," Jax said.

Through the slit in his eyelids, he could see the room he was in open up into a large hall in front of him. Thin, dark lines created a barrier where the room joined the hall.

A man was on the other side of the dark lines, crouching down to Jax's height.

"Here."

The man swung his arm out and there was a metal clang as the cup he held hit against one of the dark lines. Water splashed onto Jax and the bed. The man laughed. It was a chuckle at first, but it grew into a loud belly laugh. Whimpers and whines from the other voices around them became louder when they heard his laughter.

"Quiet!" the man yelled. His laughter stopped. "You moan like these other pieces of dirt, and you won't even get that much water."

The water penetrated Jax's clothes, bringing an icy coldness with it. His body started to tremble.

Jax's eyes had adjusted better to the light and he opened them more to see the man talking to him, blurred from his tremors. Light from above glistened off the man's dark, bald head. The face was obscured in the shadow of his brow. His clothes were a bland black, a single-piece working uniform. His plump figure bulged underneath the clothes.

"Welcome to your last home," the man said.

———

Leftover fish parts and vegetables were tossed into Jax's cell twice a day, along with a splash of water. Jax quickly learned to keep the floor clean so he could suck up the puddles.

A small blanket, reeking of Animalis, was his constant companion. It was hardly a protection from the cold, but he could at least sleep while it was draped over him. He wasn't in Australia anymore, and he missed the dry heat. Most of the people and Animalis that passed the door of his cell seemed to be speaking Russian. He'd quickly realized that his retina monitor had been removed and he could no longer rely on it for information, forcing him to use his own mind to process everything.

The first arena fight came through the ceiling as a muted audio play. He was lying on his back in the dark morning hours when he heard the sound of feet scuffling above him.

The audience started with the same primal stomping rhythm Jax had heard from the videos he'd seen. Chanting, anticipating the fight. Scavengers in the stands hoping for scraps to be thrown to them. But as the fight began, silence filled the stands.

There were occasional cheers and hisses until the end of the fight approached. Then the hoard of Animalis grew restless. Jax tried not to listen to the crowd's intermittent barks—and cries for the victim to be thrown to them.

Animals. Give them hands and a tongue, but they will always be animals. Jax never listened to another fight. When he heard the crowd start the horrible, primal rhythm on the bleachers, he tried to drown it out by using the ragged blanket to cover his ears.

Sometimes the face of the hyena came to him in those moments. Stories started to play out in his mind, reminiscent of the gruesome video games he had played. The Animalis in the stadium were cheering for Jax, and ordering him to kill more; he was so good at it. The captain was an Animalis, ordering him to kill the rat, kill the kangaroos, so that he and the rest of the company could eat the bodies.

Sometimes the face of Grimshaw came to him instead, her smile and tousles of curly red hair dangling in front of her eyes. He tried to solve the mystery of her age, her relationship with Captain Hernandez, and what it meant that they had both seen images projected into their minds. Maybe her dad had know Hernandez in the service? She would have heard all their war stories. Where was she now? If there was any way he could see her again. He would like to have known her better, or at least have said a good-bye.

Jax could hear something scampering over the floor. It woke him from his thoughts. He sat up, waiting to hear the sound again.

Moans and pleading coming from the other cages around him. Maybe he had imagined it. He leaned against the wall and went back to complaining.

The food was unbearable, the cold constantly interrupted his sleep—shaking his body with an uncontrollable constancy—and he was powerless.

Scratch scratch scratch. This time Jax definitely heard it. The sound was light, like tiny, hard feet running across the floor.

He stood up and went to the bars to look around. The walls opposite his cage were covered in dark shadows and patches of dim yellow light from the line of single bulbs overhead. Along the center of the floor was a path of golden dust that was left by the guards when they took prisoners to and from the arena.

Then he saw it. A small, white animal dashed through the hall and stopped a few feet in front of Jax's cell. It sat up on its back legs, holding a ragged sandwich in its mouth.

"Moxie?" Jax whispered.

He felt a rush of relief. Her fur reflected the light as a magical glow around her. Using a kissing sound, Jax tried to coax her closer.

"Come here, girl. Is Hank here? Grimshaw?"

She came closer and dropped the food in front of the bars. She stood again and squeaked. Her little pink hands groomed her face. Jax reached to grab her, but she pulled back and ran away. Her long body bounded in little waves down the hall.

"Moxie," he strained.

Then he heard the heavy footsteps approaching. Jax reached down and picked up the food. He left the bars and went to the back wall, holding the sandwich behind his back. Huffing, and snorting, the big rhinoceros guard lumbered past.

When the sounds of his footsteps faded away, Jax examined the sandwich. He pulled the bread away, lifted the lettuce, and looked under the cheese and layers of turkey. He flipped it over and did it again, looking at each piece, hoping to find something other than food.

Even without a hidden message, the sandwich brought Jax renewed hope. He had been found. The arena had been found. If Hank was here, he could bring a stop to the whole arena with a swift military strike.

Jax didn't mind the dirt and filth that had covered the sandwich from being dragged on the ground. Hunger pains had started after the first day from the lack of food. The sandwich was savory and delicious.

Moxie came again the next day, carrying a hearty, half-eaten bagel. She dropped it in front of his cell again and scampered away. Again, there was no message. But he devoured the bagel.

Alone in his cell, waiting for their rescue plan to come together, all he could do was wade through his memories. It was the one thing Jax didn't want to do. He couldn't afford to exercise, since the added exertion would starve him even faster, and there was little hope of escape. His mind would wander back to his parents, especially his mother—making him sit in his room without access to his wall screens when he was being punished. Getting his retina monitor had been his first act of independence when he had moved out to join the army. No one would ever leave him disconnected from the world outside, he had figured. And yet here he was, unable to access the internet now that the monitor had been taken out of his eyes.

By the end of the first week, Jax had given up hope of anything changing. The people and Animalis that walked by were always the same. The sounds from the arena, the scuffles, the cries, and the muffled cheers that came through the ceiling, were always the same. No one but Moxie ever came, keeping him from starvation.

Waiting made him furious. Why should he feel bad for what he had done to the Animalis in the warehouse? He would do it again. And if the captain was one of the Animalis in the stadium above him, looking to feast on the arena corpses, then Jax would join in. He'd eat the bodies while they were still warm. It would stop his hunger, and his shivering. It would stop the war: humans could eat the Animalis.

They were insane thoughts, but with the isolation and the hunger that tormented him constantly, they were as normal as he could manage. He realized he had never actually learned to be alone. Growing up, he had always been able to scrounge up an old portable game machine to pass the time. There was nothing for him now.

It was something worse than depression creeping in. Jax had failed, and if the pyramid really was as powerful as Hank believed, the world could crumble into chaos at any moment because of him.

Jax was naive, thinking he could change the world. Watching every video that came within his sphere of awareness had shaped his view of reality. There were so many suggestions and little promptings that had worked their way into his subconscious mind. "Join the military. Do something great for humanity. Dream big. You can do anything you set your mind to. America needs heroes." All little snippets from commercials, movies, and video games.

Was that who Jax was? A hero? Was this what life was, killing and torture and waiting to kill or be eaten? Suburban life seemed like a fragile illusion now. People walking around in make-believe, whining about pretend problems, and hoping for more synthetic enjoyment.

He wondered what Grimshaw had done to be so happy. There was a reason why she would understand Jax so well, and yet have so much hope and joy.

There was a rustle of movement in the cage next to Jax. The sound of something sliding on gravel. Jax hadn't been able to see what was on either side of him because of the solid walls of the cell.

"My babies," a female voice groaned.

"Hello?" Jax went to the bars. "Who's there?"

"I'm starving. I have to eat, or my babies will all die." It was a strange, moaning voice. Probably an Animalis, waiting for its turn in the arena.

Jax stepped back from the bars; it would have to whine to someone else. He was going to face one of the creatures around him; helping it would only make the fight harder.

The next day, the moaning hadn't stopped: "Please, please …"

Even with the blanket over his head, he could hear the pleading. *They'll send her into the arena, and I won't have to hear her anymore,* he told himself.

Jax was starting to wonder how the people running the arena could mistreat the Animalis that were going to fight. Weren't they all together? Part of the same whole like humanity? *Except that humanity has done this to itself a thousand times,* Jax realized. The arena was modeled after the Roman Colosseum, where human slaves and heroes alike fought and died to cheers.

He thought about talking to the pleading Animalis beside him again. With hours of boredom, lying on his back, then his side, then his front, then his back again, the thought of interaction became more and more of a need. *Even if it is an Animalis.*

Jax looked around his cell; he hadn't always eaten what they had thrown to him. Carrot stalks, bread that had become more mold than bread, a piece of meat that looked too similar to a human finger for him to touch. He gathered them up and slid them across the floor through the bars of his cage and into the hall, pushing them toward his neighbor.

"It's really not much, but you can have it," he said.

There was a rush of steps in the other cage. Then the crunch of gravel as they pulled the food into their cell.

"Why? I …" After a moment, the female seemed to decide there was nothing to do but say thank you. "Thank you. Thank you so much." And she started to eat the food.

"How long have you been in here?" Jax said.

"A week now," she said through her mouth full of food. "You're human, aren't you?"

"How can you tell?" Jax sat down near the bars and leaned against the wall.

"Your smell." She finished eating, and Jax could hear her pacing back and forth again.

"Why are you here? Are you going to fight in the arena?" he asked.

A low growl came from her. It could have been a "Yes." The pacing stopped, and she crawled onto the floor. "It's so hard to work. So hard now. No one will hire a pregnant Animalis. Winter is coming, then I'll sleep. But I have to have enough food to keep my babies alive. They're in me now, not growing yet. Not until spring."

Jax waited, listening to her breath hissing against the floor. "I'll win. Then I'll eat."

The chant of the crowd around the arena began to build again, and Jax left the stranger to hide from the noise.

Jax talked with her often. Her name was Misha, and she was a bear Animalis from a small town near the Black Sea, where she had once been a maid. Her parents had, as she'd put it, given her to a hotel chain. All of her schooling and training had been to clean.

It was frustrating that she had nothing else to talk about. Jax couldn't talk about sports or movies. He didn't care about stains, or carpets, or anything. But sitting with his back against the wall, listening to her moaning voice, he didn't feel so alone.

There had been another one like her, cleaning at the hotel. Another bear Animalis. And she broke all of the rules to get near him. Jax laughed to himself at the thought of the two bears looking at each other longingly, wearing ruffly, white maid's hats and aprons.

13

Misha

Eat, Misha thought. *I must eat.*

She sat on the floor in the corner of her cell, hugging her knees close to keep warm. The flannel dress she had worn for the last year didn't insulate her as she remembered it had. But the dress had kept her alive during that time. She wouldn't want to lose it.

So many humans and Animalis had been cruel to her: the shelter master, the hotel man, and now the humans and Animalis that were keeping her in this cell. All she had wanted was to have enough food for the two little embryos that were waiting for spring to begin growing. When something came into her life that was good and kind and consistent, she treasured it.

———

"Please," Misha asked. There was so much food in the old dog's bowl. Wasn't there enough for her to have just a bite?

Misha wasn't yet full grown, only two years old. Tall enough to reach her hand over the counter and pull things down, but not tall enough to defend herself. There were usually good things to eat up there, and whenever she got near the counter, she would pass her hand up over the edge. As long as one of the others in the shelter weren't looking. If she was caught, then she would run and hide. They kicked her, and said mean words to her if she didn't.

It was when her mother was away that she got into trouble. There would always be food when her mother was around. "Please," she said, and her mother always shared. But the shelter master didn't like it when Misha said "Please."

"Here. Right here. Misha, come over here," Tom hissed, calling to her from across the room. The glossy black stripe of fur that passed over his eyes like a mask glistened for a moment in the dusty sunbeam by the stairs, then he turned around and climbed up.

Misha decided to try one last time. "Please," she said.

But the old dog growled at her. "Get out of here! Scrawny babe. You're not worth the food your own mother gives you. Go!" he shouted. Then he swatted her with the back of his hand, and she fell to the ground, twisting to catch herself so that her head didn't hit hard like the last time. She decided to follow Tom. He wouldn't have food, though. He was just a pup, like her. Smaller, but older.

The old wooden stairs gave a hollow thump under her bare paws as she climbed up. Tom was near the window at the end of the room. It was hot up there, and Misha didn't like to be hot. She didn't like to be hungry. She didn't like Tom—unless he gave her food.

"What, Tom?" she said as she got closer to the window.

He kept looking out. "We've got to do that, yeah," he said, pointing down at the street outside. "Whatever he just did, look. They gave him food. See how full he is?"

Misha pushed her snout in next to Tom to get a look. Across the street was another building with a steep roof and tall windows. Humans stood by the door, walked on the sidewalk, and others rode in cars passing in front of the building.

The two humans by the door: one was yawning. The kind of sleepy that Misha had seen from new pups when they had eaten from their mother. While they watched, the tired, satisfied man pointed up at the roof of the building, and the other man looked up and nodded. Then they patted each other on the back, and the tired one got into a car and drove away. The remaining human looked at the roof again. He straightened his purple tie. He opened the door, and walked back into the building.

Misha was hot and growing more frustrated. Tom moved, bumping his elbow into her shoulder, and she nearly bit him. *Don't bite,* she knew. After the first fierce slap on her snout from her mother, she knew, *Don't bite.*

"I think it's broken, yeah." Tom tapped the window, pointing to the roof. "See the piece that moves the water away to the ground? The gubber, it's broken there." He moved back and forth, excited to leave.

Misha followed after him, still not sure what they were going to do. Downstairs, Tom grabbed a coat from the closet and handed Misha another one. It was too hot for coats. It was too hot for clothes, if the older ones wouldn't yell at her for not wearing any. But she wanted food more, so she pulled on the big coat.

"Find something that needs fixed and tell me," Tom said once they were outside. "Something broken, like that gubber. They gave food to that man when he told them it was broken. So we've got to find something that's broken, then they'll give us food."

Outside the shelter where the many Animalis families and loners stayed, Misha had to be careful. She and the others had to stay away from the humans. They did big, important, things: like driving cars, and some came to the shelter and taught Misha about planes, and space, and mummies. If you didn't do what a human told you to do, they could hurt you, or take you away, like they did to Misha's dad. So Animalis had to know a lot about the humans. Like that the tall ones were human. Adults. And the short ones were children. Small, but still human.

Misha thought she could probably stop a human child from hurting her. She could yell at it, "Stay still, or I'll eat you!" But she would be in trouble if an adult heard her.

Ahead of them, a human was approaching on a bike. Misha hurried to the edge of the sidewalk and sat down. Tom came and stood by her, his head still bending around, looking for a broken thing.

While Misha waited for the bike to pass, she looked as well. Sidewalk? Works for things to walk on: not broken. Steps to a building door? Works for getting things from low to high: not broken. Windows? Works for letting us see through them: *But I can't see into this building.* The windows were all cloudy, reflecting away the brightness of the sun.

"Those windows are broken," Misha said to Tom, and he looked where she was pointing. "Windows let you see, and I can't see through those."

"Those windows are broken! Yeah," he said.

Misha wasn't sure if they were allowed to ring a door bell, but Tom was already climbing up the handrail to reach it. Once they heard the ringing, he leaped down next to her and straightened his coat.

An adult pulled the door open, saw that there were two small Animalis on her stairs, and looked up and down the street.

"What's this?" she said. Misha thought it was a she because it had long hair. But sometimes boys had long hair. She had a skirt on, with no hair on her legs: she was a girl.

"Your windows are broken!" Tom shouted, and he held his hands out.

Misha could tell that this human wasn't mad. It seemed worried, until Tom had spoken, then it looked more worried.

She stepped out onto the porch and closed the door behind her. "Are you two alone?" she asked.

Misha looked at Tom, then back at the woman and said, "No, we're together. We were looking for broken things, and your windows are broken."

"Oh," she said. The worried look went away. Maybe that meant she would give them food now. "Which ones? Did you break them?"

Misha and Tom stepped down the stairs with her while she looked back at the building.

"I don't see anything. No, they're not broken," she said. She looked up and down the street, all the worry back in her again.

"But I can't see through your windows," Misha said to her.

The woman looked up at them again and laughed. "Oh, dirty," she said. "Those are dirty, you're right. Thank you."

When she looked back down at Misha and Tom, this time smiling, Tom had his hands out again. Misha hadn't seen the full, satisfied man do that, so she kept her hands at her sides.

"Don't you give us food now?" Tom asked.

She looked at them for a moment. "No …" she said slowly. "Are you two from the shelter? I can't give you food." She laughed. "We're not supposed to give you food." She walked back to her door. Once she had the handle turned, she looked back at them. "Were you looking for a job?"

"No," Misha said. "Broken things."

"What's a job?" Tom asked back.

It was too hot. Misha was mad, hungry, and couldn't think straight anymore. It was better to run and hide if she couldn't remember what to do. So, before Tom or the human said anything else, she had started running away down the street. The woman called to her, and she felt the urge to stay. This woman had been kind and there was love in her eyes. But if Misha stayed while she was hot and confused, she could accidentally bite her, or hurt her, so she ran faster, which made her even hotter. The sounds of cars, and horns, and humans all chased after her.

She couldn't find the shelter. In her panic, she must have run away down the wrong street. The heat was too much for her to keep running, so when she saw a dark, cold shadow under a large garbage bin, she scooted herself under it and hid.

At sun down, her mother came and carried her back to the shelter where a bowl of oats topped with a blueberry awaited. In the morning, Misha had her first job: cleaning the woman's home with Tom. Washing windows with a cloth and soap—but not too much soap. Washing the floor, dusting, and vacuuming. When each job was done, the woman gave them both a treat.

Being at the woman's house was what Misha began to look forward to. The woman wasn't like the old dog at the shelter, who constantly reminded Misha that he was more important than her. The woman was pleased to have Misha with her. And Misha loved the woman.

A week later the job was done, and the woman said they had to say good-bye for the last time. Misha got up the next day, ready to go back to her house to clean, but Tom stopped her.

"We've got to find another job, yeah," he said, standing in Misha's way.

"I don't want to have another job!" Misha cried. "I want to be with her. She needs us. She wants us to be with her."

Tom had another idea. "There was a human that brought this food here. I saw him bringing it out of a truck, yeah. I bet he gets to eat lots of food."

But Misha didn't want to go out again, wearing coats in the heat of summer, getting lost in the city. She stayed at the shelter, drowning in her sadness from not being able to see the woman anymore. While she was there at the shelter, a human came asking for Animalis that could clean. Misha's mother talked to the man, and when he left, Misha went with him. She didn't know it would be the last time she saw her mother.

The man was cold and dominating. There were several other Animalis that cleaned for him, and he had strict rules for them. They cleaned homes, and hotels, and parks, and re-strooms for the man. When an Animalis broke the rules, they were gone the next day, and the man found a new Animalis to clean in their place. When Misha's fingernails grew long, the man taught her to trim them. But when she was older, and found another boy Animalis that was just like her, she broke the man's rules.

The bear stood taller than most humans. His fur was black and glossy, flowing down from his chin under his plaid dress coat. He was carrying luggage into one of the hotel rooms.

He stopped at the doorway, turning to look at Misha. Like a bolt of lightning, awareness of her body faded. There was nothing else in the world in that moment looking at his eyes and him looking back into hers. The need to clean vanished. The need to eat was forgotten. The rules she had been trained to follow drifted out of her like particles of dust floating out an open window.

Misha broke the rules, and when the hotel man looked into her eyes to ask her why her cleaning never got done that day, he ignited with rage.

In one day, she had known love, but the next she was taken away and abandoned in another shelter. It had been six years since she had gotten her first job with Tom, and now she was alone, surrounded by strangers.

There was never enough food again. She was always hungry. The human that helped at the shelter used a machine she hadn't seen before, waving it over her body for a moment.

"This is a CT scanner," he said. "It shows me what's going on inside your body. We want to find diseases early so we can keep you healthy." The machine beeped. "Aw, it looks like there is something here. See? It's why we—Oh ... you're pregnant. You're *pregnant*."

Then he kicked her out of the shelter. Winter was approaching. Food was all she thought about. She had to eat.

That's why she had gone to the arena. After talking to many Animalis, she learned how to find the man who collected volunteers. She came as a spectator, but caught no scraps. Now she was waiting for her turn to fight.

Her belly ached again. Soon she would eat, enough food to last through the winter. She would have to say good-bye to the human in the cell beside her, and she would miss him. When she had been cold and alone and hungry, he had been kind. He had fed her.

———

Jax saved a small portion of food for Misha whenever the guards tossed in his meals. It never felt like a substantial gift, but she always thanked him with sincerity when he passed it through the bars.

Then one morning, she wasn't there. There was no scuffle of rocks when he slid the food over. He waited.

"Are you there? Still alive over there?" he called out to her.

But there was no response.

Jax heard the heavy steps of the rhinoceros guard coming.

"Get up. You're going into the arena, human," the guard said. "Now."

14
Arena

They couldn't send Jax to the arena now. Hank and the captain were coming for him.

The rhinoceros struck the bars of the cell with an electrified stick and sent sparks showering onto the floor. There were two more guards behind him, a leopard and a water buffalo.

The three guards extended their shock sticks into the cell, waving them around, trying to knock Jax to the ground. He dodged and ducked, then jumped forward and caught the handle of the water buffalo's stick. Jax jerked it free and pulled it into the cage with him. He blocked a blow from the leopard and then struck back at it. There was a sharp buzz as the stick made contact with the leopard's arm. It jerked convulsively and dropped to the ground.

"I'm not going without a fight," Jax yelled. "HA!" He struck out at the water buffalo, who had moved to pick up the leopard's shock stick.

"Give me the keys! HA!" Jax shouted. He struck the bars of the cell and sent a shower of sparks in the air. "HA! Keys! Stupid animal!" He bellowed with the force of a lion tamer. "Move! Now!"

The rhinoceros pulled the shock stick back and lowered its

Animalis

head. Jax moved closer and threw his arms out. "Now! Keys! HA!"

"Got you, mal'chik," it said with a snort. Then it jabbed in with its shock stick. Jax was too close. He tried to move, but it hit his stomach like the finger of God.

He fell, shaking to the floor, fire burning through his limbs. By the time he started to understand his surroundings again, they had dragged him to a new holding cell. A tingling sensation had replaced the burn. He could hear the Animalis audience talking and moving on the stands just above where he was lying.

Jax flexed his numb fingers.

"If you live through this fight, boy," said a smooth, deep voice from behind Jax, "I'll make sure you're well taken care of. There was only ever one human that lived through his fight, and it made people go wild to see him fight again. A shame he didn't survive that second one." The man extended his hand into the cage. "Take this. It's no guarantee, but you don't have a chance without it."

Jax pulled himself up, hanging on the bars of the cage. He could see the shard of metal in the man's hand now. The man dropped it, and it landed on the hard floor with a light clank. There was a jerk of movement that almost knocked Jax back to the floor. The entire cage was sliding forward into the arena.

It was all happening too fast. Jax wasn't ready; he couldn't even stand on his own yet. Hank was coming for him—they were supposed to break through the walls. It couldn't be happening like this; it was too fast. *Come, someone. Please,* Jax thought. But the hope he'd held onto was slipping away, replaced by a bloodcurdling panic.

"If you do win, hold your victim up and the guards will pull it to the audience. They love that," the man was saying.

"Who are you?" Jax said through his thick, partially numb lips.

Rocks popped under the cage as it slid farther out through an opening in the wall. The shard of metal lit up as the bright lights of the arena consumed the cage. It was too bright to look through the opening. After living four weeks in the low light of their prison, the light stung his eyes. Jax bent down and grabbed the metal shard.

"You can just think of me as a humble servant of Narasim-ha," the man said. "Come back from this fight, and I'll tell you more." The wall closed, leaving the man behind. Jax tightened his hand into a fist, concealing the weapon.

The cage stopped. The sound of the crowd's anticipatory rumble boomed through the arena. BOOM boom boom BOOM boom boom. Over and over again. Jax squinted, looking out to see what he was supposed to fight. Two tiny eyes peered back at him from between the bars, surrounded by a mass of black and faded white.

He heard a click, and all four walls of both cages swung open. The eyes didn't move. It was his enemy.

The Animalis turned to face the arena. The audience started to howl.

Jax looked up at the stands. *I have to get out,* he thought. Hank, the captain, Felix, and Maven, they were out there, just about to break in and stop the fight. He had to be ready for them.

He could see the Animalis moving toward him out of the corner of his eye. *Survive.* There'd be no point in rescuing him if he died before they came. He had heard they used the electric shock sticks from above the arena when someone avoided the fight for too long. The audience wanted their blood.

Jax abandoned his vigil for rescue and assessed his enemy. It was walking slowly, its arms held close to its chest. The head looked up at the Animalis watching, and then ducked back down low, looking at Jax. Its clothes were old and worn, made of a thick material that didn't have any electronics, video diodes, or internet integration.

The head was big and round, with a pudgy snout. Its eyes were small compared to the rest of its features, small and mostly black like the fur around them. On top of its head sat two round ears. A white streak of fur at the top of its chest, just above its clothes. Bear Animalis.

Jax kept walking around the rim of the arena as he examined his foe, estimating its abilities. Sagging skin, shaking back and forth on its arms, was a sign that it had lost most of its weight. The way it kept glancing at the crowd made Jax think it was nervous, maybe afraid, or even ashamed. It still had tiny daggers at the tips of its fingers, and sharp, extra-large canines in its mouth.

The Animalis were so human. Their voices, their body structure, their blood, but mostly, their will to hold on to their precious lives was the same.

"I have to, human. I have to feed the children inside of me so they can live!" the bear said in a half whimper.

It was Misha.

She stepped toward him. Jax looked around the arena: a circular dirt floor, about the size of a basketball court with walls at least fifteen feet high around it. He had seen a wall close to that height in basic training. A single person couldn't hope to get over it alone, with no ropes, stones, trees, or any other archaic equipment Jax had scoffed at back then. He noticed some scrapes and gouges, but nothing he could use to climb out with.

Misha shuffled closer. Jax glanced at the guards above the arena. Three of them had stopped walking around the rim and were holding their shock sticks ready. He'd have to face her, his friend—not with the lack of confidence of the man he had seen in the video, but with intimidation.

"Ahhhhh!" Jax charged at Misha, raising his hands above his head, remembering how intimidating Narasimha had been in that position.

She kept coming. When he got close, she swiped at him. He ducked and jumped backward. Misha's movements were almost as fast as his. The muscles looked small and weak under the sagging fur, but they were still powerful. She moved forward again with her arms spread wide.

"I have to eat. Nothing else to eat." She clapped her hands together where Jax's head had been.

He lunged forward under the arms and grabbed around her chest. Jax ended up tucked under her armpit. Misha bellowed and tried to grab at his back. The fingers slipped off Jax's smooth shirt, but the hooked fingernails cut into him.

His teeth clenched, and he groaned but didn't let go. Jax pulled his arm up around Misha's armpit and grabbed the fur on the back of her neck. He kicked his legs wildly when she bent down to get hold of one.

Jax had to get away from the claws, away from the gaping mouth. He planted a foot and tried to throw his weight around to her back. She spun with him, keeping him in the same position. Jax hit the ground again and this time threw his knee into Misha's ribs.

She let out an ear-shattering roar. Jax took the opportunity to finally get completely behind her, wrapping his left arm around her bulky neck. He wanted to tuck his left hand into his elbow to lock it in place, but the neck was just too large.

Paw-like hands slapped at Jax's back and head. He tried to bring his arms in tighter to start the choke, but he couldn't tell with all the fur and muscle if it was doing anything to her. *The knife.* Misha would die. He would make her lie down, never to get back up. Jax pulled out the shard and pushed it against the pulsing artery in the bear's neck. The tip of the metal pressed in, warping the skin around it. Soon it would puncture. Her life— Misha's life—for his own. It was the only way.

His gut went hollow, and he felt a cold emptiness remembering what the killing had done to him before. He pulled the shard away from her neck.

The walls of the arena spun around as Misha tried to shake Jax off. Claws dug into his scalp. He could feel blood trickling through his hair where she was striking his head. Jax felt his feet touch the ground as she started to lower herself. He could hear her sucking in strained breaths.

Then, in a powerful thrust, Misha jerked forward and Jax was thrown over her shoulders. His arms flailed in the air, pulled from Misha's neck. The tiny shard of metal twinkled in the light and disappeared somewhere in the dirt. Jax's legs were over his head as he came down to the floor. He tucked his head to his chest and held his arms forward as he hit, rolling.

Misha was back on him, rabid, jaws scraping against his scalp, hands beating against his chest. Jax covered his head with his arms and kicked up with all his strength. His feet caught her in the throat. She pulled back, gasping.

Jax scrambled, looking for where the shard had fallen. His hip jerked, and he snapped his head to look down the length of his body, only to see Misha had gotten a hold on his leg. His fingertips scraped against the dirt as he was pulled backward. She bit down on his calf.

"Ahhhhh!" Jax yelled.

Misha bellowed in response.

Clawed hands held onto the leg.

"I can't live without this. I have to eat, human. I'm sorry."

Jax pulled his waist up to get a hold on her, but she stepped down on his chest, pinning him to the ground. Then she bit his shoe again and started to pull.

15
Escape

Misha's weight held Jax in place, pinning him to the arena floor. Muscles twisted in his leg as she bit and tugged at it. Teeth bit into him again and again, tearing shoe, pant, and finally bits of skin.

He pounded his fists against her leg. Jerked his chest over and over, trying to throw Misha's weight off. It wasn't enough. Pain, helplessness. *Help! Please, somebody. The world still needs me, doesn't it? Anyone, help! I'm not done yet. God, help me!* He heard—and felt—a crunch of bone beneath the bear's jaws.

"Ahhh!"

Jax felt the tug of Misha still pulling at him. His body jerking back and forth under her foot. But he couldn't feel it anymore. No pain, no pressure of teeth sinking into his skin. He looked at his leg. It was still a part of him, sandwiched in her jaws, attached to his knee, attached to his thigh.

A hyena's cackle pierced through the growing excitement in the stadium.

Misha continued to pull at the leg. She jerked, knocking the wind out of Jax with the force of counter pressure on his stomach. The leg started to stretch. It kept moving out away from the rest of his body. Without the pain of it, Jax didn't understand what was happening. It was like some alien object in the bear's grasp.

Then the bone cracked near the top of Jax's right calf. The muscle stretched and tore in half, and the skin ripped apart. The lower part of Jax's right leg separated from his body. The bear stumbled back with the foot and ankle still in her jaws.

Jax scrambled backward, looking from the end of his leg to the object in the bear's mouth. *No! No, no, no, no.* This was it, the fight was over. Jax couldn't run.

He let the sick dread flood his mind and dropped back to the hard dirt floor of the arena. The lights above him were intense. An isolated thought drifted up from the emptiness: *I couldn't even kill the bear to save my life …*

A noise resonated throughout the stadium: "More! More! More! More!" It shook the walls and rumbled the ground around his head. His vision blurred, and the cries from the Animalis crowd turned into a hiss of static in his ears.

"Are you ashamed of me, Jax?"

He hadn't noticed his father come into his room. His virtual space fighter exploded.

Jax kept his eyes on the wall screen and joined another game battle. "You're not supposed to come home early," Jax said, holding back the emotion burning his throat.

"No." He could see the shadow of his father looking down at the floor. His arms shifted and the robot prosthetic disappeared behind his back. "But this is different."

Jax's ship exploded again. He started another game.

"And now I get to be here with you, and your mom. It's going to be nice."

"I didn't want you to come back," Jax said. It was part of their community, one of the laws that the heroes of the country, the warriors of the army, didn't break. Not without losing their honor.

"They couldn't use me out there anymore. I'd be no good to them, not with this." He brought his arm back around and moved it back and forth, disgusted.

Jax blew up and joined another virtual battle.

"Jax, shut that game off and talk to me. You can't think of this as failure. I lived, and that's something." His dad went to the wall to shut the game off. Jax rolled his ship to the right and caught an enemy's bullets, blowing up, just before the color evaporated, and the ships and explosions flattened out to the normal smooth surface of the wall.

Jax leaned back and looked down at the floor. His dad towered over him.

"A lot of my friends died. I was lucky to get this." He shook the metal in front of Jax. "There's not one of those men that died who wouldn't rather be back with their families. They'd be proud of me for getting out, getting to be with you."

"I'm not. And I'm not going to give up like you." Jax held still, waiting for his dad to hit him.

But he didn't. After a long silence, Jax looked up and his father was gone. He held still, listening for his footsteps.

Finally, Jax turned in his chair to look at the door to his room. His dad had stopped in the entryway and was looking back at him. His voice was soft and cold when he spoke, and the words cut permanent marks in Jax's mind:

"If you went through what I did, you'd quit. You'd be just as weak and pathetic as you think I am. You'd give up." He started to walk away down the hall. "You'll give up."

Jax opened his eyes to the sound of snarling. The guards above him were holding out their sticks, shouting at Misha: "Finish!"

Jax pushed himself up into a seated position and felt a tidal wave of dizziness flood his brain. Stone walls and dazzling lights streaked through his vision. *Dizzy ... from losing too much blood,* Jax thought. With every vein and artery in his calf ripped open, gushing its contents onto the floor, he wouldn't have long to live. *If I'm ... lucky ... pass out from blood loss ... before Misha ... before she starts to eat me.*

He stopped moving and watched the ground slowly settle. Crisp shadows from small rocks and scrapes in the floor came into focus. All a dull dusty brown color. He squinted. *Where's ... the blood?* There was no blood. None on the ground, and none on the end of his ragged, tattered leg.

"Finish!" the guards shouted again.

Misha let out a throaty growl.

Jax turned, twisting the world with dizziness again, and looked for Misha. She was still three yards away, trying to ignore the threats from the guards, to keep eating the tattered end of Jax's leg.

My body ... Yes, it must have ... pulled all the blood up ... away from the wound. He nodded to himself, holding on to the simplest—wrong reasoning for what was happening. To stay sane. No one was going to save him; not Hank, not the captain. Even if he killed Misha, he would have to fight again. *Don't give up!* his very core shouted. *Escape.*

Misha pulled the leg away from her red-rimmed maw. "Don't fight," she said. "I have to eat. I have to."

He had to get out of the arena. It was the only possible way out. But the height, fifteen feet, was so impossibly out of reach.

With the six feet of the bear under him, that could get him to the rim of the arena.

If he could jump with one leg.

With a fierce roar, Misha swung her claws down at Jax. He pulled himself forward and felt the fur brush against the back of his neck. Misha teetered to the side, catching her balance.

Jax rolled back and thrust his foot up into a sharp kick. It connected with the dismembered leg Misha was holding, and sent it flying through the air to a lifeless thud against the wall.

"That's mine!" the bear cried. "Don't let them have it. It's mine!" She started to run after it.

As she sprinted past, Jax caught her foot and yanked, sending her to the ground. He pulled himself up and leaped for the leg first.

"No! It's mine!" She scrambled after him on all fours. "Please!"

Jax threw the leg with all his strength nearly straight up.

Misha strained to watch the leg fly into the air. Her awkward scramble transitioned into a standing run before she reached the wall.

Jax rolled onto his foot beside her and got ready to jump. Seeing her against the wall, his plan looked foolish. She was big, but not a rock that would hold still.

Above them, the leg reached its apex and began to drop toward the audience. Misha would give up on the leg and turn to eat him. He had to do it, at least try. *Now.*

Instincts took over. Jax sprung up, thrusting off his left leg. As he leaped, he grabbed handfuls of Misha's loose skin and jerked himself higher. He tucked his legs against his chest and landed, uneven, on her shoulders. He grabbed the fur on her head and looked up. The lip of the wall was still so far away.

Before the razor-tipped hands could swipe for him, he leaped again. Surprisingly, Misha gripping the wall with her claws and fought the force of his jump, giving him just the resistance he needed.

Jax stretched. His arms reached. The tips of his fingers called out for something to grab onto.

He stopped.

He was holding onto the edge.

Feet scuffled close by. The guards were coming closer. *Keep going!* he commanded himself.

Jax pulled himself over the edge to find the Animalis audience thrashing about in a commotion. A large group had gone for the leg, pushing and yelling.

The leopard guard was very close behind him now, hissing out Russian.

Jax crouched down to jump away, but, when he tried to flex his leg muscles, nothing came. That was it—T*his must be the end,* he thought, and almost wanted to cry. Jax's leg lurched him pitifully onto the floor. The leopard must have expected another jump as well, because his shock stick shot out in the air above Jax's head.

He had a moment—there was still time to survive. Jax scrambled toward the crowd of Animalis.

The leopard coiled back with his shock stick. Jax rolled to his left and pulled one of the legs from the crowd of Animalis to block the attack. The hot shock of electricity sent shivers down Jax's arms as he held onto the foot. He flipped back onto his hands and good knee, letting the unfortunate crowd member fall to the ground in convulsions, and started to crawl to an opening between the rows of seats.

Animalis

Behind him, the leopard yelled. It lit up the shock stick and waved it above its head. The scared audience moved forward faster, and Jax moved along with them, dragging himself between and under their legs.

The short hall opened up into a circular foyer that ringed the arena, and the crowd began to split. Jax could hear more harsh Russian being growled out by humans and Animalis on either side of the foyer. Just above several signs on the opposite wall was a row of windows, his only hope for escape. How far was it to the ground? He could see a line of flag poles extending from the building just outside the windows.

Jax crawled to the window and got back up, balancing on one leg. He had to do it one more time, leap, and throw himself through the glass. *Jump,* he commanded his leg muscles. He felt the leg respond and he lunged forward. He put his elbows out in front of himself and tucked in his head.

Glass burst around him as he went soaring into the sunlight. His fingers brushed against silky fabric, and he snatched hold of the last handful of flag. He got a second grip with his other hand and held it, dangling thirty feet above the ground. Shards of glass struck the ground, shattering on the hard concrete below. A few pieces fell in front of a passing semi truck.

As the first of the guards reached the window above him he let go of the flag and fell through the chilled morning air. He hit the trailer with a heavy slap. The truck began to slow, another car honked behind it, and the truck kept going.

Jax rolled to his side to watch the building pass behind him. The guards were at the window. One pointed, spotting him riding away on the trailer.

They were going to follow him, find him, and kill him. Jax

182

didn't want to do anything about it. Didn't want to find a way to survive. The cold wind whipped around him. *I just want to be back in the Hornet.*

He rode the transport for a long time, letting it take him away from the horror of the arena. Even if the guards tried to follow him, it would be better to let the truck take him far away before trying to drag himself through the streets with only his hands.

Finally, to escape the cold, he dove off into a pile of garbage piled on the side of the road. The impact knocked the wind out of him, and he lay there, cold and exhausted. He had lost his leg. A cripple the rest of his life.

Lying there, partially insulated by the trash, he closed his eyes and tried not to think. The city stank, not just from the trash, but there was a chalky burnt smell saturating the air as well. A terrible ruckus hissed and grumbled all around him. The sounds were painful and abrasive.

He stayed there most of the day, waiting to be found and taken back to his cell. The sun warmed the trash, putting off a pungent, sour odor that made the burnt chalk seem pleasant. Sleep came and went, making the wait stretch on and on.

Why didn't I bleed to death? Jax wondered, still refusing to look at his severed limb. He hadn't had time to think about it during the escape. And why should he think about it now? They would come, take him back, and kill him still. He wasn't going to help end the war, or save people, or be some hero.

He had been stupid enough not to kill Misha, but she was willing to pull him apart piece by piece to eat him. If he had just pressed the shard a little harder. Deep down Jax knew he was glad not to have killed her.

Animalis came. They spoke in gruff foreign voices, probably deciding whether to stun him or not. The trash shifted and bags were pulled away from around him, and he instantly missed their warmth.

They grabbed him, pulling him by the arms, out of the pile. He forced his eyes closed. *Let them take me,* he thought, rebelling against every instinct that was telling him to fight for his life.

They stopped pulling, and left him on the hard sidewalk. He heard the sounds of bags moving and being thrown. Jax opened his eyes and saw two Animalis throwing the bags of garbage into a truck. When the pile was gone, they climbed into the front of the truck and drove away with a horrible hissing, grinding sound.

He closed his eyes and felt a powerful burning in his heart. He had made it out alive. He had escaped. The warmth of the sun was on his face, new fragrances danced in his nostrils, and the music of motion in the city trumpeted in his ears.

16
With Moxie

When Jax woke, something was tickling his ear. The sky had grown violet. It was noisy—with the sounds of car motors, beeps, and honks echoing through the streets—but the sound of the bumpy tongue sliding over his ear stole his attention.

Jax reached for what was licking him. He felt soft and silky fur. It had the warmth of caring. Jax turned to look and found small black eyes staring back at him.

"Moxie?" he asked.

The furry white animal rubbed against him.

"Moxie, no thanks to you, or maybe thanks to you, I'm alive." He laughed. "Where's Grimshaw? Where's Hank?"

The animal started to lick his face. But just when he thought he could cry out for joy, Moxie scurried away.

Jax lifted his torso up to see where she had gone. It stood three yards down the sidewalk, chattering at him. She had found him again, and Grimshaw had to be near.

"Well?" Jax asked.

She trotted back to him and licked the top of his scalp. Her soft, warm fur reminded Jax of just how cold it was. Little teeth bit his shirt sleeve and tugged. She let go and chattered again. Then she ran away.

"You want me to follow, Moxie? Wait," Jax called. He began pushing himself up and winced at the sound of bone scraping against the sidewalk.

He waited for her, unable to follow. Everything around him was so cold and so foreign. The sidewalk he was on felt like an ice cube. He wanted to get up, but every time he went to move, when he felt the resistance of this exhausted body, he gave up.

"Jax?" someone said from far away.

It was the voice of an angel. A beautiful, red-headed angel: Hurley Grimshaw. The scrape of boots running on the sidewalk drowned out the sounds of the city around them.

"Hurley? Hurley, is that you? I knew you were here," he said, quietly, to his own fears and anguish at having been abandoned.

Oh no, what will she say about my leg? he thought, and then cursed himself. *What a selfish thing to think about. If the Animalis find me now, they'll take us both to the arena. That's what's important.* Jax struggled to turn himself over to look at her.

"We've got to get out of here," he called to her. "We've got to get out of this city before they find me. They'll take us both back to the arena if you're with me."

Grimshaw fell to her knees and wrapped her arms around him, pressing her cheek against his matted scalp.

"Right, we will," she said. When she pulled her head away to look at him, there was a blush of blood left on her cheek. "Can you stand? Are you alright?"

"I'm … pretty messed up. I might need a medical car, I don't know. Is Hank with you? The captain?"

"Hank's in the Atticus, trying to find the pyramid. I can't believe you're here! After all this time. It's you, and with Moxie. I'm sorry we couldn't find you earlier. Let's get inside, then we can talk. A medical car? Are you alright?"

She held her arms under Jax's shoulders and started to pull him up but stopped.

"Jax! Your leg!" she gasped and lowered him gently back on the ground. She looked into his face, searching for more information.

Jax nodded. "Yeah, I don't think I can walk. I probably can't even stand. But I'm alive." He smiled. She was so beautiful. Much prettier than he remembered in the loneliness of his prison cell. He watched her lips move, happy to be with another human again.

"I'm so sorry. Oh, I'm so sorry." She bent to get a better look at the leg. "How long ago did this happen? It's not covered!"

"It must look pretty terrible. I've been laying in trash all day since it happened," Jax said, watching Grimshaw attempting to pull away a wrapper that had stuck to his open wound. "I made it out of the arena."

"Today? You lost it today?" She closed her mouth. Her expression was intense. "We've got enough of the equipment to take care of this," she mumbled. "Hospital is too dangerous."

Before Jax could protest, she bent and scooped up his legs. His body lifted into the air, draped between her arms.

"Hurley, wow," Jax said. It was a weak attempt to stop her, caught between feeling ashamed for needing to be carried, and being amazed that she could carry him. Maybe he had lost more weight than he thought in the arena.

Hurley didn't respond. Her eyes stayed focused on the street ahead of her, and her breathing came in heavy puffs from the strain. She was stronger than Jax had assumed. In every way, she was stronger.

She carried him through the city, winding in and out of

alleys. Moxie reappeared and led the way, squeaking whenever Grimshaw stopped to rest. Finally, they stopped at an old brick store.

Inside, books lined the walls on slender book cases. Three tables with wooden chairs sat in the space between the door and a bar counter. There were several large canisters of herbal air with little tubes dangling from breathing masks daintily propped up on a miniature coat rack. A dog Animalis stood behind the counter, watching them come in.

"Is this where the Atticus is? Is Hank here?" Jax asked. He felt as vulnerable as a baby held by its mother. Hank couldn't see him like this.

"Hodge?" Grimshaw called.

They went through a curtain on the side of the bar into a back room. There was a wall screen with a heat radiator, animating a fire burning within a coarse fireplace.

"Hodge, can you tell me what Jax needs?" Grimshaw said with a heavy strain in her voice from holding Jax.

Hodge was beginning to lift a box from a cabinet, but put it back.

"Jax!" Hodge said. He sniffed, then growled. "You were with a bear? In the arena?" He perked back up. "I'm glad to see you, very glad to see you again."

Grimshaw set Jax down in one of the soft chairs by the fire, and after a moment, he realized that it wasn't a wall screen at all; it was a real fire, giving the room warmth and an acid scent. Grimshaw pulled her hair back into a fiery ponytail before looking at his leg again. Her fingers gently lifted the tattered fabric of his pant leg. Hodge grabbed the armrest, crouching next to her.

"You got scratched up pretty good by the bear. You made it out alive? Did …" Hodge hesitated. "Did you have to kill it?"

Jax could feel pressure from Grimshaw's hands touching the stump of his leg. "I don't know what happened to the bear," he said. "After it got my leg, I didn't bleed at all. I'm not sure why. I didn't have time to do anything but get out. I know that's not normal, but why wouldn't I bleed?"

"Hodge, what do you think of this?" Grimshaw asked, not listening to Jax.

Hodge looked at the leg for a moment, and then at the rest of Jax.

"Hurley, he's fine. A lot of adrenaline, very scared. Not a lot of blood loss, still strong," Hodge said.

"The wound is wide open, Hodge! Of course there was a lot of blood loss," she said. "Smell him—focus! What do we need to do for the leg?"

"It's fine. There's nothing to do. What do you think, Jax? It doesn't hurt, does it?"

"I didn't bleed, Hurley," Jax said again, "or else I wouldn't be here."

Grimshaw scowled, looking from Hodge to Jax and back to the leg. Jax should have been in shock like her, but he hadn't had time to. In basic training, he had learned what would happen to someone with an injury like this. Blood should have gushed out. Not just from his artery, but also his bone and muscles. His body couldn't stop the blood flow with coagulation or swelling. Within ten minutes, he should have been dead.

Instead, his blood had seemingly pulled up and away from the open end of his leg. There was no good explanation for it. Unless it had something to do with the voice he had heard …

Grimshaw finally spoke: "So … the blood must be blocked. Could there be a hemorrhage in his calf? Does it hurt anywhere in your leg, Jax?"

It hurts everywhere, Jax wanted to say, but he was still thinking about the possibility of strange forces acting on his leg. Then there was what Hodge had said. He felt the burn and itch at the tip of the stump. It was annoying, but now that it was suggested that it didn't hurt, maybe he had thought it was hurting because he had expected it to.

"Yeah, it hurts everywhere, but not much in the calf. Even the stump doesn't hurt that bad. It burns, and itches," he said.

"Oh, it itches." Hodge panted a little. "Better scratch it. I love being scratched." He reached for Jax's stump in an attempt to scratch it.

"Hodge!" Grimshaw swatted his hands away. A piece of Jax's ragged skin tore off in the commotion. "Oh! Jax, I'm sorry." She turned on Hodge. "Hodge! What's gotten into you? Please, get some cream and bandages for him. And I need the CT scanner."

"It's alright, Hurley," Jax said. "I didn't feel anything. It's like all that skin is already dead." He reached down and tore away another inch long piece. "Where are we, Grimshaw?" He looked around the room. "Where's Hank?"

Hodge left to get a medical kit for Jax. Grimshaw looked closer at the ragged stump, delicately moving pieces of the skin with her finger. It hadn't bled where Jax had ripped the skin from.

"We're in the back room of an herbal air shop. The shop owner is part of a group that has been helping us while we looked for you, and the pyramid." She winced as she turned his leg to look at his calf. "If it hemorrhaged, we're going to need to cut out the clot. It can't be this main artery, or you would have bleed to death anyway." She stopped looking at the leg and started assessing the rest of Jax's wounds. "Hank is still looking for the pyramid. When the Animalis took you, he wouldn't quit, and eventually he found where their plane had landed, here in Moscow. But their plane had gone to a private airport and we couldn't trace it from there. That's when we separated. He stayed in the Atticus, and has been looking for you with whatever he does on the internet. You and the pyramid. Oh …" Grimshaw looked to her right.

Jax noticed the dog Animalis peeking through the curtain.

"And it's given us a chance to see some old friends," Grimshaw said, nodding to the dog.

It wagged its tail, and turned away to let the curtain close.

"Do you want me to get Hank? We can let him know you're back." Grimshaw held Jax's shoulder.

If Jax had counted the days right, he had been away for a month, hoping to be found and taken back to their company. What would they do with him now? Now that he had lost his foot? Would they send him home? His mind clouded over. "I …" He didn't know what to say.

"Let's get all of your scratches patched up before you move again," she said.

Hodge came back into the room with a medical kit.

Grimshaw looked into his eyes. "Jax, we don't have to do anything right now. Don't think about it. Just rest and let us take care of you."

They worked quickly to spread an ionized bacteria cream over the end of the leg and the scratches covering his body. Within a few days, the modified bacteria would help to fight off infection, and promote healthy skin growth that would leave the skin with virtually no scars.

Then Grimshaw passed the CT scanner over his leg. She stood up and walked to the curtain. "I'll use the wall screen in the shop."

When she came back, she looked more concerned and bewildered. "There was nothing in your leg. Maybe it … Well, it wouldn't make sense."

She passed the scanner over the rest of him and went back to look at the data.

"I don't see it," she said once she had returned. "There's nothing." She sat down on the footrest in front of Jax and looked at him like he was an alien object. "An inch above your shin, the blood vessels just sealed themselves. I've never even heard of that happening."

After another moment, looking at him with bewilderment, she went back to checking the rest of his body for injuries.

Jax didn't ask any more questions while they finished covering his wounds.

What am I going to say to him? Jax imagined himself standing in front of his dad, each with their own pathetic robotic limbs, and his stomach filled with a sickening dread. Jax could never use a robotic limb like his father had.

Hodge and Grimshaw lifted him and carried him down a hall and into a small, bare room. They laid him on the bed.

"I can't believe we found you," Grimshaw said. She grabbed his hand and rubbed it warmly. "You would have frozen, being out there in the cold all night."

"The people from the arena, the Animalis, they're looking for me." Jax let his head sink down onto the thin pillow.

"Then we'll stay here. You don't have to worry about anything," she said through her smile. "You're safe now."

17
ACTS

The morning light streamed in through Jax's window. Particles of dust floated serenely in the air with nothing to do and nowhere to be. The heat from the sun warmed the wool blanket on top of his legs.

He thought about getting up, but even thinking it made his head pound. He had finally made it out of his prison, but now, laying in bed, all of his muscles were useless, reduced to a body of bones and gelatin. *Don't make me move, don't make me get out of bed.*

A light knock came at the door.

"Jax? Alright if I come in?"

When he didn't say anything, the door creaked open, and Grimshaw stepped in. Her hair was already done, held in place by a colorful headband. She was holding a large glass of water in one hand and a bowl in the other.

"Don't get up," she said, coming over to him. "I have some borscht for you to eat. It's the best. Nothing will help you get back on your feet ... um, faster. Sorry. And you'll want to drink this before you start getting a headache." She set the glass on the nightstand, and pulled a chair over to sit down. "A day without water will do that to you." She waited for him to take a long drink, and then brought the bowl over.

It was a bowl of the most horrific red. Deep, thick, coagulated red. Something white floated in the middle of it.

"Beets. It looks disgusting, but it really is the best," she said.

Jax poked the white mass with the spoon. The metal sank into it easily, and as the two colors mixed, vomit pink emerged.

"So, I guess the captain just let me stay in that cage," Jax said, "waiting to die. Where was Hank—where were you?"

"I—" Grimshaw looked startled by the accusation.

Jax knew they were there while he had been in the cage. They had to be there, maybe even watching him, as soon as Moxie had shown up with food. His moment of exuberance and pride at having freed himself the day before had quickly disintegrated under the heat of his anger at having realized this.

"The pyramid. The attacks in Australia. I wanted to help. I wanted to be there to save people. Why didn't you get me out?" Jax turned away from her to hide the tears swelling in his eyes.

"I'm so sorry, Jax."

"Why would you send food in with Moxie? Why? Why not just get me out? I lost my leg!"

"Moxie brought you food?" she asked. "We couldn't find her. When we left Australia, we thought we had left her behind, run away. I would have come, Jax. Hank, Hernandez, we all would have been there if we had found the arena in time. But we weren't fast enough and I'm so so sorry for that."

Jax continued to make vomit pink by stirring the soup.

"And they didn't catch her?" Grimshaw said. "They'd have smelled her in there. And the extra food."

"She was there—definitely there. I don't know why they didn't smell her or the food, but she was there."

"I believe you," she said.

"How long are we staying here?" Jax sank back into bed.

"We can stay for as long as it takes for you to recover, at the pleasure of the ACTS: Animalis Community of Thewy Saints. They own this complex. Anyway, I'll let you get back to your rest. Sorry to have upset you."

"Thewy?" Jax scooped a spoonful.

"Yeah. It means to have muscular, or mortal strength. It doesn't mean a lot to us, but here in their community it's like an anthem. It reminds them that they have the strength to protect themselves and the ones they love. But it also makes their acronym ACTS. Like 'Acts of the Apostles.' Have you ever read the Bible?" She held the door.

"No. Are they going to make us read it, in return for letting us stay here? Is there such a thing as a religious Animalis? I mean, do they even have souls?"

She held the door, ready to walk away, but hesitated. "They do a lot here for the Animalis," she said. "It's important work." When she looked at him, her eyes moved over his face like she was searching for something. She paused for another moment, smiled, and closed the door behind her.

When she was gone, Jax took another drink of water and eased back down under the covers. The borscht would have to wait. It was more exhausting than he wanted to let Grimshaw know, sitting there, trying to make her think that he didn't need help.

But his moment of reclusion didn't last. He had to go to the bathroom.

He pulled the covers back and moved his legs to hang over the side of the bed. There it was. One good, healthy, normal leg, and one that ended in the middle of his shin. The foot, ankle, and just over half his right shin were gone. He rubbed his hand over the bandage and winced at the tenderness.

He pushed himself up and balanced against the wall. *It's just walking,* Jax told himself, *the easiest thing in the world.* He stood, breathing slowly, feeling his heart throb in his head, watching the crack of light under the old hinge-style door.

But he couldn't move. He couldn't walk. He couldn't even move to the ground without falling over. Trapped in the most normal human position, standing. The leg beneath him began to tremble, shaking under his weight.

Help, Jax wanted to whimper. *I can't do it.* Tears swelled up in his eyes, blurring the floor in front of him. He could feel a sick fear taking over his mind.

Finally, the urge to pee pushed him past his fear of falling, and he crept down the wall with his hands. There was a small thud as he landed on the ground.

Jax got back up on his hands and knees, making sure not to bump or agitate the stump of his calf, and crawled. *Please don't let anyone see,* he pleaded.

"Excuse me. Just one more minute, please. Oh, Jax, out of bed already?" Jax had swung the bathroom door wide open with Hodge still sitting on the toilet.

"Oh, sorry, Hodge. I—Sorry." Jax tried feebly to reach the handle again to close the door.

"Don't worry about it, Jax. Turn around for a second. I'm just about done."

Jax turned around in embarrassment.

"You mind locking the door next time?" Jax scolded. He heard the sound of flushing.

"The door doesn't lock, unfortunately." Hodge began washing his hands. "I'm glad to have some company. I don't understand the human need to be alone in the bathroom. It's great spending some time in a place like this. So many other people around."

Jax didn't really have anything to say. The headache was enough, and now a cold sweat was emerging from his exertion.

Without asking, Hodge scooped Jax up under his armpits and brought him to the toilet.

"Don't. Hodge, put me down!" Jax said.

"I have to help when there needs to be help. That's what I can do." Hodge was just as peppy as usual. "Myself, or others. And I wouldn't want to be alone, just helping myself."

"Yeah, well, sometimes it makes people uncomfortable when you help, Hodge." Jax waited, sitting on the toilet with his pants on. Hodge started to close the door.

"Thanks for coming back, Jax," Hodge said and closed the door. Jax could still hear him outside for a moment. "I think he likes me. I hope so. Hurley says he does, but ..." And he walked away from the door.

———

Jax spent the rest of the day lying in bed. While he was awake, he stared up at the white ceiling, trying to make his thoughts as blank as its surface until he slept again.

Grimshaw came in the evening with more food. She knocked on his door but he pretended to be asleep. The door opened and he heard bare feet cross the floor. The food gave off a savory, buttery smell. Against his will, his stomach rumbled and his mouth began to salivate. She placed it on the nightstand and took away the half-eaten borscht.

"Hodge is working on a surprise for you." Her voice was soft.

Jax held still. When he finally heard the patter of her feet leaving, he almost called out "Don't leave me," but held it back.

The next day, he avoided talking to Grimshaw. When she brought food, he turned his head away from the door and pretended to be asleep.

They hadn't told Hank he was alive yet. The captain didn't know. He felt like he would never be ready to contact them again. Once he told them he had lost his leg, it would be enough for them to send him home. The leg would be enough. He wouldn't have to tell them he couldn't even kill the bear. They had to discharge him from the army. He was useless to everyone if he couldn't kill to save his own life.

When he thought of being discharged, like his father had been, he turned his face against his pillow and cried, or screamed, or bit it, furiously.

Jax found a Bible in a drawer on the nightstand and flipped through it. He found a touch screen attached to the back cover containing references, a search function, and a rudimentary message board with:

1 unread message

Jax tapped on the note and a password box came up. He quickly typed in ACTS, and received an access denied message. He considered other words that might have significance to these Animalis. He tried thewy and the message appeared:

> 11/2/2091 – 4:00 a.m. - Meet for plan of attack.
> What weapons will be needed, etc.

The date was for tomorrow.

———

Jax woke early in the morning with the stub of his leg throbbing. It was still dark. Jax pulled the covers back and felt his leg. It stung under his touch. There was something different about it. He unwrapped the bandage and brushed his hand over the tip. The ragged skin flaked off easily, and the rough edge of the bone had been covered in something. He'd check it again in the light of the morning; he couldn't tell what it was in the dark.

"Are you done feeling sorry for yourself, Jax?" he whispered. "Whining about losing a tiny little foot? You're weak. Hank needs you, and you're just lying in bed. You can do this. Get back up. Don't quit."

He slid off the bed and started prepping his body for a workout.

He didn't want to keep struggling to stand. He didn't want to lay down and give up. He didn't want to keep fighting in this confusing conflict with the Animalis. He didn't want to be sent home to live a life that didn't make a difference. More than anything, he didn't want to be powerless.

The floor creaked outside his room. A light came in through the slit at the bottom. There was a light tap, and the door squeaked open.

"Jax?" Grimshaw asked. She stepped in quietly and held a small hand lamp to light her path. Her eyes were wide awake, her hair was done, and she was ready for the day. "You're up? Did you fall out of bed?"

Jax had stopped at the top of a sit-up. He dropped his hands away from his head and started to get up.

"No. I'm fine. You're up early," he said. *You'd have to be for a 4am. meeting.* He turned around to straighten the blanket on his bed.

The light of her lamp pulled his shadow down onto the bed. Her hand touched lightly on his back. His muscles tensed.

"I can't imagine what you must be going through right now, Jax. The arena is one of the things I despise most in this world. The Animalis, turning themselves into demons, forcing everyone around them to sink down with them." She reached down and helped pull the bottom corner of the blanket straight.

"Hurley," Jax said. With a quick turn, he caught her wrist and held it while he whispered to her. "What are they planning to attack? Are these militants?"

"What? Militants? No, Jax, never."

When she didn't try to pull away from him, he let go of her arm. "How could you help them, Hurley? They're killing people."

"It's so much different here," she said.

She sat down on the side of the bed and held the light on her lap. Jax finally raised his head to look at her. Eyes twinkled with the lamp glow.

He reached for the Bible in the nightstand. "I saw a message in here about weapons. Are you killing people to save Animalis?" Jax set the Bible back down and saw that his hand was shaking.

"That's something that we have to constantly watch out for," she said. She leaned forward and placed her hand over Jax's. "These people here wouldn't be helping anyone if they resorted to killing. You should come with me to the meeting, just to see what they have to go through. Jax, they've been hurt and taken advantage of, and it's not easy for them to keep letting it happen. Sometimes they want to fight and kill, like the militants. But it would only make it worse."

Jax nodded. "Why do they need weapons, then?"

Grimshaw let his hand go while he eased himself back onto the bed.

"Well, it's going to be exciting," she said and her green eyes twinkled. She stood and helped him swing his legs onto the bed. Then she gasped. "Oh my gosh, Jax! Your leg."

Grimshaw set the lamp on the bed and crouched down to get a better look.

"What is this, skin?" she asked.

Jax turned his knee so he could see the end of his stub. A film of semi-translucent skin had spread over the ragged bone and tissue.

"That's not normal?" Jax asked. Of course it wasn't normal, but he didn't want it to be getting worse. He tried to rub his hand over it gently, but the sensitivity was too intense.

"No, I don't think so. Not this fast," she said. Then she turned her head to the door and muttered, "Hodge, what's wrong with you?" She turned back to Jax. "Maybe we should have taken you to a hospital. It looks like there's new skin growing over the bone, but if there's any bacteria, or infection starting, that could be serious."

"But what about these Animalis here?" Jax said. "Running around with weapons isn't 'exciting,' Hurley, it's illegal."

It took a moment for Grimshaw to stop gaping at the leg, but when she did, she let out a long breath. "You're right. It is illegal, but I don't know what else they can do." After another moment of silence, she looked into his eyes. "Come to the meeting. They could use your input. I need your input."

Jax was relieved she had changed the subject. He didn't want to think about the leg. *It's just skin—that's a good thing.*

"I could try," he said.

After a moment, she put her hand on Jax's knee and held it. "No one else could have made it out of the arena. I don't know how it would be possible not to give up." She picked the lamp up and started walking to the door. "I still want to get another scan of your leg, though. Would you mind?"

"Okay," he said.

"Good. The meeting is in ten minutes. I'll come back and take you to it."

Grimshaw watched him for a moment before closing the door behind her. The light in the room was gone. He sat, staring into the darkness with his thoughts swirling around him.

Maybe the Animalis he was with were militants, maybe not. He shouldn't have been so angry with Grimshaw. She was only helping. And his leg, what was happening to it? The one explanation that came to mind was the voice that had promised to protect him.

18
Meeting

Jax held onto Grimshaw's shoulder, standing against the wall in the secret meeting room in the basement of the compound. The light came only from the ceiling, radiating from three long panels. The room lacked windows or wall screens, and the only furnishings were six long benches.

Jax was wearing the clothes the priest had given him. Thick, tan canvas pants that tied in the back, and a gray wool shirt that was very warm—and very itchy. Seated around on the benches were a dozen Animalis, who all took turns glancing nervously back at him.

"These homes are built into the mountainside. They're part of the rocks, very genius, very clever for their day," a hairy dog Animalis said. "They have fresh water that comes from the melting snow and heat is directed from surrounding rocks to grow gardens—very clever."

Another Animalis in the crowd stamped its foot, startling the dog.

"Yes, well. Not all of it still works," the dog said, shifting away from the noise. It began pacing in front of the room. "The three families that have stayed there will freeze when this storm hits at the end of the week." It stopped in front of a ram Animalis.

"Gaspard knows the mountainside there, and will be leading the team down to the transports."

The dog walked to a goat Animalis. Jax strained to look past a tall horse to see what the goat was holding. The goat stood and held up its prizes for the group to see. They were sleek gray rods with two thick rings of blue plastic at their tips.

Jax squeezed Grimshaw's shoulder and gave her a questioning look.

"Sonic inhibiters," Grimshaw whispered. "Farmers use them to herd animals."

"I know. How did they get them?" Jax asked.

The goat at the front of the room was saying something about marauders in a canyon.

"There's more sympathetic humans," Grimshaw said. "They see how the Animalis are treated so they want to help. Those two inhibitors are a few years old and were being sold cheap, so someone in our network picked them up." She turned and looked at Jax. "Would you speak to them? Tell them why they shouldn't bring the inhibitors?"

Jax turned back to the room and watched the Animalis talking. He watched their arms, giving recognizable gestures. He watched their faces. They were all so familiar: dog, goat, cat, raccoon. He had seen these faces his entire life, but was only just coming to understand the thoughts and emotions going on behind the faces.

After a moment, he nodded.

Grimshaw reached up and squeezed his wrist. She turned back to the group and stepped forward.

"Excuse me," she said loud enough to get everyone's attention. "Jax doesn't want us to bring the inhibitors."

Jax stayed leaning against the wall, afraid he'd tumble to the ground without the support. He felt all the eyes on him. Most of them had never seen him before.

"I joined the military to stop Animalis that threatened humanity," he said. "There are groups that have bombed, shot, and mauled humans. Led by monsters like Narasimha."

Some in the group nodded at this. But he also heard the name "Narasimha" echoed by someone in a reverent whisper.

"If you go out there to help, but break the law, or look like a threat in any way," Jax said, "you are doing more harm than good. If you save these families by force, you're only going to bring more trouble to the Animalis." Jax took a deep breath to pace himself.

While he was exhaling, one of the Animalis spoke up. "We could be killed by marauders! These humans are willing to attack other humans. No one will care if we protect ourselves from thugs."

"Quiet, please," Grimshaw said.

"It doesn't matter," Jax said. "They could be the worst humans, but as soon as you use force against them, any attack from Animalis is an attack on humanity."

The goat at the front of the room lowered the inhibitors and began murmuring. Jax could hear bits of conversation like, "Protect ourselves" and "Why die for new families?" coming from among the crowd.

Grimshaw took the lead: "We have to help these families. It'll be dangerous; it always is. How many of you would be here if someone else wasn't willing to risk their lives? I'm going out there today to bring back these families. If our group gets attacked by the marauders, it will still be worth it. I can't bear to see the innocent die. No human can." She turned to Jax. "No human can."

And no human can bear to be the cause of innocent death, Jax thought. "You're going?" he asked.

She nodded.

The thought of a dangerous gang in the mountains jumped to the front of Jax's mind. Marauders wouldn't just kill Grimshaw. Men willing to kill were usually willing to do much worse. Jax looked around the room again. It was what all of these conspirators would be facing. And he was telling them they couldn't defend themselves.

Grimshaw was strong. She had been trained in the military. But Jax didn't want her to go.

"I can't come with you, Hurley," Jax said. "I'm no good, I can't even walk."

She looked at him with a surprised, skeptical look. "Well, maybe you can come on the next one."

Jax closed his mouth, realizing what he had been suggesting. He wasn't ready to volunteer his life for the Animalis just yet.

The meeting continued. Animalis discussed plans, and Grimshaw continually forced them to come up with backup plans. If all went well, it would be a fast operation. The group would leave before breakfast and be back for lunch.

When it was over, Grimshaw helped Jax get back to his room.

"While I'm gone," she said, letting him steady himself on her shoulder as they entered his room, "try not to tell Hodge what I'm doing. He'd want to come, and he'll worry to death if he knows it's dangerous."

"Alright," Jax said.

Before he knew it, she had wrapped her arms around him. "Thanks for coming back in one piece."

Jax didn't know what to do. The coals in his chest heated up.

She started to laugh. "Oh no." She stopped hugging and held his shoulders, giving a sympathetic frown. "Mostly one piece."

Jax smiled.

"I'm sorry," she said between fits of laughter. "It's not funny."

Jax wanted to laugh with her, but the humor was lost to him.

A tear leaked down her cheek. She covered her mouth, trying to hold back another burst of laughter, but it came out anyway.

"I'm sorry. I'm really sorry. This is terrible. It's not funny. I don't think losing your leg was funny." She wiped the tear off her cheek. She seemed to gain control of herself as she reached the door. "They'll have breakfast ready soon, if you want to join Hodge."

"Alright," he said. As she left, closing the door behind her, Jax could hear the laughter escape with a restrained snort.

19
Regeneration

Jax kept finding himself gripping his fork too hard during breakfast. Grimshaw was in danger and there was nothing he could do about it.

Once he had cleared his plate he headed back to his room to give his mind a rest. When he left the group of Animalis cleaning in the kitchen, he got down on his hands and knees to crawl. The knot in his left calf had stretched down and was starting to cramp up the middle of his foot. His stump hadn't stopped throbbing, either.

Once in his room, he took out the pins that held the folded end of the pant leg and pulled the fabric back to reveal his stump. The skin really had moved in fast, hadn't it? And there were several tiny lumps that had formed near the center.

Jax sprawled out on the bed, trying not to imagine either Grimshaw's or his own gruesome death.

There was a knock at his door, and Jax realized he had fallen asleep.

"Jax?" Grimshaw said. "Hodge has something for you. You're not going to believe it when you see it."

He sat up before she came in. Her shirt and pants were a vibrant blue. Two multicolored strips of fabric started on her chest and flowed up over her shoulders and came together in a billowy arch just above the small of her back. It was unique, out of fashion, but completely adorable on her.

"Everything went well?" Jax asked, trying not to show his relief. "You're back—everyone made it back?"

Grimshaw nodded but held her finger to her lips and glanced at Hodge, who had followed behind her holding something behind his back.

"I'll tell you later," she said.

"Now, it's not going to be very comfortable. No, I wouldn't like it at all. I don't even like these clothes. Tore off my first clothes when I was a pup. But I hope you like this, Jax. I hope you really like it." Hodge's tail was flipping back and forth through the air.

He pulled his arms out from behind his back, revealing a mass of harnesses and a robotic foot. Beneath a semitransparent plastic outer case were motors, gears, and power cells, crammed together into an intricate reproduction of human muscles.

Jax dropped his hands away and stared at it with a blank expression. He felt hollow.

Grimshaw took it from Hodge and brought it to the bed. She knelt down and held the piece of metal up for Jax to see.

He pulled away from it. "No. I don't need that." He tried to laugh. "That's ... I couldn't use that."

"Do you want to try it on?" Grimshaw's face sparkled like it was Christmas.

"It's just ... The end of the leg is still so sensitive." He looked at Hodge. "I can't use that, Hodge."

They both held on to their excitement. Grimshaw looked at Hodge.

"There are lots of designs to choose from," Hodge said. "This one is specific for sensitive limbs. See these cables?" Hodge pointed to thick, vertical lines starting from varied heights on the harness, and extending to varied depths on the robot ankle. "Those all capture the weight of your body, and bypass the tip of the leg."

Jax chanced another glance at the robot limb and felt his stomach acid curdle. He did want it. He wanted it to make him normal so he could walk, run, jump, and pretend nothing had ever happened. And it was that desire that made him want to throw it.

"Are you alright?" Grimshaw asked.

Jax kept the prosthetic dangling in front of him. He could just wear it, not think about it. There wasn't anything to fight against anymore. It wouldn't hurt to wear it. He could just give up again and let it happen.

"It's … Can you show me how to put it on?" he managed to say.

Grimshaw glowed with excitement. "It'll be easy. Maybe you'll forget that you ever even lost it."

———

Walking on the robotic leg hadn't seemed like a challenge until Jax had to move to avoid the young Animalis scurrying through the cramped courtyard within the ACTS compound. The weight was unnatural, and threw off his sense of balance. But it didn't aggravate the sensitive tissue at the end of the of severed leg, which made it bearable.

Grimshaw had volunteered him to help with a small winter carnival.

The walls of the courtyard created a space fifteen feet wide, twenty feet deep, and three stories high. Warmth came from the commotion of excited Animalis bouncing up and down, pushing each other to get closer to the activities Grimshaw had designed. Their voices were high pitched, quickly squeaking out Russian and English.

One of the larger children pushed past Jax, knocking him to the side. "Watch it!" Jax shouted. His prosthetic limb caught the ground and he began to tip sideways.

"Got you," a hand gripped his and stopped the fall. "Hold onto my hand." Grimshaw stood above him with an even more childish face than the ones running around them.

He let his hand wrap around hers and felt her pull him up. He tried to pay attention to the instructions she was giving him, showing him the bean bag toss where he would be giving out bracelets to winners, but the feeling of her hand in his overwhelmed his senses.

"And I'll be giving rides with this." Grimshaw held up the black flight suit he and Hank used before.

She left him on a stool with a pile of bean-filled sacks on his lap. He watched her move past Hodge, popping popped corn, to where she had placed a table to take off and land from. Jax turned away to find an army of faces waiting for him. His first customer was a small horse Animalis, her thick blonde hair was held in a continual French braid down her neck. Her eyes were large and glistening, and there was a ring of white around her nostrils where snot had dried.

"Pozhaluysta," she said.

Jax tried to remember the rules Grimshaw had told him. He handed her the three bags, and pointed to the line she had to stand behind. "Don't cross that line." Then he pointed to the wooden board propped against the wall with three holes in it. "You have to get at least one bag through a hole." It seemed reasonable, but he wasn't sure that's what the rule was. He jingled the bracelets. "Then I'll give you a bracelet."

The little horse nodded. As she pulled the first bag over her head, her large tongue poked out and held tight to her upper lip, as if it aided her balance. She threw the bag, and it flopped to the ground in front of the board.

She threw the second one harder, and it slapped against the wall and slid to the ground.

Her eyes looked at Jax, scared that she might not get the prize. He raised his eyebrows.

The third throw was a mix of concentration and what looked like an effort to draw on magic powers. She kept her eyes on the board, held the sack with both hands, crouched like a tight spring, and then pushed up and out. The bag flew into the air and hit the side of the board. It stayed for a moment, then plopped to the ground without going through any of the holes.

Jax shook his head. "So close."

The horse looked down at the ground, twisting her bare toes against the dirt. The next child, a badger-looking creature, ran past her and gathered the three bags.

Slowly the horse stepped back, and other children moved in front of her, waiting for their turns.

He handed out the bracelets while watching Grimshaw. It was unbearable not to know how she felt about him. He wanted her to like him. She had gone out of her way to see him rescued, that was significant.

The child at the front of the line whinnied. "Pozhaluysta," the small voice said.

It was the horse again. She held her hands up to take the bean bags.

Jax almost laughed at her stubborn determination to get the bracelet. He gave her the bags and watched her fling them in increasingly desperate maneuvers. The third one skidded across the ground and stopped when it hit the board.

Her breath was heavy, puffing out in quick bursts. The next child pushed past her and gathered up the bags. Jax could see tears swelling, glistening in her eyes. She disappeared behind the crowd that was starting to grow smaller as the afternoon crept nearer.

Jax gave out his last bracelet to a spotted deer Animalis, and the last of the children, some of whom had already gone for rides with Grimshaw, turned to leave.

The horse stayed standing as the others moved back into the building. Jax stood up and walked to her.

"You tried hard," he said.

She kept her eyes on the board with holes in it.

He held his hand out for her to take. "Can I take you for a ride? Puzalshta?" He tried to use the word he assumed was please.

She looked up at him. Her eyes were wide with surprise. After a big sniff, she wiped her eyes and took his hand. "Spasibo," she said. She started to run, pulling him toward the table.

"I think it's my turn to give a ride," Jax said.

Grimshaw had landed and was letting a wide-eyed bird Animalis out of the harness.

"You want to?" She looked down at the horse. "Alright, it'll just be a minute."

Jax climbed into the straps and stuck the little diodes to the

213

back of his neck. Below him, he could hear Grimshaw talking to the horse in Russian. The horse said something and Grimshaw laughed and looked up at Jax shaking her head. "Nyet! ... Nyet." She stroked the little horse's braids, "Ready?"

With the horse strapped in, Jax started to feel her excitement. She couldn't hold still, looking up into the sky and bouncing in the harness.

The fans hummed to life, and the two of them floated off the table. The horse gave a squeal. He started to imagine what was in her mind, the thrill of riding up, free from gravity, into the air. *I'd want to go fast,* Jax thought.

He increased speed, quickly climbing to the top of the three stories. At the top, he stopped and felt the weightlessness turn his belly over. They started to drop.

"Eeee! Nyeeeet!" the horse cried. She pulled frantically on the harness and kicked her legs in a wild panic.

"Oh, stay calm. Stay calm, It's alright." Jax stopped the drop and stabilized in the air. He held her shoulders and kept trying to soothe her. "We're okay. We're not falling." He hadn't want to frighten her to death, poor thing. She was still struggling in a panic.

"Oh, I have to sneeze!" he said loudly. "Ah-choo!" And he flew backward as if the fake sneeze had pushed them. "Wooo! That's better." He kept his voice loud, trying to occupy her attention.

She stopped kicking, but was still breathing hard.

"Do you get sneezy up here, too?" Jax asked.

She looked up at him, still scared.

"Like this? Ah-choo!" he said, and pushed them back a tiny bit.

She nodded. "Ah-choo."

Jax pushed them back a few feet. "Wow! That's a big sneeze!"

Her head turned up again with a timid smile. "Ah-choo," she said with a little more enthusiasm.

Jax flew back again, turning to avoid the wall. "You want to go back down?" he asked.

She nodded.

"Alright, grab this rope." Jax pretended to hand her a rope. "And pull us down. Like this." He pulled his hands toward his chest, as if he were tugging on a rope, and made the fans lower them closer to the ground.

She nodded, as if convinced that it was the only way for them to get back down. Her eyes concentrated down at the table, and she pulled.

Jax slowly descended. By the time they reached the table, the little horse was bouncing up and down in the harness again, bubbling with excitement.

Grimshaw helped her out, and as the horse ran back to the building she called out, "Spasibo! Spasibo!"

When she had gone, the courtyard was empty except for Jax and Grimshaw. She smiled up at him. "That was so much fun to watch. I'm sure she feels like the most special kid here."

Jax frowned. "I nearly made her cry. I guess I don't have the same magic touch that you do with the Animalis."

Grimshaw held her hand up to help Jax climb off the table. Jax took her hand, and said, "Do you want to go up one more time? With me?"

Her eyes sparkled and the dimple appeared on her cheek. Her hand held tighter around his. She leaned forward to climb up, but then stopped. Jax could see her smile flatten. She paused, gazing at nothing. She let go of his hand.

"We'd better go in for lunch. You know how fast the food goes here. Come on, I'll clean this up later." When she looked back at him, her smile was back, but the sparkle had left her eyes.

Of course she wouldn't go up with him. He had fooled himself into thinking they could pretend it was an innocent ride, like the Animalis children on their carnival ride. But being so close to her, held together by the harness—he could already feel the butterflies, moving around, brushing their delicate wings against the insides of his stomach. She didn't feel the same way, and wasn't about to lead him on.

"Yeah, I'm starving," he said, sniffing the air.

"Maybe another time," Grimshaw said, taking his hand again to help him down. She winked and squeezed his hand warmly.

He used a boost from the flight suit to ease off the table, letting Grimshaw's hand guide him to the ground. While he took the harness off, Grimshaw kept talking.

"Do you think it's time to tell Jesus, and Hank, that you made it back?" she asked delicately, but the reminder was abrasive for Jax to hear.

He didn't want to have to think about it. But she was right: he had to tell them. He stayed silent but nodded.

20
Tessard Minette

Jax stood in the small herbal air parlor facing the lone internet-connected wall screen. It was growing late. Outside the small windows, the streets were lit with a warm electric glow. The dog Animalis that manned the shop was slouched over the counter. He drifted in and out of sleep.

Hollow nervousness squeezed at Jax's lungs. He had been able to hide for the last week, but now he had to tell someone he was alive. Even though it was Hank's call icon stuck on the wall, waiting to be dialed, he couldn't lift his hand to connect.

What if the leg isn't enough? Will he make me stay? He tried to imagine joining Hank again, holding a rifle, raising it to his shoulder. *I can't hesitate again.* But he wasn't sure he would be able to. In the arena, with the bear's neck in his arms, he couldn't do it.

He felt ashamed and terrified to admit it. For most of his life, he had accused his dad of cowardice, sure that he would never be like him, sure that there had been weakness in his father that he could find in himself—and eradicate.

But he hadn't. By the time he could finally see the root of what he was so scared of becoming, it was too late. Now they were just alike, pretending they hadn't quit, walking around with a robotic crutch.

It felt like there was a wall in front of him, just as impassable as in the arena, and he couldn't get over it.

He moved his hand to the wall and began typing. He removed Hank's name and typed in *Tessard Minette*.

The computer brought up a new icon. The face was as hard as stone. His eyes were thin, like Jax's.

Why had he pushed his father away so far? The face embossed on the wall could have been a stranger from the way Jax had treated him.

Now that I need him, how could he possibly forgive me? Jax thought. He held his finger above the *Call* button. They were a hemisphere apart: while the sun had just set for Jax, it would just be starting to rise for his father in the foothills of Colorado.

There was no one else he could ask. No one else knew the wall Jax had come to. He pressed the button to activate the call.

The icon faded away, melting with the rest of the menus, and a bell began to ring. After a moment, the bell clicked off and a new image emerged. His father squinted, peering up at Jax. There were streaks of black across his cheek and on the tip of his nose. His eyes widened briefly, and he ran a black-tipped hand through his short, thin hair. He stood in a garage, with pieces of an antique car spread out behind him. The dim morning light had turned the mountains in the window a pale purple.

He let out a heavy breath. "Jax?" He sounded surprised. "Is your mother not answering? Do you want me to go tell her to pick up?"

Jax coughed and shook his head. "No, Dad." He turned his head away from the lifelike replica of his father on the wall. He didn't know how to talk to him. "I wanted to talk to you."

Tessard blinked a few times, then he sat down at the desk and pushed his chair closer to the screen. "Alright. What's going on? Are you enjoying the army? Still able to hang around with …" He looked up for a moment. His hand clenched into a fist.

"Hank," Jax said.

"Hank, that's right," Tessard said, striking the table. "How's Hank?"

Jax nodded. He took a deep breath and let it out with a frown. "I'm sorry, Dad."

"Oh, no, is he alright?"

"Hank's fine. I'm sorry … that I didn't believe you. That I treated you so bad. I didn't know." Jax stopped before his pain turned into tears.

"Slow down," his dad said. "What are you saying you're sorry about? Did you do something wrong out there?"

"No," Jax said on impulse. He didn't want his dad to think he had broken the law, or gotten in trouble. But he was in trouble. "I …" *What am I trying to say? What did I want him to do?* "… I want to come home."

Tessard scowled. "You want to come home? It's too soon for leave time, isn't it?"

Jax didn't want to have to say it, but he would find out eventually. He put his hand against the wall for balance and held up the robotic foot. "I lost my leg." He flexed the toes and heard the whine of the electric motors working inside it. "I haven't told my captain yet."

His father looked stunned. "Your leg?" He kept looking at it and began shaking his head. He knew not to ask what had happened.

"I ..." Jax put the leg down and stood straight again. "I'm sorry I didn't understand." How could Jax expect him to care about him now? "I'm sorry I thought you were ... weak."

His dad looked through the wall screen into Jax's eyes with the same expression he always had when sizing up an old motor part that might keep his antique car running. He blinked again and looked away, seeming to decide that the part was just out of his budget.

"I'm sorry I let you," he said.

Someone called out in the background, "Tess?"

Tessard turned to the side. "Yes, hon. I'm on a call."

It was Jax's mother. He didn't want her to see him. It would be too much now, to see her reaction to his leg. *She'll cry,* Jax knew, and that would make him feel even worse.

"Let me finish. I'll be in for breakfast in just a minute." He turned back to Jax and shook his head. "She's always worried something like this will happen to you."

Jax nodded.

Tessard ran his hand through his hair again. "You want to know if coming home is the right thing to do? If I think I was right to come back?"

"Was it?" Jax asked. His hand moved unconsciously, rubbing the thick wool of his shirt between his fingers.

His dad looked up at the ceiling and rocked back and forth in his chair. His eyes closed when he spoke: "I guess I never tried to get you back, you know, make things right between us, because I hated myself, too. Maybe I thought you were right. I knew I could have stayed and finished off my commitment to the military." He brought his robotic arm up onto the table and looked down at it.

"You wish you would have stayed?" Jax felt his dread resurface. If he stayed, he'd feel the terrible fear over and over again, that he could die at any moment, that he would let everyone down by failing again.

"Part of me did. Part of me knew there was more I could have done. Every time I used this arm to do something I'd never thought I'd be able to do again, I felt guilty." He gave a reluctant smile. "But I was able to be home. Watch you grow up into the man you are. I don't think I've ever told you, but I'm so proud of you, Jax."

There was a sting inside Jax's chest, followed by a soothing warmth that began to spread out. It crept into his throat and went for his eyes. Jax swallowed. He felt his chest starting to shake.

"What hurt, was that my company had just been attacked. Lots of guys died, and I got away with just loosing my arm. But it was the start of a push that the Animalis were making on the city we were in. For a long time, I beat myself up for not staying." His dad nodded, as if to acknowledge the truth and the pain of what he was saying.

Jax pushed his fist under his eyes and wiped away the tears that were about to break over his eyelids. "They gave you a choice?"

"Once they got the wound sealed up," Tessard said, "they had me do some tests, some physical and some mental. I don't really know how they came out, but after it all, they just asked if I wanted to go home, and I said 'Yes.'"

Jax nodded.

"You said you wanted to come home ..." Tessard looked at Jax with a serious expression. "... but don't run away from someone that needs you. You're strong, and you're stubborn, and it takes a lot longer to get over letting yourself down than to give it everything you've got. You don't lose your responsibility to the people you leave behind; you only lose your ability to serve them."

Jax nodded again.

"Tess?" Jax's mother called again from the house.

"I'd better go." His dad stood up, tapping his human fingers against the tabletop. "I'm glad you called. It's so good to see you, son."

Jax held still, not ready to let go of the feelings that had opened up inside himself.

His dad started to reach for the wall to end the conversation. Jax took a deep breath. "I love you, Dad."

Tessard stopped and smiled cautiously. He moved his hand over and delicately pressed it against the wall in front of him, where Jax's image must have been. "I love you too, Jax. I'll be glad to see you if you decide to come home."

Then he ended the call. The wall flattened out.

Outside, the sky had grown completely black. Jax stood for a moment, gazing out the window, feeling a calm, steady peace. When he was ready, Jax brought the menu back up and put in Hank's name.

———

Hank knelt on the hard floor of the lab with the black shadow of the pyramid making a thick X on the floor in front of him. Every half-second, his body shook with a powerful beat from his heart. An intense urge to vomit passed over him, but he held it in. His skin was cold and damp with sweat.

The symbols engraved on the surface of the smooth metal

shook with the pounding of his heart. He could hardly keep his vision straight to make a clear mental image of them.

An eerie creak echoed through the lab. Hank's eyes bulged and he held his breath. The hammering pulse in his chest seemed to scream for everyone to hear: "Intruder! Someone's here! Kill him!" A drop of sweat that had been building at his hairline cascaded down his forehead and dripped onto the floor—SPLASH!

Hank was on the verge of fainting from the strain of his secret, self-imposed mission: take advantage of the lack of security to prove the pyramid was the powerful DNA-altering machine that he claimed it to be. According to his observations, he had another fifteen minutes before he would come close to a possible encounter with one of the Animalis who worked in the lab. Except that creak sounded like someone was coming right now.

After another minute in a state of frozen panic, Hank let his pulse drop from the two hundred beats per minute range and returned to his task at hand. There were many ways he could prove the machine worked—but altering a small test animal's DNA would do. Something like the last time the machine had been used. But Hank wanted to do something *more*.

His index finger crudely traced the symbols on the metal beam. "Where is your interface?" he mouthed silently.

A melodic chime shattered the stillness around him, nearly sending Hank's heart to three hundred beats per minute. The sound was everywhere! He was caught! Doomed to die a short, pointless, insignificant, wasted life. He shouldn't have come!

Then Hank saw the icon floating in front of him, an image of a dusty-brown-haired boy with cheeks and a jaw that could have been carved from stone. The chime had been ringing in Hank's own head from his retina monitor's connection to his earpiece. And the face was just as ghostly and ethereal as the sound.

Hank weighed the risks of taking the call. He would have to speak aloud, which could ruin his stealthy mission. But there were no microphones in the room to record his voice, or else the many conversations he had spied on through the security camera would have given him more information. The call would take up valuable time. But if it really was Jax ...

The icon disappeared, and Jax was suddenly standing in front of Hank, four feet away, as a figment of Hank's augmented reality. But the call was real; the person on the other end was Jax. He hadn't died.

Hank's mouth trembled, still processing the shock of seeing Jax alive. He was wearing strange clothes. The pants were thick and fuzzy, and the shirt was woven with threads that could have been spaghetti strands. His weight was distributed disproportionately, not the way Hank had remembered him. The hips were shifted to hold weight off one of his legs, like he was injured somehow.

"Jax?" he whispered, so quietly that it didn't reach his own ears. "Jax!" he finally whispered again, a decibel louder. "You ... You look like ..." He sucked in a breath. "Like ... a preternatural ghost. Where are you? What happened?" He consciously pushed the fear out of his voice.

A smile spread across Jax's cheeks. He glanced left and right, as if expecting Hank's face to appear for the call, but without the thousands of tiny cameras embedded in a wall screen, only Hank's voice would come through.

"Hank? Are you there? I'm alive, but just barely," Jax said. "Can you see me?" He held up his leg for Hank to examine.

"Is that a Richester print? Looks like one of his prosthetic designs" Hank could see a metallic sheen where Jax's skin should have been, causing the alteration to his posture.

"It's what's left of my leg. I got sent to the arena, fought a bear, it bit my lower leg off, and I've been hiding out at a weird Animalis religious community building." Jax set the leg down and waited like a child expecting a punishment.

Hank started to sort the information into a timeline in his mind, but stopped at the Animalis religious building. Was he making a joke? "And you're staying with the bear?" he asked, coaxing the punch line.

"No, not with the bear. Hank, it's good to hear your voice again." Jax started to undo the buckles on the harness around his strange leg.

"After being alone with nothing but Animalis for two months, I'd hope so," Hank said. He checked the time—down to ten reliable minutes.

Jax pulled the attachment off and lifted the severed tip for Hank to see. His leg stopped almost halfway down his shin. Hank started to shake his head back and forth, still not wanting to accept the story Jax had told him.

"No, Jax. I'm so sorry. The bear—you really lost your leg. In the arena," Hank said. He could see the red around the rim of his eyes, too. "Your eyes—they took your retina monitor, too."

Jax went through the story with him, vividly describing the amount of blood and the stench in the cage. He told Hank he was staying with Grimshaw and Hodge, and gave him the location of the herbal air shop.

"You're with Grimshaw?" Hank asked. How could Hank have missed the signs of her lying? She had sent a video message earlier that day, and she was saying something about a … She and Hodge had been … No, that's right, she had told him, nearly a week ago, that her updates would be more infrequent. Hank had assumed she was giving up the search. He knew he should have kept track of her in secret, to make sure she wasn't taken to the arena as well.

"Good. That's good," he continued. "I'll let the captain know you're back."

Jax had gone through the arena, held prisoner by the Animalis. He must be tortured inside.

"We'll get even," Hank said. "We'll make the Animalis pay, end the arena forever."

After a short delay, Jax nodded.

But Hank knew that Jax didn't believe him. He didn't understand what Hank meant. "With the Ivanovich Machine," Hank said.

Now Jax looked even more confused. Hank decided not to elaborate, his time investigating the pyramid was running out. With the last five minutes, he would have to escape the lab and the building. He didn't regret taking the call, but it had been very unfortunate timing.

"You're alive!" he reiterated. "I've been busy, Jax. The pyramid, I've almost got it. I think so. It'll be in our hands soon."

Jax nodded. "Good. They haven't used it to kill everybody yet."

"No. Can you stay there? With Grimshaw? I'm not sure when I can come get you," Hank asked.

"Yeah, I think so."

"Good. Check your messages a couple times a day." Then he realized how distant he had sounded, trying to keep his nerves under control. "I'm glad you're alright. We are going to end up being heroes, Jax. I can't do this without you."

He ended the call. It would be good to have Jax with him again. He had made it out of the arena alive. The information was finally sinking in. *Incredible.*

———

Jax walked quietly through the curtain and down the hall back to his room. The hard plastic floor and colorless walls didn't seem as far from his normal life as before. Without contact from Hank, the building could have been light years away, on an alien planet.

Now he was back on Earth. He was in the army, under Hank's command. They were waiting for their chance to take back something that Hank believed was a terrible weapon. But there had been something so strange about the conversation. Hank had been disconnected, on edge from something.

Jax remembered the painful indifference from a dream about Hank while he was in the prison cell at the arena. Were they drifting apart?

His original question had been answered: Jax would stay put. People needed him; Hank needed him, and maybe the Animalis needed him. He wouldn't give up trying to help.

21

Gold Teeth

A week later, Hank still hadn't come for Jax, but the last message had left him feeling uneasy:

> I think I've got it. I think I've figured out how the pyramid works. Expect a message from me within three days. ~Hank.

It wasn't much to go off, but the promise of returning to the fight in just three more days made Jax anxious again. He hadn't told Hank yet about the details of the arena, or that he was struggling just to fulfill his commitment to the military. Jax's leg continued to ache, and the skin seemed to be growing thicker. Most of the time he could get around with the prosthetic, but it would never be the same.

In the meantime, the Thewy saints got another lead. A young mongoose Animalis that was a rising sensation as a lightweight boxer was in danger. The gym he trained at had discovered his mate was pregnant. The Animalis at ACTS expected some kind of public disgracing, something that would show that even popular Animalis had to follow the rule not to perpetuate their species.

This time, Jax was eager to get involved. He could go with Grimshaw on the mission, and it had something to do with fighting. Not just fighting, but boxing, the sport Jax had fallen in love with in high school.

"Two thousand UCs? That's a good down payment, but for what he's done, he's worth way more to me if he fights," the man with three gold teeth was saying. "His last fight tonight is going to be unforgettable anyways. There's no way I can let him go."

Jax stood beside Grimshaw, talking to the owner of the gym. Jax gestured to the boxing ring behind the man. "Is this where the matches are?"

The man smiled, revealing a fourth gold tooth. "Yes. This is where it happens. The crowds fill this entire room and it transforms. It comes to life." His thin chest rose with pride. The man was short and tightly built. His arms were covered in animating tattoos, and his blond hair was braided tightly to his scalp.

Jax looked around. The ground was worn colorless, and sections of plastic were beginning to roll back to reveal the deep blue foundation. Around the perimeter of the large warehouse, Jax saw sparring robots, weights, ropes, and a dozen humans and Animalis in little clusters. There was a sharp *slap-slap!* from padded fists striking at one of the robots.

"Four thousand, then," Grimshaw said.

Jax snapped his attention back to the conversation. He tried to match her bluff: "He's obviously not worth that much, but you can consider part of it as a donation for your gym."

"Ha!" The man turned and spat on the floor. "We bring in twice that much, every fight." He folded his arms and looked Grimshaw up and down.

Jax glanced at Grimshaw. She had tried to dress down for

the meeting, coming alone with Jax to barter for one of Mr. Gold Teeth's fighting Animalis, but the way she stood, spoke, and moved still revealed her classiness. Gold Teeth wasn't even paying attention to Jax anymore.

Jax elbowed Grimshaw in the side and pulled his head toward the door. "Let's go."

She frowned, but when Jax started walking away, she stepped in beside him. As they walked farther away from the gym owner, they heard him whine, then mutter "Bah." But he didn't give a counteroffer.

When they were a few yards away, Grimshaw whispered, "We can't walk away, Jax. They're going to take everything away from Rikki tonight—his children, and any possibility for future children."

"He's just trying to suck money out of you, Grimshaw. There's no way this place gets eight thousand UCs a fight."

"Well, he makes enough that he's not desperate for the money," she said.

Jax thought about it, slowing his walk. "It's not the money he's interested in," he said. "He loves the fight. It's everything to him. Even if you give him eight thousand, he's going to ask for more. This is a mongoose Animalis that we're rescuing, right? Mr. Gold-Fang back there has got to be upset that he can't use him anymore. He's losing a fantastic boxer."

"Maybe, but he's going to be an even better father when his mate's litter is born," she said. "Hmm. He only cares for the fight?" Within the next step, she slowed to a stop.

"That's it!" she said and turned around to walk back to the gold-toothed man.

"What's it?" Jax asked, struggling to catch up.

Ahead of them, the fourth golden tooth appeared on the man's face as his mouth widened into a grin. He unlaced his arms and stroked the braids that ran along the top of his head.

"Two thousand, and you get me to fight in his place tonight," Grimshaw said as they approached.

The man scowled. "No, eight thousand." He looked at Jax. "Why, who is she?" He looked back at Grimshaw. "Who wants to see you fight?"

Grimshaw launched her fist at the man's face. Jax didn't have a moment to react, and the man was even more caught off guard. His eyes went wide before her knuckles drove his head backward from the solid impact. He staggered backward.

"Wha—" he said. When he looked at her again, his eyes were alight with passion.

Her hand relaxed and went back to her side like nothing had happened. "I think people will want to see me fight."

Gold Teeth brought his hand up to his face, still looking over Grimshaw like she was a winning lottery ticket. "Two thousand?" he asked.

Jax held still, as surprised as the man, but not as thrilled. She should have volunteered *him* to fight. But the man wouldn't have reacted the same way if Jax had punched him just now. If this was a bluff on Grimshaw's part, he didn't know how they were going to get out of it.

"What weight class are you?" the man asked.

"Featherweight," Jax said, before she had a chance to look to him for help. If she was going to fight, it had to look like she knew everything about boxing.

Grimshaw looked back at the man.

"We don't do featherweight here. You're either lightweight or bantamweight." The man looked up and down her body again. "How much do you weight?"

She looked at Jax. He swallowed. He had guessed at her weight, aiming low to make sure that her opponent wouldn't be too heavy for her.

"One twenty-five," Jax said.

Grimshaw frowned with an offended look. "One thirty-four," she said.

"You're too heavy for bantamweight. You get bumped up into lightweight. It's a deal." The fourth golden tooth slowly emerged again. "Oh … and you'll be fighting me."

———

Later, while Grimshaw and Jax rode back to ACTS in an automated taxi, Jax couldn't hold it in any longer: "Why did you do that? You don't need to fight this guy, Hurley!"

"You said it yourself," she said. "He wouldn't accept more money. He wanted a memorable fight."

She had been quiet since the deal was made. Her knees were pulled up under her arms while she watched buildings pass outside the taxi's window.

"Can you really box?" he asked, rubbing his hand over the fabric covering his stump.

"Did you see the way he looked at me?"

Jax tried to pull up the visual memory but felt the sting of realization that his retina monitor was gone. He struggled for a moment to push his mind into the past. The moment after she punched him had left an impression on Jax; a look of intensity. He knew the look disturbed him, but he didn't know why.

"I nearly broke my hand when I hit him," she said. "I don't know anything about boxing."

As he watched her, Jax sat back in his seat. Ice cut through his heart. Something had happened to her. Her spirit and her zest for life was gone, like an animal that was resigned to die in its cage.

"Let's call the deal off," Jax said.

She continued to watch out the window and didn't respond.

Jax joined in watched buildings pass by and let his mind rest. There were no solid ideas, only restless worry. They passed a sushi restaurant that had a giant purple octopus with long, suction-cupped tentacles on its sign. The next building was a print shop, glowing neon orange—Hank's favorite color.

Jax sat up. "Maybe you don't have to fight," he said. Then he commanded the automated computer, "Taxi, turn around. We need to stop at that print shop back there."

"I want to fight him, Jax," Grimshaw said.

Jax hesitated. He knew she was strong. She was strong enough to carry him through the city. But she didn't know boxing. If she went into the ring, she was going to be beaten, and probably knocked unconscious.

"I know a way we can fight him together," he said.

"How?" she asked, a spark of her former self coming through again.

"Do you have sixteen hundred UCs?"

22
Fighting for Control

Jax ascended the stairs to the boxing ring, but it wasn't his body moving. He looked around at the crowd of people that filled the warehouse, marveling that the gym owner was right: it was completely packed.

He tilted his head to watch the live wall screens that would display the action of the fight to the back of the crowd. The person in the ring was Grimshaw. He looked down and saw thickly padded gloves at the end of her lean arms.

The newly printed strips of fabric that controlled her movements were placed over her entire body and blended in perfectly with her skin. Each sticky diode was latched onto her skin, sending the signals from Jax into her muscles as powerful electric impulses.

Jax was actually reclined in a chair—back in the herbal air shop at ACTS. His body was sedated, so that the commands from his brain were only being broadcast from the diode latched to the back of his head to the suit controlling Grimshaw. When he commanded his knee to lift up, the signals were picked up by sensors, and Grimshaw's knee rose up. His own body lay perfectly still on the chair.

"Everything seems to be working alright," Grimshaw

whispered. Her voice came in clear above the constant buzz from the crowd.

Jax had no way to respond to her comment except to nod his head in agreement, which forced Grimshaw to nod her head.

She still had free control of her face and voice, since the diodes stopped at the base of her skull. Otherwise, Jax could control everything, as long as he was careful not to let his concentration lapse, which would mean that Grimshaw herself would be back in control.

"Tonight's fight," a booming voice said throughout the warehouse, "has an unexpected twist." The chatter from the crowd fell as the lights faded. Spotlights filled the ring. "Our mongoose, Rikkitikki, seems to have a human admirer. She stands before you now, promising an even better show than what you were expecting."

Jax raised Grimshaw's hands over her head to draw cheers from the crowd, but he received only disappointed boos.

The voice droned on, "Behold, the reigning lightweight champion of Ireland …" But Jax was stressing about the fight. The last thing he wanted was to let Grimshaw be knocked out, especially while he was controlling her body. He would be responsible for every hit she took. Her body—her safety—was in Jax's hands.

"The reigning champion of Ireland?" Grimshaw muttered. "Just because I'm a redhead?"

Jax shrugged her shoulders.

Across from them, the man with four golden teeth, now glowing through a clear, plastic mouth-guard, slid between the ropes into the boxing ring. He looked a pale white with his shirt off. His muscles were small, but dense. Jax guessed that he really was in the lightweight class. He was thin and wiry.

The announcer went through a condensed version of the rules. "Don't hit below the belt. Strike with the front of the glove only. No kidneys, rabbits, or hits to the spine. Knockout is a count to ten, and there will only be four rounds of two minutes each."

A referee emerged through the ropes and walked to the center of the ring. Jax felt Grimshaw's body start moving to the center. He had lost concentration, and she was in control. It felt like she was walking his body toward the ref.

Jax carefully synced his movements with hers again, not wanting to topple her with two incompatible commands pushing parts of her body in different directions. He had to feel her arms moving, and begin moving his in the exact rhythm, until the two became one. He had to feel the muscles in her stomach, hips, and legs, while they constantly rebalanced to keep her standing. As he took control, her thighs first pulled his thighs forward, then his pushed hers back. He slowed her to a stop at the middle of the ring.

Gold Teeth met the two in the middle, facing Grimshaw with a dominating stare. His eyes slowly moved over her body.

Jax could feel her reaction. Her stomach tensed, and her breathing restricted.

Jax clenched her fist. He wanted to punch the man so bad.

The ref whistled, a bell rang, and the fight began.

"Oosh!" Gold Teeth shot forward, punching a quick jab at Grimshaw's head.

Jax hopped backward, keeping distance between them. Jax suddenly felt struck with fear: How could he force himself to put

Grimshaw in danger? Every blow that he delivered, she was sure to get hit in return.

Gold Teeth leaped forward again, pumping his fists out with hisses of breath: "Oosh, oosh!"

Jax backed away, letting the swings hit harmlessly against her boxing gloves. But he could feel her pushing his legs forward, stepping him toward the fighter.

Boom-boom. Two jabs connected with Grimshaw's gloves and forearms.

Jax could feel her body tense from the impacts. He couldn't feel the pain of it, but he could imagine it. All he could think about was that each strike he let through was his fault.

"Eess, eess!" Jax pumped Grimshaw's fists forward, forcing out two strained hisses from her mouth.

Gold Teeth blocked and Jax hopped her body out of range.

"I can take a hit, Jax!" Grimshaw said between breaths. "Go after this guy."

She started to push her body toward the fight again.

Gold Teeth was coming at her for more. Jax blocked another blow and hopped to the right, jabbing twice.

"Eess, eess!"

Her arms were knocked to the side with a quick block, exposing her face and chest to attack.

"Oosh!"

Grimshaw's head snapped backward. Jax could feel her muscles go limp for a moment. She was off balance and disoriented from the hit. *Stop it!* he wanted to shout at her. *Let me do the fighting!* Jax forced her arms back in front of her face and stepped back.

The punches kept coming. "Oo-oosh! Oo-oosh! Oosh, oosh!"

Jax had to step back. The jabs shook her arms, slamming her own gloves into her face over and over. Her body was tense. He had to fight past her urge to turn away from the punches and curl up.

Jax had no panic-stricken, adrenaline-fueled response happening in his mind. He was separate and safe from the fight. He could see what was happening in real time, and respond with a clear and calculated attack.

Jax dug Grimshaw's right leg into the springy surface of the ring and shot her fist through the oncoming punches. The jab connected with Gold Teeth's nose, sending his head backward with a streak of blood arching up through the air. Glowing particles of dust swirled in little tornado patterns where her glove had plowed through the air.

Gold Teeth staggered backward with a confused look at Grimshaw. His most recent punch trailed out uselessly in front of him. The crowd was taken by surprise. The only sound coming from the warehouse seemed to be the powerful beat of Grimshaw's heart.

From the neck diode, Jax could feel Grimshaw pulling muscles that connected around to the front of her jaw. She had to be smiling.

Gold Teeth wiped the blood leaking from his nose. When his glove came away from his face, his eyes were on fire. Jax could feel Grimshaw's body retreat away from the man's lurid face again.

"That's more like it," he said.

The bell rang, signaling the end of the first round.

The two fighters retreated to their own corners. Grimshaw sat on a stool where one of the ACTS members waited to massage her muscles and force-feed her water.

Around them, the crowd hummed with anticipation for the next round.

Gold Teeth's eyes didn't stray from Grimshaw.

"Jax," Grimshaw whispered. "I don't care about being punched, It doesn't hurt. All I want is to beat this creep,"

Jax slowly nodded her head.

The ref called the two fighters back to begin the second round. It would be two more minutes before the next break. Two minutes to block his punches and keep her safe.

The bell rang and Gold Teeth came at her swiftly.

Before Jax knew it, Grimshaw was pushing herself toward the oncoming punches. A fist swung at her from the side. Jax ducked to the right. Another fist was coming at her from the other side. Jax knocked it away and pushed forward to get inside the attacks.

Jax could hear the man's hot breath now. Gold Teeth was holding her before pushing her out to where he could swing at her again. Then there was a sound of wet sandpaper sliding on her skin, and every one of Grimshaw's muscles locked up. Jax lost control. He tried to move her away, but her body wasn't responding.

He licked her? Jax was dumbfounded. How could he let that happen to her? *Never again.* He could never let that happen again.

Gold Teeth pushed her away and Jax immediately hooked him in the side of the face. The man responded with a full onslaught of jabs. This time, Jax was the one to drive Grimshaw's body into the fray.

Jax knocked a punch away and hooked him in the side of the head again.

Another punch knocked Grimshaw's glove back into her face. Jax fainted left and jabbed again. "Eess!"

Pop-pow! Grimshaw was thrown backward with two powerful counterpunches.

The second bell rang after another minute of fierce punches.

When Grimshaw sat down on the stool, she gasped. "His breath. I can still smell his breath on me, Jax."

He could feel her chest constricting. Her whole body moved with the force of her breath. The movements triggered emotions inside Jax. He could feel her sense of powerlessness. He felt like he was nothing. He could feel defiance in her movements. She was trying to demand her opponent acknowledge her, but another emotion was telling her not to resist.

All Jax could do was bring her gloved hands up to cover her face.

After a moment, she pushed her head up out of the gloves and said, "I'm okay. You're doing great, Jax. Most of the time, I can't tell what's going on. But I love when my arms shoot out and I hit him in the face."

The third round began, and Jax dove into the fight.

Jax didn't hold back. He stayed close and jabbed and threw hooks over and over again. Grimshaw took more hits, but she landed more hits, too.

Her breathing was strained. He could feel her muscles tingling from exertion.

Halfway through the round, Jax got too close. Grimshaw's head ducked under a wide hook and came face-to-face with the man's eyes.

She pulled control away from Jax, and this time took a step away from him. Her foot caught on the mat, and their body tumbled to the ground. In a flash, Gold Teeth was on top of her. Her muscles locked up, and Jax was powerless to pull her out of it.

"What are you going to do now?" his chilling voice said in the confined space.

"You can do it," Jax called to her in his mind. *"Fight it. You have to stop him. Don't let him do this to you."*

He could feel the two battling emotions inside her. Part of her was completely terrified that the man would kill her, the rest of her was calling for retribution. He was treating her like an animal ... no, like an Animalis.

"You're stronger than him ... and he knows it," Jax whispered in his mind. It was the last feeble way for him to communicate with her. *"He's just a creep that wants to control you, but you've got to fight back!"*

"Did you want me to—" Gold Teeth began saying, but he wasn't able to finish.

Jax felt a surge flow through her body and her fist shot up into his jaw. His teeth cracked together, and his head snapped back from the force of it.

His eyes lost their focus as his body went limp and fell to the mat beside her.

Jax had seen that look before. There was no consciousness in those eyes.

KO.

Knocked. Out.

Gold Teeth was out of body and out of mind: in a dream land that could seem to last longer than a full night's sleep. In reality, he would only be unconscious for a few seconds, but when his consciousness returned, he would have to figure out

241

where he was and why one of his golden teeth was lying on the mat next to him.

Most people, Jax knew, couldn't catch up with reality within ten seconds of losing consciousness.

The crowd held their breath to listen to the ref count.

"One!"

But Grimshaw apparently hadn't seen the look as Gold Teeth had crumpled to the ground beside her. She was already scrambling to throw another punch into his face.

"Two!"

As his eyes began to open, her glove smacked him down into the floor again. His head bounced and he scrambled to his feet to get away from the attack.

The referee stepped in and stopped her from hitting him again.

The bell rang, signaling the end of round three. Gold Teeth looked around in confusion until one of his team members ushered him to the stool in the corner.

"Did you see that?" Grimshaw asked when she got back to her stool. "He doesn't have that look anymore."

Jax wished he could have been there. He wanted to be yelling, "YES!" and throwing her up on his shoulder.

The crowd started up a chant: "I-er-land! I-er-land! I-er-land!"

Jax took control of her arms and wrapped them around herself. It was strange, but he could feel his own arms around her, and he could tell that she could too. The muscles around her jaw pulled into a smile. Her head leaned to the side, pressing her cheek in a warm caress against the shoulder Jax was controlling.

Across the ring, Gold Teeth looked at Grimshaw with wide eyes.

Jax reached up and patted her on the back. The ACTS member behind her took it as a signal to massage that spot and began rubbing between her shoulders.

When the ref called them back up to start the final round, Grimshaw was ready. Her body hopped back and forth, like a natural boxer, pushing Jax into the movement.

Gold Teeth shook his head and strained to focus a glare at Grimshaw, but when the bell rang, he cowered away from her.

Jax gave up control and felt her arms pop the creep in the face a few times before the end of the final round.

People around the ring started up the chant again. They all knew who had won. When Jax raised her hands into the air when the fight was over, they burst into a cheer.

It had worked. Somehow, they'd pulled it off. The mongoose and his family would be safe now, which Jax felt good about, but he was more focused on Grimshaw.

She'd made it through the fight without getting hurt, and that made him feel even better.

————

Two days later, Jax got another message from Hank:

> I was wrong. I need more time to understand how to operate it. Give me another week.
> ~Hank

23
Changed

Jax kept busy, learning about the Animalis. But as the days passed, he realized that something was wrong with his leg, and it was getting worse. He woke several times every night from the intense throbbing.

It terrified him to see what it was becoming, but it also filled him with hope. Something was wrong with him, he knew. No ... not wrong: he was ... different. He wasn't a normal human. But maybe he was better than human.

The change in his leg forced him to stop using the robotic leg. He and Hodge found some crutches to use instead. He kept it a secret as long as he could.

———

The one person he could trust was Grimshaw. She knew both sides of him. She knew the army side, he had a commitment to serve and protect, and she had shown him the nature of the Animalis.

No matter how much he came to know her, there was always more. They would talk with each other for hours into the night, until one of the human deacons that helped enforce rules within the living quarters would send them off to their own rooms. It seemed like Grimshaw could talk about anything.

Then on Christmas night, as Grimshaw was blushing from remembering when they had tried to smuggle chocolate into the kitchen and hid for an hour in a storage room under the stairs waiting for the cook to leave, Jax kissed her.

She let herself be pulled into it. Jax felt the furnace inside his chest blazing. They sat, frozen, lips barely touching.

Then Grimshaw pulled away. Her ears were almost as red as her hair. She held her eyes closed with a shy smile on her lips. When she looked at Jax, her face lit up for a moment, then her eyes went wide.

"No," she cursed. "What's wrong with me? Ugh." Her clenched fist went to her forehead. "This is so stupid. *I'm* so stupid!"

"Hurley." Jax felt a knot forming in his stomach. He had completely misjudged the situation, and now she was angry with him. He got up. "I didn't mean to upset you."

Jax's hands jerked as he was pulled back down.

"I'm not mad at you, Jax," Grimshaw said, "I'm mad at myself." Agony twisted her face. "I'm sorry. I don't know why I didn't tell you, or how I let it get this far, but I can't kiss you. I really like you, Jax, and I want you to be happy, but we can never be a couple; it's impossible. We can never, ever, be more than friends."

"I'm sorry. I should have asked," Jax said. He had always stayed distant from girls in high school, reminding himself that he would have to say goodbye once he joined the army. Now, the one girl he was willing to throw the army away for was saying they could never be together. Ironic, maybe, or karma, but mostly acid-on-skin-unbearable. *Impossible?* he questioned in his mind. She was at the door, trying not to look at him.

Of course, she was older than him—less than a decade—and

that wasn't such a big gap. He had thought about their potential differences plenty of times. Silly things: would they hate each other's music, would they always wear clashing styles of clothing, would Hodge always be there?

When he reached the door she gripped his shoulder, still not looking at him.

"I'm not what I look like," she said. "I mean, that's not what I'm trying to say. I'm just me, but now, I'm even more of an idiot. I'm … a coward, too. I'm old. Alright? I'm old."

"I know," He said. He wanted to ask *"Why does it matter?"* but stopped himself. She was wrong. It wasn't impossible for them to be together.

"No, you don't know," she said, and the words sliced into Jax with an unexpected sting. "You're so new, Jax. Barely in the army. I thought I wanted to protect you from the lifetime of misery I had to go through to learn. I could see how much you cared about the world and about your friends, just like I did. You're so much like me. And you don't know what's right around the corner, because you don't know how life works like I do."

She let go of his shoulder, and looked at him with a hollow smile.

Jax's emotions had built to a breaking point. It wasn't his fault he was young! Who was she to call him young, anyways? It wasn't like she had been through much more than Jax had, she was barely older than him. He certainly didn't need her to protect him. Fighting was the one thing he was good at. He had escaped the arena!

She continued watching him while he stared back into her eyes. The shades of green within her iris layered like blades of grass. Closer to her shimmering black pupils, the green faded.

It was so subtle, but it gave a Jax the impression of depth and wisdom.

So she didn't like him. Fine. Then why did she spend so much time with him? Why had she come to Russia to find him, and why had she stayed with him? If he hadn't thought there was a chance to be with her, he would have already joined Hank.

He was ready to close the door on her, but he couldn't. She was still the one person close enough to care about him.

"Hurley, before you go. I need to show you what's happening to my leg." The words were out before he could reconsider.

"Your leg? What is it?" She stepped back into the room.

Jax hobbled back to the chair and took a deep breath. The caring tone in her voice worked to numb the sting he was still feeling from the conversation. "Close the door for a minute. I … don't know what's happening. I should have told you earlier."

He pulled up his pant leg to reveal the shape of what looked like a small foot inside his gray sock.

Her eyes went wide. "Jax, what is that?"

He pulled the sock off. The intense sensitivity had diminished as the leg had grown. It was pink, only four inches long, shriveled and hideous, like a quarter-moon raisin with toes.

It was wrong to show her. It was wrong to hope it was really growing. Looking at it now, showing Grimshaw, Jax became ashamed of himself for wanting it to grow back. He had seen exactly what he wanted to. Now, with his self-deceptive spells being broken by another person's intrusive eyes, it just looked disgusting.

"Oh my gosh! Your leg," she gasped. "It's your foot. It's … I don't understand. Does it hurt?" She crouched in front of him, afraid to get too close to the leg. "What happened? I just … don't understand. What did you do?" She stopped herself from touching it. "Did you have one grown? It's only been a few weeks!" Her voice broke, then returned as a whisper. "Why is it pink?"

"I haven't done anything. The leg grew itself."

She looked at him with an eyebrow raised.

"Every morning," he continued, "it seems to have grown a few centimeters in the night. I didn't know what was happening, but I didn't want to give up the hope that it was real, and have someone cut it off." He stretched out his toes and wiggled them gently.

"There really isn't any seam is there?" She was looking at the transition from his upper calf into the skin of the pink leg. "No scar tissue. I can't believe it. Does it hurt?" She held her hand over the leg, asking permission to touch it.

"Not as much." Jax reconsidered and said, "Well, it doesn't hurt, but it is sensitive."

"That's incredible," she said, as the tip of her finger sent tingles of sensation through Jax's nervous system.

"You think it looks normal?" It hadn't deflated. It hadn't shriveled and fallen off now that someone else had seen it.

"It's hard to tell. I mean, it looks fine, except for being a little red and small. Have you walked on it?"

"No. I've been terrified that any pressure might destroy whatever growth is going on. And I don't want a doctor telling me it has to come off, or be turned into a lab rat because I'm some kind of anomaly." He started to pull the sock back over it.

What was he doing? She was done with him, she didn't want anything to do with him now that he had tried to kiss her. Here he was, trying to get her to care about him again. He had to let her go, like she wanted.

"I've wanted to ask you for a long time now," Jax said, "about the pyramid you saw, back in Australia. Do you remember? When Hank mentioned the pyramid, you said you had seen it."

He nearly slapped himself in the forehead. He was just dragging on his own agony.

Grimshaw scowled "Yes. Did I mention that? I did see the pyramid, just a flash of it in my mind. Why do you want to talk about that?" she asked.

"I ..." he stammered. "I have a theory for why my leg grew back. You seeing the pyramid, I think the same thing happened to me. Tell me what it was like," Jax said. The connection was elusive, but it was the only thread of explanation for his leg he had thought of.

"Well, it seemed like an answer at the time," she said. "Before Hodge and I got Jesus' message about flying you and Hank to Australia, I had been asking myself if I could do more for the Animalis. More for humanity, and more for the Earth. Then, in Australia, I saw the pyramid and I remember being struck with this feeling that this was my opportunity to help, like I'd asked."

Jax considered the possible connection between the two. "I saw a yin-yang the same way," he said. "It was weird, almost a hallucination. The next day I saw Moxie and Little Hank floating in the air, wrapped together just like a yin-yang. But I heard a voice, too, that said if I helped it, it would help me. I think that's what this is." Jax gestured to his foot. "I think something saved me from bleeding to death in the arena, and now I'm growing my leg back."

Grimshaw didn't say anything for a while. She watched as

the last of the pink leg was covered by the sock. She slowly stood up. "Alright. I guess you're right about not walking on it. Probably best to let it grow, if it's growing."

"You think that could be it? Something saved me?" Jax asked.

"I don't know. It would be incredible, but then so many things in life are, and I've seen most of them. I've seen money fall from the sky when someone needed to pay for food, I've seen a diseased siblings note appear suddenly when her sister needed it most. Life is an infinite mystery. This just shows how important you must be, Jax. Something beyond our world can see it. I can see it."

"But who?" Jax asked. "Who's beyond our world? God? Angels?"

"That, I don't know," Grimshaw said with finality.

Jax continued pinning up the end of the pant leg in an uneasy silence.

Jax stood up, putting the crutches under his arms, and walked to the door with her again.

"I can have Hodge look at my leg in the morning," he said.

"You must have been reading my mind." She held his hand lightly. "Good night, Jax."

And she kissed his cheek. Then she walked out into the hall. Moxie circled around her legs and went with her into her room.

Jax stood still, more confused than ever. He didn't want to move, for fear that the sense of her lips against him might vanish forever. *Just friends.*

———

By Jax's birthday, January 20th, the leg had grown back to its full length. It had been two months since he had fought for his life in the arena. That time had started as an agonizing eternity of suffering, but now he didn't want it to end. Finally the fight came back for him. When Hank showed up, it was time for Jax to decide.

24
Pulled Forward

Jax was surprised by Hank's appearance in person. His eyes had signs of lost sleep. His hair had begun to form a curly nest on his head. A freshly printed set of clothes and a pair of shoes were tucked under his arm. He panted and finally said, "I figured out the pyramid. We have the perfect opportunity to get it, right now."

"Now?" Jax said. "Today? But—" What was there for Jax to say? That he was impossibly in love with Grimshaw, that maybe he didn't have to help fight against the Animalis anymore? He looked at Hank and tried to make words come out, some explanation for why he couldn't help anymore, a plea that Hank, the captain, and the world would understand that he couldn't be a tool for useless violence anymore.

He could see his reflection in Hank's eyes, and in it, he looked foolish. The time had come to fulfill his commitments. Back to saving the world, helping end the war, pretending there was such a thing as a hero.

"Jax," Grimshaw interrupted.

She had stood with her arms folded ever since Hank had come in. The Herbal Air shopkeeper had brought Hank to the ACTS building a few moments before, and now Hank was standing at the door to Jax's room, waiting for him to come.

"Have you told Hank about your leg?" Grimshaw asked.

"What?" Hank looked at Jax. "That you lost it?"

Jax nodded. "Well, it's going to be hard to believe. I don't understand what's happening to it." Jax pulled up his right pant leg, revealing the new foot. He lifted his leg and started to pull off the sock.

Hank stared at the leg. "What happened?"

Jax finished pulling the sock off and the pink foot hung bare. Hank cringed at the sight of it.

"Is that your foot?" he asked. He looked mad. "I thought you lost it, Jax."

Jax wiggled his toes. "I did. I don't know what's happened to it. But it … it's growing back." He started to pull the sock back on.

Hank looked at Grimshaw, skeptical. She nodded.

"Well …" Hank stepped back from it, staring into space for a moment. He shook his head. "We don't have time to talk about this. Can you come? You know I can't do this without you."

That was all Hank was going to say about the leg. Jax had expected some kind of awe from him, marveling at the novelty of it. He was acting panicked and disheveled.

Jax stepped down, slowly putting his weight on the new foot. It tingled against the ground, but the sensitivity had gone away. It felt solid and held his weight. He was almost normal.

He wasn't ready to leave Grimshaw, but he could never use that as an excuse. He had a duty to Hank, and the army, and humanity. Even if he wasn't sure either side deserved to win.

"Are you sure you want to go?" Grimshaw asked.

Jax looked at her, and back to Hank.

Did she want him to stay? With her? He was repulsed by the

desperate feeling of hope that had exploded within him. *Impossible*, he repeated to himself.

He took the clothes from Hank.

————

Their automated taxi dropped Grimshaw, Hodge, and the two little ferret animals off at the Atticus. Then, on the way to the pyramid, Hank told Jax he had been living in the Atticus, tracking down surveillance footage of the plane Jax had come in on, hacking private networks for more footage, and he had found the pyramid. He watched it being sent from building to building where Animalis and people took turns looking at it.

"And today, I read an article that made it click," Hank said. "I know how to use the machine." His eyes looked at something in front of him for a moment, then he looked expectantly at Jax. "Oh," he said, "no retina monitor. Well, the article was about repairing damaged cells with your brain, it's been fringe science for decades. It basically explains why medicinal placebos work. Why some people can kill off a tumor with a sugar pill. It's all about frequencies."

Jax didn't know they were trying to figure out how to make the machine work. He was about to ask more about the mission when Hank held his hands out to demonstrate. With his left hand, he started moving it up and down in a wave motion, while his right hand held still.

"So, say this hand is the cell that needs repaired." He indicated his stationary right hand. "And this hand is the wavelength of your brain." He waved his left hand. "Now, if the brainwaves fall into the same frequency as the cell here," he said, moving the left hand to form a line with the right hand, "then the thoughts can dictate instructions to the cell. Normally the wavelength moves up or down, meaning higher frequency and lower frequency, depending on the amount of cerebral activity.

"If you're in a panic, filled with adrenaline, or stressed with a test, then you're going to be way up here." He lifted the wave up. "When you're sleeping," He dropped his hand, "it gets really low. I think the pyramid is like this cell here. It's almost like a lock: when you get your brainwaves into the right frequency, your brain becomes the key, and you can open it up."

He folded his arms and sat back in his seat again. "I don't know what they've been doing with it. While I was watching, there were a couple Animalis, and people, that went inside it. Nothing seemed to happen. There was that lioness, she came just a few days ago and the pyramid was put into another truck. And it's just sitting there. I don't know what they're waiting for, but it isn't guarded."

"And what kind of building is it in? How are we going to get in?" Jax asked, focusing in on what mattered: finishing the mission.

"It's not in a building." Hank tapped his laser tool against his leg. He hadn't stopped moving and twitching since he had gotten into the car. "And I found some tutorials for how to get one of those trucks to start without a key. With a laser tool, it should be pretty easy."

"And we drive it to the Atticus? Is there storage on the Atticus?" Jax asked. He was growing uneasy about the mission.

"No. There's not quite enough room for it on the Atticus. But we don't need to jump it, not yet. I rented a storage garage to keep it in, and we can rent a truck to transfer the pyramid into before we go there."

The uneasiness finally had a name in Jax's mind. "Why are we alone in this mission? Won't the captain send another unit?"

The speed of the tapping increased, and Hank's legs began to shimmy back and forth subtly. "This might be our only chance," he said. "I've been here, alone, for almost three months, tracking this thing down because the captain wasn't willing to divide his resources. He needs proof. But we've got to get it first. As soon as the captain finds out we've found you, he's going to pull us back, and we'll lose our chance to get the machine."

"What? The captain doesn't even know we're going after it right now?" Jax asked. "Come on, Hank! We can't do that. We're going to get killed. Or worse, sent back to the arena."

"No!" Hank shouted.

Jax shrank back from the angry outburst.

Hank lowered his voice: "I'm not going to let it go. And I'm going to use it, at least once. Don't think I'm being selfish, either. We're doing this for you, too, Jax. They have to pay." His green irises tunneled into Jax's eyes.

Jax hesitated. *Why am I fighting against him again? Hank needs me.* "We're going to use it?"

Hank's stare grew less intense. "If we get an opportunity … once we get it out of their hands."

The car came to a stop. Outside, the sky looked dim, covered in heavy clouds, rimmed with red and orange, hinting at the sunset hidden behind them.

"You look good, Jax. I can't believe you were in the arena," Hank said. "They never posted video of your fight—but then, with an escape like that, I'm sure they don't want anyone to see it."

It disturbed Jax to see Hank acting so strangely. Hank had

always been a constant. Had he really just forgotten that Jax lost his retina monitor? Jax had the feeling it was related to his plan to use the pyramid to demonstrate its power to the captain. He just couldn't figure out why using the pyramid would scatter Hank's mind like this.

They stepped out of the taxi and into the chilly air. Beside them stood the remains of a crumpled, partially demolished building. Old bricks still formed a short wall along the sidewalk, and beams protruded from the rubble into the sky.

The city block was divided in half, with a shipping access road between the ruined building and the warehouse where the Animalis truck was parked. Down the skinny road, to the right, would be the shipping bays.

"How is it walking with your new foot?" Hank asked, his voice joining the rumble of machinery and combustion engines spread throughout the city.

"It's uncomfortable, but it's working," Jax said.

"You really lost it?" Hank asked.

Jax had no interest in talking about it—not right now. They had to be focused, watching and listening for anyone that might catch them. Maybe Hank was acting strange because of the danger that lay ahead, like in Australia.

They turned down the alley. Footsteps echoed off the walls of the buildings. They could see the trucks parked in the loading bays now. Lights on the side of the building had turned on, beacons for the coming darkness.

"Do you see that one?" Hank said. "The third one down. Not from the end, from where we are. I'll have to check the license plate, but I'm pretty sure that's the truck we want."

"Alright," Jax said.

About fifteen yards separated the alley from where the trucks were parked. Once they started crossing that distance, they would draw the attention of anyone watching. They'd have to be fast and direct.

"This doesn't seem suspicious to you?" Jax asked. "They just left it here, out in the open?"

Hank kept walking, pulling his chin down into the collar of his coat. "It won't matter if we can just get to it. Ready?"

They quickened their pace as they went for the loading bay. Jax reached door to the cab and tried pulling it open. He was surprised to find that the door wasn't locked. He was about to climb in when he heard the sound of another door opening, and then felt the truck shake.

Jax whipped around, expecting Animalis, but he saw no one—not even Hank. His heart pounded in his chest, and his stomach turned over at the thought of an ambush. Jax moved to the back of the truck to investigate.

"Hank?" he whispered.

The back door of the truck was open and Hank stood in front of it, looking in. Jax looked up and down the loading area, still nervous that they were being watched. When he looked back at Hank, he felt his stomach drop. Hank was climbing into the back of the truck, where the plain, metal pyramid stood from floor to ceiling.

The idiot was going get them both killed. They had to leave—*NOW.*

"Stop!" Jax hissed.

Hank jerked to a stop, hanging on the edge of the cargo truck.

"What are you doing?" Jax took a step closer to him.

"I can do it. I just need a minute," Hank said. His breathing was fast and loud. "Help me up." He turned his head back to look at Jax, scowling. "Come on!"

"We have to get out of here, Hank." Jax checked the area around them again. He grabbed the door to close it. "Let's go."

"Leave me back here while you drive," Hank commanded. "I have to see inside it. I want to know how it works. To see if it can undo what it did before, and make the world right again." His hand blocked the door.

No, Jax's mind reeled. Was that it? Was that his plan all along? Destroy the Animalis? The Animalis were a part of this world now. Jax had struggled with their existence, along with the rest of humanity. He had thought they were a mistake at first. Now he was starting to understand what Grimshaw knew: the Animalis were vital for humanity. They were an integral part of humanity's journey: progressing, becoming better as a whole. They couldn't be destroyed. Jax wouldn't let it happen.

Did that mean he and Hank were on opposite sides now? Was Jax an enemy to humanity? It didn't have to be that way. He wasn't against either side. That wasn't the question. The question was, how could he keep Hank *and* the Animalis safe. Right now.

"You're the only one that knows how to drive a vehicle like this—and you know where we're going," Jax said. "Please, Hank. If we're ever going to be able to use it, we have to go!"

Hank blinked, and shook his head. "Right, we have to get it out of here." The hatred was gone, leaving his face pale with fear. He let go of the door, and Jax closed it.

They quickly went back to the front of the truck and climbed in. They didn't even have to hot-wire it; the keys were still in the ignition. The truck rumbled to life. A horrendous grinding noise came from the front of the truck.

Hank held the wheel in front of him with his left hand, and with his right hand, he was trying to shove a stick forward and backward. There was another grinding noise, then the truck lurched forward.

"Hey, wall!" Jax wanted to reach for the wheel. Hank looked up and saw the wall of the next building coming toward them.

"I've got it. Is there anyone following us?" Hank spun the wheel and the truck started to turn.

Jax looked in the little mirror that hung on the side of his door. He had to move forward to get the reflection of what was behind them. Everything about this vehicle was alien to Jax, but strangely visceral.

"I can't see anyone."

Hank straightened out, driving down the alley to the road ahead. A few dozen yards and they'd be out on the street.

"Lion!" Hank shouted.

The lioness stepped in front of the opening to the alley. The fur on her head, shaking in the breeze, had turned golden-red from the light of the setting sun. Her arms were relaxed, hanging by her sides.

"Can we go faster?" Jax asked. "If she doesn't get out of the way, run her over!"

It was definitely Narasimha; Jax could see the short tail. She seemed so calm, watching them come at her. Then he noticed a gadget in her hand. She lifted it up and started to squeeze her finger on the trigger—but it wasn't a gun.

Jax's subconscious mind had put it together before the trigger was fully compressed. He arched his back, thrusting his hips up and away from the seat. It was a trap, and they had sat right on top of it.

Hank convulsed in muscular spasms, as electricity shot up through the seat. The wheel spun as his arms flung wildly out of control. The low wall of the demolished building appeared in front of them.

Jax held his body away from the seat, rolled to the side, and kicked Hank's door open. He pushed the two of them into the alleyway just before the truck smashed into the bricks, sending a cloud of dust into the air.

The pain of the impact was hidden beneath the adrenaline shooting through Jax's veins. Through the confusion and pain, Jax managed to put together one coherent thought: *Narasimha isn't my enemy.* She had been waiting for them to come. The truck must have been rigged with shock wires that held the same incapacitating force as shock sticks.

Jax pushed himself to his feet. Narasimha was coming, but she was still a dozen yards away. More Animalis were joining her, coming from around the front of the warehouse.

They had to get away. Jax had to get them away. He couldn't go back to the arena, and couldn't let Hank be taken to that evil place.

Jax lifted Hank's torso off the ground and pulled him onto his back. He turned around, but more Animalis were coming out of the shipping bay. He looked back at the truck. Where it had hit the wall, the bricks had collapsed down onto the front of the truck, opening up into the jungle of metal and plastic of the demolished building.

Jax held onto Hank tightly and ran at the truck, leaping off the tire and launching up onto the loose bricks. His foot skidded, lost his balance, and the two of them landed hard on the bricks.

Jax rolled over and stood up again. The Animalis were running at them now, holding out long shock sticks. Hank let out a light moan as Jax pulled him back up.

A shock stick buzzed past Jax's head. Jax dodged to the right. Another stick let out a *crack* as it struck the bricks. Jax kicked a brick down at the attacking Animalis dog.

Hank jerked away from Jax's grip. Another Animalis—a leopard—on the other side of the truck was pulling at Hank's leg.

"No!" Jax yelled. He hefted another brick up and threw it hard at the leopard. Hank slipped out of Jax's grasp and fell off the truck.

Jax couldn't leave him. The dog was reaching with the shock stick again from the other side, and the leopard was standing over Hank. Jax dove off the truck at the leopard. The shock stick was ready, catching Jax in the side.

His eyes were still open; he could see Hank lying in the rubble next to him. Jax's ears were ringing, and the rest of his body was frozen in electric spasms. The leopard struggled out from under him.

"I hoped you'd come," someone said.

Jax couldn't move his head to see who it was, but he recognized the growl of Narasimha's voice. He knew he had muscles in his jaw and in his tongue and lips, but they were lost from his mind, consumed in the electric flames that gripped his body. *Move,* he commanded himself, *get up.*

"Was it you in the pyramid? I saw how you survived in the arena. The way you were torn apart without any blood. No blood. And I thought, humans bleed. Even the Animalis bleed. It's part of us—part of our DNA."

More Animalis had come to the cargo truck, pulling Hank

away from Jax's view. Jax struggled to cry out, *"Stop! You can't do this! Narasimha, you don't know what you're doing!"* but his muscles wouldn't respond. He was sick with failure.

The world started to shift as Jax was lifted away from the ground as well. He tried to move his jaw again to force out a desperate plea, and felt an icy tingle somewhere on his face. Lips. He could feel his lips.

Narasimha's voice followed him as he was carried. "Do I need to keep both of you alive? Or do each of you know how to use the pyramid?" Her voice caught. "What are you—your lip, human. I've never seen someone move so soon after the shock."

The rough pad of a finger rubbed over Jax's lips. He wouldn't have felt it, but the icy tingles multiplied with the pressure.

"Take them to my plane. Make sure they're secure," she said to one of the other Animalis surrounding them.

A blindfold slid over Jax's head and the world went black. Narasimha stopped talking. The sounds of the Animalis carrying him, grunts, mumbled Russian. It was all that was left to him. And a chittering. Moxie? He tried to listen for it again. Grunts, mumbles, the slide of fabric.

The sounds around him stopped. He was closed up inside something. Was Hank still with him? It was impossible to tell.

Minutes later, he regained feeling and muscle control. He was being moved and bounced around in something. He tried calling out, but Hank wasn't with him, or was unable to speak.

Movement, shaking. Someone unstrapped the harnesses that were holding him against the floor.

"Don't struggle, and I won't shock you," said a snorting voice.

He struggled, and was shocked again.

———

When he found his senses, he was in a standing position, held against a wall by tight straps. He could hear movement nearby, but couldn't see anything. Everything was a perfect black, which meant he was blindfolded.

"What is your name?" asked the deep, penetrating voice that he had come to know well now: Narasimha.

"Mnnnaaah," Jax said, letting out more of a moan than a word, along with a dribble of saliva. The rest of his body was tingling and starting to tremble with fiery tremors from the shock.

In a flash, the blindfold was pulled from his head. His eyes stung in the light. Narasimha stood in front of him. He saw nets, boxes, and maybe a cargo hold behind her. It looked like the inside of a plane. Jax tried to turn his head, but it was strapped tightly to the wall.

"Jakth?" said a higher-pitched voice to Jax's right.

Jax pushed his eyes as far as they would go in that direction and saw the outline of someone strapped to the wall beside him. The figure had a sharp nose and chin, and was wearing an outdated coat. It had to be Hank.

"Yes. The two of you together," Narasimha said.

"We have permission to jump from the tower."

Jax strained his eyes to see who was talking, it sounded like the warthog.

Narasimha turned and bowed her head. "I'm ready," she said. She seemed patient and controlled through the interruption. After a moment, she turned back to Jax and Hank. "Humans used to think they were the only creatures that could demonstrate self-control. Did you know that? It was what they glorified themselves with. And if a man couldn't control his behavior, he was a beast, a mongrel, giving into his animal nature." She start-ed to strap herself into a harness for the takeoff.

Jax tested his restraints. His fingers could wiggle, but his hands were held together tightly behind his back with a strap that also held his wrists together.

"Animals. Mindless," she continued. "Only kept alive for as long as they were useful to a human. Are you my animals, hu-man? Do I have the self-restraint to keep you alive only for as long as I can use you? And then what? Eat you?"

"Don't," Hank said with a slur.

"What would be so terrible about having a meal? We all have to eat. Some species are meant to be hunted. Humans are my prey." Her voice broke into a self-amused laugh.

"Please," Hank whispered. "Please don't eat us."

Narasimha took in a deep breath, listening to Hank plead. The corners of her mouth pulled up into a smile.

She had left their mouths free to talk. She must want them to help her use the pyramid.

"I terrify you, don't I?" she said. "Why? Is it my eyes? Or my fingernails? That I'm stronger, faster, and more deadly than you could ever hope to be?" She closed her eyes, "Or is it that you cannot see my thoughts." Her breath held the vibration of a deep purr. "I don't know that you have thoughts, human. Should that terrify me?"

"I have thoughts!" Hank said.

"What do you need from us?" Jax demanded. "Why did you keep us alive?" He hopped his courage would ease Hank's fear.

"Do you have thoughts?" She had looked at Jax when he had spoken, but ignored him to answer Hank. "Even when the An-imalis were revealed to the world—walking, talking, thinking animals—humans continued like they always have, like mindless robots, enslaving and controlling."

"The world is becoming more like Australia. Australia didn't control the Animalis!" Jax shouted to get her attention.

"Australia wanted tourism!" she hissed. "They didn't say anything about the slaughter of tens of thousands of what they considered 'unpredictable' Animalis that flocked there for safety." Her voice was like thunder. "In India, they welcomed the blessed cow Animalis, but in America, they were enslaved."

"There aren't any—" Jax started to say, but he was cut off again. She was becoming more impassioned.

"There are no cow Animalis in America?" she scoffed. The plane started to move, getting in line for the launch shaft. "In America there is no difference between a common heifer, and a mother cow Animalis. They perform all the same functions that the humans want from them: birthing, milking, fattening. The farmers only look at the price tag. They'll take the heifer if the price is lower."

Jax tried turning again, straining to catch another glimpse of Hank. As he struggled, the words sank in. It churned Jax's stomach. After living only a short time with the Animalis, his understanding had shifted. The Animalis weren't human, but they weren't animals, either. She was telling them all her reasons for attacking the humans. Jax was leading the conversation now. Where did he want it to go from here?

"What are you thinking now, human? That they are right to? That we should continue to be subject to the humans? That our tongues should be cut out, so you can no longer hear our protestations in your own language?" Her growl layered into her voice: "I am Narasimha. The man-lion. I defend those that cannot defend themselves."

The bones in Jax's chest trembled from the deep vibration in her voice. So she thought of herself as defending the Animalis. Then maybe Jax could steer her using that.

"It's your attacks that put the Animalis in danger!" he said. "You want to be seen as an equal with humanity? Then stop killing us!"

Hank joined in: "Don't kill us. Let us go."

Narasimha barked out a loud laugh. "I have the pyramid. And one of you knows how to use it."

"It's you, Narasimha," Jax tried again. "How can humans treat you with kindness when you are their greatest enemy?"

"Approaching the launch shaft," the warthog's voice said over a speaker.

"I didn't know what it was, when you came for it the first two times in Australia," she went on, ignoring Jax. She had returned quickly to her normal state, calm and unemotional. "But you made me think, maybe it was the pyramid you were after. That's when I learned about the possibilities, that it could be the ultimate conduit of revenge. And when I saw your leg come off in the arena, I finally knew what it was." She rested her head back. "Our key to survival, to genetic superiority."

The buzz of the electromagnetic shaft let them know they were about to launch. Jax flattened momentarily against the wall.

Once the acceleration had evened out, Narasimha unbuckled and walked out of view.

"Now that I've seen your leg … Jax, was it?" Her voice bounced around the cargo hold of the plane. "Amazing. The foot is completely grown back. I know that one of you can use the machine. It doesn't matter which one." She came back into view holding a syringe. Her golden eyes moved between Hank and Jax. "You will do."

She approached Hank, lifting the syringe.

25
Atonement

"No! What is that? No, please. Stop!" Hank cried.

Jax could hear him struggling under the harness.

"He doesn't know! I'm the one!" Jax shouted.

Narasimha checked the needle.

"Do it to me! I can help you," Jax said.

She didn't listen to either of them. The needle went into Hank's arm. The plunger compressed. When she pulled it out, Hank spat at her. He screamed and cursed.

"That's not a full dose," she said. "No, not like the one you gave to my Rema, my hyena. You remember Rema? She couldn't say very much when we found her in that hospital. No, poor Rema will be crippled for the rest of her life. But she is strong. Not like a human." Narasimha slid the syringe into a recycling duct. "If this doesn't kill you, then I will give you the full dose."

Jax could hear Hank struggling in his restraints. The straps would hold back the grotesque distortions his body would be trying to make. Jax could already hear him sucking in spasmodic breaths.

"Aaahhhhh!" Hank's scream rose to an unbearable shriek.

Narasimha walked to the other side of the cargo hold and began manipulating a small section of a wall screen.

"It's the … DN … DNA. All in the … in the DNA." Hank rambled in between pained gasps.

With Narasimha's back turned to them, Jax caught another movement inside the cargo hold. Something white. Moxie slid over a box and came across the floor to Jax. Jax felt both relieved and frustrated to see her. She stood and rested her paw on Jax's leg. He started to struggle in the harness.

"Please, Moxie," Jax whispered. He kept watching the rest of the compartment, hoping Grimshaw would appear as well. "Straps. Chew the straps."

Moxie turned and scurried back into the boxes. No, it was too much to hope for. But how had she gotten into the plane? Maybe this time she had only come to watch them be tortured and killed.

Narasimha turned around from the wall screen and started to approach Jax and Hank.

"No … controls," Hank mumbled. "No way … to access the computer in the … pyr-pyramid. eeeeEEEEE—inside yourself! The peptide … transmitters."

"So weak," Narasimha said to Hank. She turned to Jax. "I would rather have seen you under the drug. Could you have fought it?"

"Nara, our third warehouse has just been attacked," the warthog said from where it stood in the doorway to the cockpit. "Krishna—he was killed!"

Narasimha snarled. "What?" She looked at Hank, then back to the warthog. With another growl, she turned and went into the cockpit.

Jax heard the scratch of Moxie climbing over boxes toward him again. She came quickly to his side and began biting the straps.

"Good girl, Moxie," Jax whispered. "Hold on, Hank."

"Destroy … we have to destroy—" Hank looked like he could barely breathe from the tension in his body.

The first strap ripped apart, and Jax felt his knees loosen. Moxie was quick to break through the second strap, and Jax's weight pulled uncomfortably at the last strap around his head. He pushed with his toes while he reached up to undo the last strap.

While he fumbled to undo the strap, he looked around the room for something that could stop Narasimha. A weapon, something. He saw a storage compartment in the floor, possibly containing supplies, maybe a laser tool.

The strap released and Jax expected to crumple onto the ground, but they were moving into orbital freefall. That meant the plane had reached its apex and was gliding through space. Now he didn't need to support himself.

"Moxie, can you get Hank?" Jax asked.

Moxie rubbed her soft fur against Jax's cheek before bounding over to Hank.

Jax heard a sound from the cockpit. He had to hurry. The low gravity would at least help him move quickly through the cargo space. Jax leaped, and soared several yards. He could see the outlines of the compartment on the floor. He grabbed the handle and stopped himself before pulling it open.

This was a much larger compartment than he had expected, holding space suits, straps, nets, and shock sticks.

The door hinges to the cockpit creaked; Narasimha would be coming for him soon. He snatched a shock stick, and then launched through the air, pushing down on the hand grip and lighting up the electric tip.

The door to the cockpit folded open just as Jax reached it. But it wasn't Narasimha in front of him.

"Nara!" the warthog grunted.

The hiss of the electricity shot forward with Jax's jab. Narasimha's hand came from the side grabbing the end of the stick. She body took the impact of the blow, shaking and convulsing. Her hand had clamped, out of control, to the shock stick. As her body jerked and twisted, the stick was pulled from Jax's hands. The electricity stopped abruptly once the handle was out of his hands.

"No!" the warthog cried, grabbing the shock stick.

"Nara!" the warthog shouted. "No, get away!"

It lit the shock stick and jabbed at Jax, who moved away to get out of range. Narasimha's body floated in the air.

"I'll flush them out! Open the door and flush them out!" the warthog yelled. The cockpit door folded closed with Narasimha inside and the lock echoed through the cargo hold.

Jax looked at Hank. Moxie had chewed through his straps, releasing him from the harnesses, and he was floating into the air. It seemed like the serum had started to fade, easing the painful expression in his posture. Jax needed to get the space suits, just in case the warthog really was crazy enough to open the cargo bay door.

Jax pulled two of the suits from the storage compartment and went to Hank. His breathing was starting to normalize, but Jax could still see waves of pain tensing up his body every few minutes. Jax pushed Hank's legs into the suit first. Then he pulled the second piece over his head and arms. Once Hank was tucked inside, he sealed the suit together.

The alarms began wailing through the plane and Jax felt

his stomach churn. In case he didn't have time to get a suit on himself, he helped Moxie crawl inside Hank's suit. He put the helmet over Hank's head and sealed it with a hiss.

An icy wind began to tug at Jax's skin. No—too late! The door was opening, the death of space creeped in. He had his suit legs on when his fingers began to freeze. Arms in. He lost feeling in his feet. His gloved hands pressed the two pieces of the suit together between violent tremors. Might be sealed; he couldn't tell in his panic. Helmet on. He shoved a dial on the front of the suit. Oxygen. He breathed.

Jax bumped into the ceiling. His limbs had become rigid, and his mind was swimming in a cloud of partially evaporated blood. But now the air inside the suit was staying, and he hadn't died. Not yet. This might be their one chance to escape. Jax tried to grasp fragments of a plan.

Hank had been beside him, hadn't he? Jax twisted, searching for the floating limp body.

Jax pushed off the ceiling to reorient himself. He saw a movement toward the tail of the plane and turned to see Hank floating toward the open cargo door. In a few moments, he would be drifting out into space. The rush of air escaping had pulled his weightless body with it.

Jax didn't have time to do anything but act. He thrust his legs against the ceiling and shot down the length of the cargo hold. His plan hadn't included taking their chances drifting into space, but even if he was able to get a cable or strap anchored to the ship in time to snatch Hank and pull him back into the plane, they would have to face Narasimha and her militants, maybe more torture, maybe the arena and death. Hank's ramblings might have been enough for them to discover how to use the pyramid, and then it would be over for the entire human race.

The pyramid—gleaming metal, nine feet tall, the four sturdy beams of the base strapped to the floor of the cargo hold—caught Jax's attention. Take the pyramid! He couldn't let it slip out of his hands again. If their bodies were going to burn a fiery streak in the atmosphere, then the pyramid was coming with them.

Jax shifted his position to prepare to redirect his momentum toward it. He caught a section of shelving and sent himself toward the big metal pyramid.

The vibration of the nylon straps slipping out of their holds shook Jax's gloves. He had it free in a few moments. As he wrapped his arms around the big metal beam, Jax felt it: consciousness, life. The pyramid was alive. The feeling was strange to comprehend. It didn't move, or react to his touch, but within Jax, he felt some awareness from the metal, reacting to him. The pyramid was cold and unmoving, but it was alive.

He pulled, slowly dragging the heavy mass into a powerful thrust of momentum, then held on. It was too late to stop now; Hank had cleared the lip of the bay doors.

The inside of the cargo bay drifted by: textured metal floor, flashing lights. There was silence within the space suit, except for the air moving in and out of his own lungs. Jax thought there should be a sense of doom coming over him, a pit forming in his stomach, but there was nothing.

Jax rode the pyramid like a Ferris wheel ride over the earth. His legs dangled over the edge of the bottom beam, and he wrapped his arm around one of the four vertical beams. It was actually pleasant, the pyramid keeping him company. The blue glow of the Earth filled his vision, spreading out over the horizon. Rippled, swirling, vivid clouds gave a depth to the globe. Even the stars felt within his reach.

What would Grimshaw do with the rest of her life now, without him? Living by her side for the two months with the Animalis, Jax had wanted to pretend it could last forever. If they had tried to join their lives together, would they wait until his commitment to the military had expired? They could have had a child together: Hodge and Grimshaw taking care of the baby while Jax spent far too much time working. He didn't even know what Grimshaw did for her income. It seemed like it was something she never thought about, like her life was a series of adventures. Jax's heart burned with the desire to experience all of those adventures. Whatever their life could have been, it wouldn't have been normal. But he wouldn't have had it any other way, if she had felt the same way.

Hank's body was slowly coming closer. Maybe he had already died, overcome by the thralls of the painful drug. It wouldn't matter in the next few minutes anyway.

A white star caught Jax's eye, hovering just beside Hank. It could have been right next to him; in the vacuum that surrounded them, there was no haze from the atmosphere to scatter and blur the light coming off of it. Clarity made the distance hard to distinguish. It was solid, and pearly white. But it wasn't really a star …

It was a beautiful white plane.

It was moving toward them, growing in size. In just a few minutes, it would be on top of them.

26
Collision

The Atticus was getting closer. Hank was getting closer. Narasimha's plane was drifting away behind them. Maybe this wasn't the time for Jax to die after all.

Hank started to move—he was alive! A crackle sounded inside Jax's helmet.

"Hello? … Hello?" Hank said in a pained whimper. At least he had managed to turn on the suit's communications.

It crossed Jax's mind that whatever was said could be transmitted to the plane they had just escaped from.

"Hank. I'm sorry, it's hard to explain. How are you feeling?" Jax asked.

"Who-Who is this?" Hank asked.

"This is Jax. I'm floating behind you. Can you see that plane in front of you? It's the Atticus, Hank!" Jax realized he was speaking to Hank as if he hadn't just felt like he had had his insides ripped apart.

"Jax?" Hank sounded confused. He hadn't lost his memory, had he? "Where's the pyramid? The lioness." He choked with what sounded like an echo of the pain.

Jax breathed a sigh of relief. "I've got the pyramid. We made it out. It was Moxie. Somehow she followed us and made it onto the plane with us," Jax said. "She's in your suit with you. I'll have to tell you what happened when we make it back to Earth alive."

"That's Grimshaw ... coming toward us?" Hank asked.

The plane was getting big now. In reality, they were all cruising around the Earth at nearly the same blistering speed: the Atticus, Jax and Hank, and Narasimha's plane. The relative difference between the movements was subtle, and felt like a slow-motion ballet.

"To the rescue," Jax said.

"I might be able to shift channels ... to communicate with her plane over the headset. Do you know how to do that?" Hank asked.

"I don't have my retina monitor anymore. I don't see a way to manipulate the suit," Jax said.

"There's a pad on the back of the helmet; it should link to your brainwaves for controls. What does it say in the heads-up display?"

"No, I don't see anything." There was no HUD. The helmet must have been malfunctioning somehow.

"Alright, I'll come back to this channel in a minute," Hank said. There was a pop, and the soft hiss from Hank's microphone went silent.

Jax was alone in his head again. Narasimha had probably gained control of her body by now. What would she do when she found out they had taken the pyramid out into space with them? It was possible that her plane, or at least she and the warthog, had weapons. Would they turn around and come after them?

Jax pushed his awkward, suited body around to get a view of the plane. It was only about twenty yards away. The cargo hold was still open, with the warning lights still blinking. If it slowed down, just slightly, it could scoop them right back up into its terrible belly.

The sound of breathing came back into Jax's helmet.

"Alright. Well, we've got some backup coming," Hank said, sounding more alert. "When she saw us get captured, she got a hold of Captain Hernandez. Sounds like he is coming to intercept us!"

"Hank, I'm worried we don't have much time," Jax said. "When we got out of the plane, I was able to hit Narasimha with a shock stick. But she has to have gotten movement back by now. She might even be listening to this now. Can Grimshaw, I dunno, bump us away from the other plane?"

"I'll tell her," Hank said, and was gone again.

Jax got in a position where he could look back and forth between the two planes. Grimshaw was very close now. He could see little puffs from thrusters that maneuvered her plane while at the edge of space. Jax looked back at the militant plane. It was closer, much closer than before.

"Hey! I see you! Grab my hand. Jax, get me!" Hank shouted like the sound of his voice was separated by the physical distance that their bodies were. Jax looked around. Hank wasn't in front of him anymore.

"I'm just under you!" Hank said.

There he was, floating just below the pyramid. Jax clenched his legs around the base beam he had been sitting on, and swung down to reach him. His hand stopped just four inches away from Hank's. Jax loosened the grip on the pyramid with his legs, and tried to hold on by squeezing his calves against it.

It worked. Jax clutched Hank's hand. Hank's face looked gaunt, the strength sucked from it, but his eyes grew excited, looking past Jax to the pyramid.

"Pull me in!" Hank said.

Jax moved to get a better hold on the pyramid, getting ready to pull Hank up with him.

"Hurry. I just need to be inside it," he almost pleaded.

Jax stopped. Hank wanted to use the pyramid so desperately. It made Jax uneasy. Hank was losing control of himself, forcing them to peruse the pyramid in an obvious trap, hiding Jax from the captain. Jax could feel a cold dread, and kept his arm straight, holding Hank at a distance.

"Jax?" Hank looked at him, confused and angry.

The view below Hank changed. The blue and white and green of the Earth were being covered with dark metal. The cargo hold of the Animalis plane was swallowing them again.

Grimshaw's plane was so close; the white reflection filled the glass of Hank's helmet. The two planes were going to collide, with them right in the middle.

"Hold on!" Jax yelled.

Silently, the nose of the Atticus smashed into the tail of the other plane. Pieces of metal crumpled and drifted away. The open bay began to move again, shifting up and away with the impact. The floor came swinging up at them. Jax could hear the sound of the impact first through Hank's microphone picking up the vibrations sent through his suit. Then Jax was hit. The two of them were pinned between the swinging door and the pyramid. The pressure was intense as the momentum of the pyramid was redirected.

When the edge of the door finally released them, the situation reversed. The door hit them like a baseball bat, flinging them out into space. Jax's grip on the pyramid was slipping as it pulled away in a crazy spin.

"Hold onto me, Jax!" Hank gasped.

The weight of Hank's body, moving at a different angle from the pyramid, was ripping his hand away from Jax. The fabric of the gloves slipped, and Hank fell away, disappearing as the pyramid spun Jax's view away.

The pyramid rotated away from where Hank had slipped off, taking Jax with it. In a moment, when the pyramid rotated back around, Jax might be able to reach him, but the pyramid was starting to slip away from his grip as well.

Jax fought the centrifugal force, hugging his body to the beam of the pyramid. The muscles in his arms burned with the effort. He pulled himself up on the beam, climbing toward the center of the pyramid. Finally, the force pushing him out decreased as his mass came into alignment with the pyramid's. He pulled his body into the center of the pyramid where he could relax his muscles.

He wanted to close his eyes; the Earth, stars, and planes were spinning around him. Until something stopped him, he would keep flipping head over feet. After a moment, the Earth came into view and he watched what was happening to the planes for a few seconds. Then the stars rotated back around and it was back to watching space.

The two planes were slowly moving together below them. Grimshaw's plane was beginning to turn sideways, sending more chunks of debris drifting as its bottom dragged against the tail of the other plane. The Atticus was in a much better position to keep flying than Narasimha's plane, which was drifting down with its nose pointed at the Earth. Then the stars swung back into view.

Hank was a foot out of reach of the pyramid now. But soon

it would be two, and then four, and then a thousand, as the two minutely different paths continued to diverge.

"Hank, I'm sorry! Don't worry, Hernandez is coming. Felix and Maven will be here to pick us up," Jax said.

The view of the planes was swinging back into his vision.

"And my Animalis will be here to meet them, Jax," Narasimha's voice growled in Jax's helmet. "The pyramid is not something I'm going to give up easily."

Now Jax could see the planes floating above the Earth.

"Jax?" Hank asked. "Who is that?"

"The lioness," Jax said. "Narasimha."

"I'm glad you remembered my name," she said.

Jax could see another plane approaching where the first two had collided. It was much larger than the Atticus and Narasimha's plane.

"It has significance to me," Narasimha said. "Are you familiar with Hindu deities, human?"

Why was she speaking to them like this? Wasn't she trying to reorient her plane into a position to either come get the pyramid, or to escape?

"There have been many incarnations of Lord Vishnu, the god of this world. But none has been loved by the humans throughout the millennia like Narasimha."

The Earth and planes were rotating back into view. The third plane was gradually getting closer, and now a fourth plane had appeared. It was sleek and black, with wings that ended in sharp points. The rear stabilizers were nearly as large as the wings—not one of their planes, so likely Animalis. Neither of the two most recently arrived planes looked like fat, weaponless, cargo planes. They were military. But Jax wasn't paying attention to the planes anymore. Something small was floating above the planes now. He couldn't see what it was before the stars were back in front of him.

"Half man, half lion," Narasimha went on. "He protects his faithful subjects who call on him for protection. My subjects are those who have been maligned by the belligerence of mankind."

The four planes came back into view. The thing above the planes was bigger now. It was moving toward Jax and Hank. A space suit? Was it Narasimha? Jax tried to keep the figure in view, but the movement made him sick and dizzy.

"Hank? Jax? This is Hurley! Are you on this channel?" Grimshaw said over the headset.

"Hurley!" Jax felt his heart leap at the sound of her voice. "We're floating out into space, above the planes."

"Jax!" she said.

"For every creature, Animalis or animal, which is killed by man, I will exact justice for the crime," Narasimha continued.

"Oh, who is that?" Grimshaw asked.

"In the world to come, we will use the name 'human' as a curse."

"That sounds pretty serious. Jax, I'm not sure if I approve your choice of friends," Grimshaw said. "Right there, Hodge. I see you, Jax. We're coming to pick you up."

The Earth rotated back around. The floating figure was closer. It wasn't moving very fast, but it was faster than Jax and Hank. And it wasn't Grimshaw in the suit. Jax could see the face wrinkled into a snarl, golden yellow fur, and intense feline eyes. It was Narasimha.

Grimshaw's majestic white plane was maneuvering around now, moving toward them. Maybe she could bump the lioness and send her tumbling out into space.

Animalis

"Hello? Hello? This is US Border Patrol Reinforcement, Battalion 6 attempting to contact Catcher 6 Actual. Anyone on this channel? Catcher 6 Actual if you can hear me, please respond." A new voice came into the conversation.

"F-Felix?" Hank asked.

"Yes? Who is this? Jax? Hank? Are you guys there?" Now Jax recognized the voice of Felix. Jax could see that the third plane was his company plane, the Hornet.

"Yes, we're here," Jax said. "We are stranded in space suits. Maybe two hundred yards above where you're at now."

The second Animalis plane was starting to arch up behind the Atticus. The Hornet fired a burst of machine gun rounds as a warning.

Jax strained to watch. The Animalis plane fired a rocket. It flew through space at the Hornet. A flare sprung from the nose of the Hornet, detonating the rocket a second before impact. The bright point of light sent shrapnel flying in all directions, pushing the Hornet with the force of it. The scene spun out of Jax's view.

"Wow!" Felix cried. There was a sound of him bumping into something, being thrown with the impact. "What was that? Maven? You alright?"

"Yes. I was clear of it," Maven said. Her voice came over the speaker. "They shot a missile at us. More incoming."

"We're alright. This bird could probably take a direct hit and still be alright. Wow!" Felix yelled with another barrage of noise. When the noise had settled, he spoke again: "Maven, did you hear Jax? Can you move to them?"

"Maven? Are you in a pod?" Hank asked.

"Yes. Coming to get you," she reassured.

The scene was coming back around for Jax.

"Hurley?" Jax said. "You should get out of here. That black plane coming up behind you has rockets."

"We can handle ourselves," Grimshaw said.

The blue glow of a shock stick lit up in Narasimha's hand. She was very close now. On the next rotation, Jax would have to face her.

"Hodge, let out some drone mines," Grimshaw said.

Two dozen tiny balls floated out of a compartment that opened up on the bottom of the Atticus. Each of them had their own thrusters, and they spread out in a pattern behind the plane.

A rocket shot out of the black Animalis plane. One of the mines moved and exploded in front of it, consuming the rocket in a second burst of light. The mines rippled from the radiating force of the explosions but the thrusters countered, and they flew back into formation.

Blue spilled into the reflection on Jax's helmet. He pushed away, swinging from a beam, avoiding the shock stick strike. Centrifugal force jerked at him once he was out of the center of the pyramid's spin. Narasimha grabbed onto the nearest beam and joined the spin. She held on with one powerful arm and thrust the shock stick at him again. Jax hooked his feet between two adjoining beams and escaped the attack by drifting backward. Even with his suit on, the shock was designed to pass through thick Animalis hide, and could easily pass through the suit's insulation.

The black Animalis plane fired more rockets—five, ten rockets—streaming out and flying at the Atticus. The field of mines came to life, moving into the paths of the rockets. Tiny puffs of gas propelled the rockets into unpredictable spirals. The first rocket spun and ducked but exploded with a burst of particles when it collided with a mine at the front of the mine field. Debris bounced off the next two approaching rockets that were swimming through space in parabolic waves.

The mines moved like a horde of angry insects as the rockets began to break through the front lines. Another mine exploded with a burst of light and the surrounding mines were pushed outward from the perfectly spherical force. The next three rockets shifted and dodged and exploded. Mines began moving back to form a column of destruction with explosions erupting within it.

A rocket broke free of the column and spiraled away, coming for the Atticus.

"They're getting through!" Hodge's voice said.

"Detach the cockpit," Grimshaw said. "Send the rest of the plane back at them."

Jax saw a flash, and the front of the Atticus separated from the rest of the plane. Thrusters on the wings of the headless plane threw it backward at the oncoming missiles and enemy plane. Balls of light silently tore chunks away from it. Sparkling particles flew in every direction. As the walls were torn apart, revealing the complex metal skeleton, Jax could see the warm interior flash and go dark. The bulk of her plane remained, and the enemy was too slow to maneuver out of the way. The two planes crumpled into each other, sending the Animalis plane spinning in a new direction.

Jax moved to avoid another strike. The stick sent a vibration through his boots when it struck the pyramid near him. Jax had to keep the lioness on the outside of the pyramid, where she had the disadvantage of having to fight to hold on as well. Her hind legs wrapped around the beam she was on. Jax kicked down on her gloved hand. She let go and snarled. The sound was mixed with the rest of the voices crowding the frequency.

"Hank. I'm moving in beside you," Maven said. Her pod spun and crept slowly up to Hank's spinning body. The hatch on the side of the pod opened. "When you spin back around, you need to grab that handhold." Hank did, and it stopped his spin. The pod readjusted to stop the pull of his momentum and they both straightened out. Hank climbed in with Maven.

"Why haven't you used the pyramid to destroy me, Jax?" Narasimha asked. She reached into the pyramid but Jax kicked the hand away again. "It would end the fight swiftly and permanently. Would it not?"

Hank seemed to perk up at the mention of using the pyramid: "Jax, you're inside it! You can do it—activate it!"

"Is it the same reason you spared the bear in the arena?" Narasimha asked.

Jax went to kick her hand away as it reached for his boot. Narasimha swung the shock stick. Jax couldn't pull his leg back, but managed to avoid the attack by pushing his body into the centrifugal pull. The stick hit against a beam, leaving her vulnerable. Jax fought against the pull and pinched her hand against the beam with his foot. He had wanted to stomp on it to knock the weapon from her hand, but couldn't pull his body in fast enough.

"I'm not you, Hank. I don't know anything about DNA," Jax said.

Narasimha reached to grab the extended leg with her other hand. Jax shoved his foot down, sliding her hand along the beam, pushing the shock stick in a cutting motion at the reaching hand, forcing her to pull back.

Hank and Maven were flying back to the Hornet. They went in a wide arc to avoid the debris and mines that were left from the Atticus. Maven spoke before Hank could answer Jax.

"Felix? Why is the plane moving away?" Maven sounded concerned.

There was a click of static before Felix spoke: "Maven? Get back here as soon as you can. That rocket explosion must have hit one of the thrusters; we can't maneuver to pursue. We are going to have to return to normal airspace as soon as we can."

"Jax?" Grimshaw spoke.

Jax reached for the shock stick. When he pulled it from the lioness's hand, it shut off.

"We don't have very much fuel in this pod," Grimshaw said, "and when we open the hatch, our oxygen is gone. We'll only have whatever is left in our suits."

It wasn't the best news Jax had ever heard. His own suit only had forty minutes left before his own carbon monoxide asphyxiated himself.

The black Animalis plane with rockets had recovered. It began gaining altitude again.

"Hodge, are any of the mines still active? Send it over to one of their wing tips," Grimshaw said.

A tiny speck sat motionless while the plane moved over it. With a sparkle of thrust, it shot to the right wing and exploded. The tip shattered and the plane started to swerve to the right. The plane began to drop down, doomed to an explosive re-entry in the atmosphere.

"Felix, we've docked with the Hornet," Maven said.

A new voice came into the frequency: "This is Captain Hernandez. Hurley, are you alright? Who all is out there with you still?"

"Good to hear you again," Grimshaw responded quickly. "There are five of us in total. I have three with me in my plane's cockpit, Hodge and I, and Little Hank here. Jax is holding off one of the leaders of the Animalis militants. They're in the pyramid, and their trajectory isn't good."

"We'll send another plane now. I'm sorry we can't get you ourselves. Can you two hold on?" Hernandez asked.

"This is Jax. I can, sir," Jax said.

Narasimha had managed to pull her upper half inside the pyramid. If she made it in just a little farther … Jax waited.

"Hang in there, Jax," Hank said. "I'll see you when you make it down safe."

Narasimha was finally in a position to come after Jax, and she thrust herself toward him in the middle of the pyramid. In a quick motion, Jax lit the stick and shoved it into her. She shook, and began to drift with the pyramid rotating around her. The corner opposite Jax was swinging in line with the rotation of the pyramid. He pushed her gently, and the force of the spin pinned her into the converging point of the pyramid. It would be cruel, but he would have to shock her again every few minutes to keep her from gaining control of her body and attacking him.

The captain's plane descended slowly out of view, leaving the five to wait for rescue. Although, the cockpit of Grimshaw's plane should have been designed to re-enter atmosphere. Jax suspected, or maybe just wanted to believe, that she was staying to be close to him.

Jax tried to calm his nerves now that Narasimha was

unconscious. The adrenaline had tunneled his focus again. Clouds of crimson and gold nebulae swung by with an infinitude of gem-like stars overwhelming the spaces in between. A mist of white hung in the view beside him.

The mist wasn't stars or a nebula. Jax twisted his waist to get a better view of it, but the mist continued to spray just beyond his helmet. It was flowing out of something on him. Right at his neck, where the helmet should have sealed to keep his oxygen in.

Jax pushed his head against one of the beams of the pyramid and felt the last of the seal click together. The lights of his heads-up display sprung up on the glass of the helmet, giving him an altitude readout, guidance lines to objects in view, and, amidst the rest of the information, his oxygen supply and an estimation of how long he could expect to keep breathing:

12 minutes remaining.

"Can your cockpit re-enter the atmosphere?" Jax asked Grimshaw. They were drifting farther and farther away from the pyramid, but he could still see her and Hodge through the cockpit window. Both of them had their suits on. Grimshaw smiled when she saw him looking at her, then his rotation spun them out of view.

"It can," she said. "But we aren't going to leave you."

"Good." Jax tried to sound positive. "It feels like I'm already back on Earth, with you so close."

"Hodge?" Grimshaw said, but her voice was distant, talking to Hodge in the cockpit. "How long can we last?"

Hodge's voice echoed into her microphone, inaudible to Jax.

"We've got forty minutes," she said to Jax. "What's your oxygen at?"

"I ..." Jax debated lying to her, telling her that he could wait for the rescue plane. "I've got twelve minutes left."

"Say again?" The fear in her voice cut into Jax's heart.

I should have lied.

"You can still make it back to Earth, Hurley," Jax said. "With Hodge, and Little Hank, while you've got oxygen."

"No, Jax. Not without you." Her voice switched to Hodge: "Put Jax's location in."

Jax already knew what she was going to find: it would take five minutes to get to him, and once they opened their hatch, they'd have to rely on their suit's own oxygen, then it would be another fifteen minutes to hit the surface of an ocean and get open air. Jax would still die halfway through the trip, and the rest of them would be at risk.

Her breathing grew panicked.

"Thank you for being my friend, Hurley," Jax said.

"What if we do it manually?" she was saying to Hodge. "Burn full throttle the whole way?" Hodge gave an inaudible response.

It could be almost an hour before someone came to rescue them. Even their tiny reserve of cockpit oxygen would run out by them. If they left now, they might be able to make it back to the Earth without suffocating. She couldn't let herself die for some crazy kid who thought he loved her after just a few months of knowing her. He couldn't let her.

The ocean of stars swept past him, streaming though his vision in brilliant clusters of color and depth. The crest of the Earth came into view, the rim glowing hot-yellow, red, and orange, refracting the light from the sun and dividing the colors in the clouds. Lights from a thousand cities gave life to the dark and separated the land from the sea. It was all so pretty.

"Jax? What are you doing? Why are you breathing like that?" she asked.

Jax's oxygen was coming out in a slow trickle, and he had begun breathing slow, shallow breaths. "I cut off my oxygen supply," he said. It hadn't taken long for his head to start getting light. "You're always so happy."

"Turn your air back up!" she shouted, obviously not happy.

"I ..." He had to talk slower. He couldn't catch his breath. "I thought maybe I could ... be one of the reasons ... you were ... are so happy."

"Not if you're dead, Jax! Come on, we can't stop fighting," she pleaded. "Give me a chance to save you."

"Please, Hurley," Jax tried again. "I'm the one ... trying to save you."

The speaker was quiet for a minute. Jax listened to the sound of his lungs filling and deflating. The glass of the helmet catching the noise and reflecting in, as a steady hiss, into his own ears.

Jax thought of Hank, that he had let him go. If he had held onto his hand, and let himself be pulled away from the pyramid, he could have gone back to normal life.

"You saved us," she finally said. "Even if no one else on Earth knows it. I love you, Jax."

Jax could see her looking at him through the window. It was the one time he had ever seen true helplessness in her expression. It was painful to see. He could feel his own heart breaking with what he was forcing her to do. Hodge said something to her.

"Yes, get a return trajectory ready," she said, then she spoke to Jax again: "Don't give up, Jax. Please don't give up."

Hodge hit the thrusters, and their pod shot away.

———

I've let the one person go that might have loved me. Hurley's eyes held onto Jax's small figure spinning farther and farther away into the certain death of space. His back rotated past, and for what might have been the last time, she saw his face. *He's still trying to smile.*

Her cockpit, the last remaining piece of her beautiful space plane, continued to descend past the wreckage of the battle. As the distance between her and Jax grew, the space was left empty. A void, deprived of heat, energy, life, and breath. And she hated herself for the choice she had made. *You foolish old woman,* Hurley scolded herself. *You stop thinking for one second and ruin the rest of your life. You ...*

"... fool," she whispered aloud.

But it was done. Nothing she could do now would save Jax—or herself.

"Hodge?" she asked, voice trembling. "When did I become an aimless people pleaser?"

Hodge, though, said nothing, leaving Hurley alone with her thoughts.

Make a difference, save the world ... That was what Jax had wanted most. And hadn't she let him have it? He had dragged Narasimha and the pyramid—humanity's greatest threats—out into the depths of space. It was heroic, right out of a storybook. She should be so happy for him, so proud of herself for aiding him.

After another moment without a response from Hodge, she tilted her head to look at him. Hodge was belted into the co-pilot's seat beside her, his fur drifting in beautiful waves without gravity to hold it down. His eyes were wide, still looking out the window at where Jax had disappeared. His ears stood up above his head, twitching back and forth, searching for the sounds that were no longer coming through their cockpit speakers. She could hear his nose cycling the air of the cramped cockpit, searching for scents that might as well have been a universe away.

"Maybe he'll make it … I think he'll make it," Hodge finally said, and he sounded genuinely hopeful. "Don't you?"

Hurley swallowed down the ache building in her throat. "Yeah," she said. "I hope he does."

And she tried to smile, but cried instead.

27

The Ghost of Doctor Ivanovich

Jax was alone. Maybe Narasimha would regain control of her body soon and she would kill him before the carbon monoxide building up in his suit did. Unless she lost consciousness …

He pushed himself over to where Narasimha was pinned. He reduced her stream of air. It would either kill her, or keep her in an unconscious state until someone was able to find them.

His heart was still beating rapidly; he would need to calm it down quickly to cope with the new atmosphere content in his suit.

He closed his eyes and focused on his breath. Slower. In, and out. In, and out. Ten seconds on the intake, hold. Ten seconds on the exhale, hold. He could feel the rhythm slowing in his chest. Eleven seconds in, hold. Eleven seconds out, hold. He continued up to sixteen-second intervals.

After breathing slowly for a minute, he felt his body relax. The surface of his mind settled like a calm undisturbed lake. A tingling sensation started to creep into his feet. It spread up his legs with a pulsing rhythm. Maybe his body was shutting down from the lack of oxygen.

No. Not more than five minutes had passed; his brain couldn't already be shutting off unnecessary functions.

Something else was happening. His eyes were closed, but he could see the eyelids and the muscles attached to tendons that extended up under his scalp and back into his skull. Everything stayed frozen.

Jax realized he wasn't breathing anymore and tried to gasp but he didn't have a mouth to move. He jerked his eyes open, or what he thought was his eyes, and what he saw twisted his mind to the point of breaking.

Before him was Narasimha, pinned at the end of the pyramid. Her space suit was ghostly translucent, like a wisp of steam held in its shape around her. Her body pulsed and shifted beneath it, constantly moving in and out of focus in a blur of colors and shapes. As Jax scanned her face, he could see her snout lengthen and contract, her teeth vibrate in three directions, and her eyes squinting, scowling, bulging, crying, in an endless display of possibilities.

Jax shut what he thought was his eyes in confusion. *What's happened to me? I can't be dead!* He glanced down at his own body. He could see it, as if under both an X-ray and a microscope, sitting perfectly still. His space suit was gone now, too! The only thing he could see was his naked body suspended in a void of … well, it wasn't black, star-filled space. It was as if his body were as big as the entire planet. He could look for miles and miles on the surface and not see the end of it.

The vision he was having was more than his imagination, he knew. He was experiencing his body in a way he didn't understand. As he realized this, every part of him expanded out in his awareness, spreading like a blanket of possibilities. Muscles, tendons, bone, veins, blood—more depth of sensation than he had ever known—all frozen in time, but alive in memories and futures.

It wasn't light he was seeing, he realized. It was all of the possible shapes and sizes and colors that his body could be.

He looked out to Narasimha once again, trying to understand more of what he was viewing. It was like watching the countryside from inside a speeding rocket. He could see everything, but it was all a blur. His focus held for a moment, there, and expression of pain, gone with the blur.

The longer he focused on her shifting form, the more Jax felt himself becoming a part of the blur. He could feel a new experience. It was like suddenly recalling a forgotten memory. Her inner makeup spread before him. The hard, pointed nails were his nails. The golden fur was his fur. The tail, extending out of the base of her spine, was his tail. And the short tip of the tail triggered memories flowing into him. It was a story more rich than the lioness had experienced herself.

The pain of the flesh separating under the knife. Blood working to seal off the open wound. Each cell obediently following the instructions dictated by its DNA. Jax remembered a pain before the tail had been cut from her body, more potent than the physical shocks of nerve signals. The scene filled with the living matter that connected to that moment of pain. He saw, or experienced, another Animalis—a breed of house cat—whose lineage was also somehow contained in Jax's awareness. Her tail had been removed, sliced off by a laser rifle, in an attack on a group of humans that had been breaking Animalis for farm labor. Jax could feel the sting of Narasimha's pain, guilt for not protecting the cat, and remorse for the Animalis having to give life and limb for their cause. He could feel the deep connection that Narasimha made with those around her. Her love was simple, natural, and more potent than what Jax had felt, even for his own parents. Narasimha had cut her tail off and gave it to the cat, as a token of her love and for her sacrifice.

Jax pulled himself out of the experience. He wasn't dreaming, not this vividly. Somehow he was seeing and living through someone else. He knew what a dream felt like, and this was definitely not a dream.

Jax pushed his awareness out farther, and found the pyramid, locked in his new timeless reality. It shook him to come in contact with it. As his mind began to spread out with what made up the pyramid's existence, Jax wanted to tremble, to cower back and hide from it. The history of life over the entire planet. More than that, every element of emotion—joy, triumph, remorse, sadness—were now within his sphere of experience. What he had seen from his own eyes, and heart, were less than molecules in the cosmic expanse of the reality that was life. What he had known as love was a tiny fragment of what had been experienced in the pool of life. He wanted to hide every moment when he had thought his life was too hard, and disown every time he had thought he had achieved something great, for fear that this accumulation of existence would crush him with some immeasurable laugh at his own insignificance.

At the same moment that he realized he was a speck of nothing, a warm, comforting sense of purpose filled him. This thing, this access point of all life, had brought him here. Like a two-sided mirror, Jax's focus had expanded out to the entirety of life, and the focus of life had been brought down on Jax. *Don't move. Watch him,* it seemed to whisper. *What will he do?*

He could feel it now; he was inside the machine. He had

activated the pyramid. He hadn't been using his eyes at all, but instead, paying attention to different parts of an immense tapestry of DNA. It was more than DNA that he had power over now; he could see the history of the world, and every detail as it existed in the now, and fragmented trails of possibilities and probabilities spread out into the future. It was all kept within the DNA, and as it passed from life to life, it accumulated a record held as a code in the very atoms of the DNA molecules. Jax could see the pyramid reading subtle differences in the subatomic particles within the atoms, reading it like the binary of a computer. A feeling of immense power came into him, and it scared him.

This was the machine that had created the Animalis.

Jax wanted to understand it. He started to follow histories that were contained in the DNA around him. His own path had connected with Narasimha, Hank, Grimshaw, and at each of the points of connection, he could transfer from his DNA to theirs.

When he found himself holding Moxie and pushing her inside of Hank's space suit, his curiosity became excited.

Moxie's DNA spread out its secrets before Jax.

"Hello," a strange and inhuman voice said.

Jax froze. The voice hadn't been in the history. It was immediate, something in the endless time he was experiencing. He tried to mentally answer *"Who's there?"* but the thought didn't extend out of him like the voice had.

"You made it, Jax," the voice said again. *"Are you looking at our body?"*

The history of Moxie was still spread out in Jax's mind.

"Thank you for keeping us safe. You protected us."

He tried again to find the source of the voice. There was a connection in his thoughts. Jax could sense the entity at the other end of the connection, but it wasn't part of the DNA. There was no arrangement of electron spin for the pyramid to decode to show its history. It was on a different plane of existence. Jax's mind struggled to envision how it could exist outside of the realm of reality that everything else was in.

Although it wasn't DNA itself, it had a permanent connection, spreading down into two bodies. Jax followed that connection and found himself at Moxie again, and Little Hank. The entity was spread throughout the two creature's entire existence. It was them, or controlling them, or manifesting itself through them. The thought of clay came to him: maybe the creatures of DNA were like figures of clay, and this entity was like a hand reaching down to move and control the clay.

"Now, you are like us," the entity said. *"You can make changes."*

He could make changes? *"How?"* he wanted to ask, but his thoughts stayed within his own mind. Changes could be made in this strange realm, just like clay. Even he might have been changed. That's why he was different. That was why his leg had grown back.

Jax dove through the ocean of information and found himself in the arena. His DNA history linked with the bear's, and hundreds of spectators. He focused down on the DNA describing his leg, moving back to the moment Misha had pulled back, bit down, and held him to the ground with her foot.

Before the leg was torn off, he came across a gap in his DNA's record. It wasn't a big gap, just a difference between what it was before, and what it was after. Before, his leg would have gushed blood, killing him within minutes of the incident in an explosion of pain. After the gap, his leg had been altered to cut off its blood circulation, and deaden the nerves. Not only that, but the cells immediately began rebuilding the leg.

The change, the gap in the DNA, had come from something. Maybe Moxie and Little Hank, Jax couldn't tell; the trail of influence drifted off without leaving a record. It hadn't come from the pyramid, or anyone using it.

Jax was growing excited. The machine held answers he wanted to know.

He brought his focus through time to the moment the machine had been conceived by Dr. Ivanovich. From the present, Jax followed the life of the pyramid's DNA back to its formation. He was surprised to see Moxie and Little Hank beside the pyramid the entire journey.

Before the machine had been loaded onto the rat Animalis plane, it had been locked underground in the frozen tundra of Russia. Moxie and Little Hank had been its sentries, keeping humans away from the device for nearly one hundred years.

Jax followed the path of its existence back to the very beginning. He could see Dr. Ivanovich injecting DNA that had been taken from the two ferret creatures. That was the moment of its birth. But Jax could see gaps in the doctor's own DNA. He had been affected by the entity, or entities. After each gap came a burst of inspiration in the production of the pyramid.

Jax saw when the machine had first been used. He could feel the body within the pyramid: Dr. Ivanovich. He sat, legs crossed, hands resting at his knees, in a meditation pose. His breath was under control. His heart slowing. There was a spark, and the story only existed in the thoughts that had been in the doctor's mind as he traveled through the strange reality of DNA.

Jax watched as Ivanovich stretched his consciousness to six

potted plants he had prepared on his desk: three identical flowers and three freshly planted seeds of the same type. Jax could see the first plant change under the influence of the doctor's mental focus; instead of red petals, this flower would be changed to blue. Jax saw the projected future of the plant change. The cells would shift their behavior based on the new instructions given by the DNA. The plant would turn to blue within a matter of a few minutes once Dr. Ivanovich returned to normal reality. Then, within a day, the plant would return to its default red color.

They moved to the next plant. Jax felt the doctor pulling in traits from other plants. He wanted to see, when time resumed, if this flower could be transformed into an entirely different species of plant: a tomato plant. The projection of the future changed, and the plant deformed, trying to take on the attributes of the new plant. As well, within a day, the plant would return to the red flower it had been, but with damage that would take several more days to mend.

The third plant's DNA was given instructions to change into a bird. The projection ended in the plant's death, cells tearing apart before another structure had taken their place. It would die within an hour, incapacitated by the quick deterioration taking place within it.

The doctor repeated the process on the seeds.

The first seed projected a natural life as a blue-colored flower.

The second projection showed a fully functional tomato plant. If nourished, it could bear fruit, reproduce, and even form new hybrids with other plants.

The third plant grew as an abomination. Never fully functional as either a flower or a bird. It would die within a few days.

Dr. Ivanovich left the machine and watched the projections come to fruition. After the plants' alterations had run their course, the doctor continued his experiments, and eventually created the Animalis.

Jax returned to the awareness around his body, itching to try it himself.

He focused in on himself, on the instructions that dictated his eye color. It took some trial and error, but as he touched pieces of the DNA, he could see his eyes shifting from brown to yellow, to red, to blue. He stopped on blue, and watched the projected change take place in his eyes. They would shift in a matter of minutes, and remain blue for a little less than twenty-four hours.

He shifted the DNA back, and the projected change vanished.

He could do it: change the world in whatever way he wanted. He could cure every human embryo growing in its mother's womb of genetic defects in an instant. Or find every sick person and strengthen them with a twenty four hour burst of God-like immunity. Was that why he had been brought here? Would that ruin some global balance? There was no one to guide his action. The question echoed through his mind: *"What will he do?"*

He searched for Hurley. She was frozen in time in the atmosphere, Hodge and Little Hank at her side. Jax could see her spreading out before him, her possible future, and her accumulation of past experience. She would make it to the surface, and she would look for him. It made him happier than he had expected, to feel her love for him. He felt her flutters of joy when she had been with him at ACTS. Her rage was his rage when Hank had tortured the Animalis hyena, her anxiety was his, that someone might ever hurt Hodge. There was an innocence and

301

purity in Hodge that she knew was better than her. More honest. If he was hurt, there could be no justification for it. Jax saw the fear she felt when she allowed herself to want to be with Jax, unsure if he would see her as lovable, desirable, beautiful, or good. He felt her anger at herself for her cowardice and inability to tell Jax her secret.

In Jax, she saw a young man, full of potential, just like Jax saw, ready to change the world. Not knowing the depth that would come from living a long life as she had. A long life. If Jax had had full control over his body, he would have staggered at what he found hidden in the history of Hurley's DNA. Her history, her life, seemed to go on and on. She had lived for seventy-five years.

Jax reeled again. How? She looked so young! Seventy-five? Almost twice as old as his own mother, even older than his grandmother. Yet her body was still vibrant with healthy tissue. She had done what she could to remain in her youth but even she didn't know the real reason her body had defied the deterioration of age.

Disgust built up inside him. She had lied to him. She was so much wiser and accomplished than he had ever imagined. She had a trust worth over a million credits. She headed a foundation for the Animalis. Here Jax was, an inexperienced, underwhelming child before her.

But she loved him.

She had to have been changed. Jax scanned through her past and began to notice slight changes in her DNA. He followed the wisps that had affected her. Tiny fragments of DNA had been influenced, shifted by something, like his leg had been. The trail faded off without a record from the mysterious entities.

He opened his vision wider and began to see more wisps. He could almost make out a pattern spread through history. Changes, leading to more changes, building in importance. It was like an intelligence flowing through life itself. Something big was coming in the future. It looked like the entities were preparing to transform the balance of coexistence within the sphere of life. She had been saved to come into contact with his own life, but the reason eluded him. Perhaps he had been brought here for this. So that he would be here, to use the machine.

The question came back: *"What will he do?"*

He could end the war, like Hank, Hernandez, and his father wanted. He could destroy the Animalis.

His body compressed with the resonance of the answer that the focus of life gave to his thoughts. His physical body contorted with the agony of it. He could feel all of the suffering contained in those few words: *destroy the Animalis.* The sorrow of genocide from the past locked in the memory of the DNA felt overwhelming. Jax was sucked down in it, incapacitated, drowning in the pain. There was a whole eternity of suffering. But it wasn't the physical pain that would stay with him forever; it was the betrayal each individual—animal, Animalis, and human—had felt. A hand that could extend love and mercy, had lashed out instead. Where friendship could have been, should have been, there was cold, indifferent cruelty. Fear, mistrust, and separation were the result.

He tried to flee the experiences, and the guilt of having been a part of it, focusing back down on the one twinkle of kindness he could think of: Hurley. Within her mind was the hope he needed to feel. Kindness, trust, faith in those around her. She loved Jax. She loved Hodge, Little Hank, and Moxie. Jax could even see the compassion she had for Hank, even while he had been torturing the Animalis, but how?

He noticed another rift in Grimshaw's DNA that caught his attention. Jax tried to bring it into focus. It was strange, remnants of pain and regret, but he saw some sections were out of his reach. He had thought the secrets of all DNA were in his control, but not this. He started to form an idea of what had happened, guessing from what came before, and what came after the gaps.

28
Hurley

Hurley's DNA displayed her life to Jax. From an early age, the Animalis stood out in her mind.

"The census from last year was unaware of the groups of Animalis living in northern Mongolia," a news reporter had said. "This could increase the estimated population by tens of thousands."

"A new study is underway," said another reporter from her memories. "Researchers are hoping to find the answers to the question: 'Just how human are the Animalis?' Many theorize that their brains—like their bodies—are half way between humans and animals."

Conversations from her childhood friends drifted through Jax's awareness: "If I could have any Animalis, I'd want a dog. I'd train him to clean my room, go to the bathroom in the toilet, and he would guard our house."

The dream of owning Animalis was quickly quelled. Protective Animalis rights groups held popular sway within the United Nations and laws were passed to prevent ownership and mistreatment. With the world economy doing well in the twenties, the Animalis were welcomed into the work force. When the economy collapsed in the thirties, the Animalis became despised.

Her father had been in the military, and it was a natural choice for her to follow in his footsteps. She hated the training, the mental games, and the manipulation, but she made it out of boot camp, alive, but hardened.

Jesus Hernandez was there, joining the military several years after her. He was young and cocky, like Jax had been, ready to save the world. He was younger than her, too, ten years younger. In the present, he had aged far more than she had. She knew that he was attracted to her, but her attraction to him wasn't the same. She needed someone to share her fears with, and Hernandez was always willing to listen. Letting the other men in the unit think they were dating helped to quell most of their own ambitions for courting her, but it seemed to fuel a dangerous protectiveness in Hernandez.

The Animalis started attacking humans. Not just the random bitings, but deliberate, planned assaults on humans. There were political discussions about if they should be controlled, registered, if their population should be limited. Then she was deployed.

"What?" the voice of Hernandez echoed to Jax from the DNA memory. "They're splitting up the unit!" He didn't have much of a temper, but it was coming out now.

"I'll be online most nights," Hurley tried to reassure him. "That robotics company, Nano Wrimo, might actually have their robot avatars ready for public use within the year, you know. I'll rent one and come walking with you."

He didn't want to hear it. "I should be coming with you. I'll put in a request. I don't care what they have planned for me."

He kept it up for the two days leading to her departure. But when the time came, he had never sent in the request, afraid to have discipline come down on him. He said good-bye.

They were sending her into the heart of Siberia, where the bulk of the Animalis had built whole cities of nothing but Animalis. Apparently they were going to be helping reduce excess Animalis population. She didn't know what it meant, and wanted to imagine it would be a clean euthanasia of an overcrowded animal shelter. But it wasn't.

The first mission was frightening: Animalis in an urban environment, talking, playing, curious at the troops forming barricades and buildings for themselves. Jax felt the anxiety she felt; it was not an animal shelter. The Animalis were just as alive as the humans who had come to eliminate them. It was sickening how willingly the Animalis obeyed. They came to the buildings, Hurley worked at the desk, helping them fill out paperwork before being led, one by one, into another room, never to come back out. One week at the desk, the next week in the room the Animalis were led to.

Jax came to the first gap in the DNA's records. It wasn't a subtle change, like Jax's leg had been. There was a small piece of time and space that had been clipped out of the universe, and then sown back together. After the gap, Hurley was different. She had closed off a piece of her emotions. She thought she should feel bad about something—gap—but everyone seemed to think they were doing a great thing. It was important, they were protecting the world, and she was a part of it, playing an important role.

One of the weeks while Hurley was working at the desk, Hernandez walked in. He was smiling.

"Hey, firecracker. Did you miss me?" he asked.

"Jesus!" She ran to him. She needed someone familiar, she needed someone to tell her she was a good person. She needed an ally. Jax felt the relief of being held in familiar arms.

"Hernandez, your first shifts are going to be back in this room." Another soldier broke up their reunion.

"Let's catch up tonight, alright?" Hernandez said.

"Alright," she said, smiling.

The two men started to walk to the other room.

"Watch it, freak," the soldier warned one of the Animalis.

Hernandez laughed. "Ugly aren't they? Back off, apestoso." He pushed the mole to the ground with the Spanish insult.

Jax felt Hurley's hope pull back. Hernandez hated the Animalis just like everyone else. She wanted to say something; the unspoken words were all a part of the DNA's memories:

Leave it alone. It trusts us with its life, and we are crushing that trust under our feet. The least we can do is let it enjoy the last few moments of its life. I thought you were kind. I thought you would see the pain we were causing and want to put up a fight with me, refuse our duties together. But I can't say any of this to you because you'd say I was wrong. You'd push me down, just like that Animalis.

When they met later, she found she couldn't open up to him anymore. He thought they were still a couple, and didn't seem to notice that it was only him speaking when they were together.

When the Animalis began to suspect that their friends and companions weren't coming back, they became hostile, refusing the demands they had given into before. Hurley and the others were ordered to use deadly force if an Animalis showed signs of defiance. She was sent into the city to escort Animalis that hadn't come at their appointed times, and then there was another gap. The gaps were not in her memory, there was nothing there to remember.

The disconnection from her emotions widened, robotically

obeying commands. But something was trying to get out from inside her. Jax could feel doubt building, with every gap in the story that he came across, but she held it back. She held onto any justification she could, trying to shield herself from the guilt.

She broke down in the third city they were ordered to reduce. Standing in the room where the compliant Animalis were being taken to die, she held the syringe in her hand. It was meant for the Animalis, but she, and Jax, caught in the experience, were going to turn the needle on themselves; they were the ones that deserved to feel the deadly prick of it. She couldn't get away from the military. She couldn't disobey, or run away, or feel sorry for what she was doing. There was no way for her to escape. The dam she had built, between herself and her feelings of guilt at betraying the trust of the innocent Animalis, broke. Jax passed the last gap.

Hurley was put through a rehabilitation program and discharged from the military. She had known what she was doing, and had chosen to ignore the voice that had called out from inside her. The deaths of thousands of innocent Animalis weighed on her conscience. There was no way to ask for forgiveness, no way that the debt could be lifted from her shoulders.

Jax started to feel peace replacing the shame five years later in her life. She sat in her apartment, sinking into an ever rising layer of trash on the floor. She stared at the ceiling thinking, *I want to do better. I want to fix what I've done. I won't stop until it's made right. I won't stop until the Animalis are safe and the world is at peace. I just need this pain taken away. I know everything will be alright.* There was a sudden shift in her mind as all of the gaps in her past were created and the weight lifted from her shoulders.

There was an opportunity the next day to join a group that would be living with and helping Animalis, and she took it. The more she came to understand the Animalis, playing with them, helping to reinforce human mannerisms, the more she found she loved them. The more she loved them, the more she never wanted to see another Animalis hurt the way she had hurt them. Jax had already experienced glimpses of the quality that she cherished so much in them: innocence. But seeing it through her eyes revealed the depth of their innocence.

The Animalis hadn't known lies, and hadn't known betrayal. They were all little children, and like children, as they were abused, taken advantage of, and belittled, their trust grew thin and fearful. Their instinct of self-preservation took over, and they would lash out in violent ways when provoked.

29
Awakening

Jax slowly receded from Hurley's life; she should have some privacy left to her past. He had been seeking solace in her life, but had found more than he could comprehend. He had needed to know that there was more than misery in the world, and he had found it.

Jax pulled himself back to the DNA that had trails connecting to him in the present. His body floated in the timeless present. He couldn't die. This couldn't be the end.

Strands of possible futures trailed off in front of Jax. He was surprised to find that, within the next five minutes, he and Narasimha would almost certainly be picked up. The plane he had been on, Narasimha's plane, was still in the upper atmosphere. The warthog that was flying the plane had waited for the others to leave, and was going to be returning.

The arena again! Jax thought in despair. He checked inside of Narasimha and found that there was almost nothing he could do that would stop her from taking him back to that horrible place, and killing him herself.

He could feel the focal point of life still watching him, waiting on him, before it would continue on. He wished there was someone to just tell him what to do. Hank, Hernandez, Hurley—

Let them decide—and he would be the tool in their hands. What price would he have to pay if he made the wrong choice?

He could use the pyramid to stop Narasimha and save himself and countless others she might kill. Just one life.

But his mind trembled again from the answer the pyramid gave: *"NO."*

Something shifted inside his mind. Lessons from Hurley's life, and his own, combining and taking root in him. He cared for the Animalis, he realized. He couldn't leave the war and bloodshed to continue unabated. This was his opportunity to make a difference. If he flexed his will within this realm, nations could fall, lives could be changed. If only he knew the right change to make.

They have to choose, Jax realized. It wouldn't change anything if he forced a change on the Earth. That had happened plenty of times in the past and the result was always the same; resistance and regression to even more violence. The people had to choose it for themselves. *Ten billion people? How...*

Narasimha was the key. He couldn't hope to change everyone's mind without force, but maybe one. She was the catalyst for the Animalis. It would be the beginning of a change for the better.

Narasimha's life spread before him once more. He had to know what was motivating her. If he could understand her, then maybe he could change her.

Jax absorbed her life in giant gulps. She had been a mother. She was the last of her kind. Her parents and her children had been killed one by one by humans. She had suffered and lost everything and attributed all of her suffering to humans. She had a need to hunt and had convinced herself that humans were prey.

But behind all of that, Jax found her need to belong. She wanted to have a place in the world. Someone had to want her.

It was a simple thing, but impossible to achieve. She had demonized and debased humans down to the lowest and most insignificant creatures in her mind. How could Jax possibly make her believe that she was important to a human?

He would help Narasimha to change because he loved her. He wouldn't stop until he had found a way to connect with her. He would dedicate his life to her.

Slowly a plan began to form in his mind. Jax worked with a new found passion. Jax spun the gears of his mind coming up with ways to keep himself alive that were more and more ridiculous and awesome. If Jax could have grinned in this strange place, he would have been radiating giddy excitement.

When it was done, Jax brought his focus back to the pyramid, and to his body spinning within it. Before he tried to pull himself from the experience, he thought of Hank again. His best friend, driven crazy, knowing what the pyramid might be capable of, while no one had believed him.

Jax quickly found Hank's DNA and watched it spread out before him. Hank sat, in the present moment, inside the company's plane, within his small cabin, still aching from the near fatal dose of serum. Jax was blown away by the complexity and power of Hank's mind, but there was something wrong.

Hank's mind was split, torn between his faith and friendship with Jax, and his hatred for the Animalis. The split was creating a chasm. His mind was a whole world of thoughts and information, carefully organized and cared for.

When the split had started to form, three months ago, the force of his emotions had pushed his actions out of alignment with his ideals. He was doing things that he knew were wrong. Instead of fixing the incompatible actions, he was creating mental blocks, meant to stop his moral judgment from condemning himself for what he had done to the hyena. The mental blocks had started to fragment his mind.

It was painful to see. On one side, he was taught to honor life, and on the other side, where he had hidden his grief for his mother, was a boiling volcano of vengeance ready to explode with a deadly wrath. The pyramid had been the ultimate tool.

Pain shot through Jax's heart to see the chasm cutting through their friendship.

Jax was growing weak; he could sense the strain of using the pyramid for too long building up inside his body. He had to get his mind out soon. He wanted to do something, give Hank some satisfaction that the pyramid was the Ivanovich Machine.

So he planted a seed in Hank's mind as he sat in his cabin, linking their memories in a way that would give him an echo of Jax's experience in the pyramid.

Then Jax was back, focusing on himself; what his breath had been. Breath in, hold. Breath out, hold. In sixteen seconds, out sixteen seconds. Time was starting to continue. He felt his legs and his arms. The synapses finished firing in his brain and his eyes cracked open. The Earth spun into view, the blue glow so beautiful to him now. The pyramid continued to rotate, and the stars came into view. He was alive. In: one, two, three, four, five, six, seven, eight, nine, ten, eleven, twelve, thirteen, fourteen, fifteen.

He could feel something shifting inside his body, sending out a sound of gurgling fluids. Something popped, but he didn't feel any pain. His changes were happening! Everything was going to be different. His excitement burst onto his face.

Fatigue washed over him. In the eternity of the machine, he hadn't had to hold all of the information flowing through him. Now the enormous wave of knowledge was crashing into his limited body. His muscles ached, his eyes leaked, and his mind started to forget. The wealth of information slipping away like a dream. His consciousness began to drift as he slipped into a recovery sleep.

———

Jax woke up strapped to the wall of the plane. His space suit was off, and he could hear the rumbles from sound waves propagating through the air again. His head was still pounding, and his left hand was numb. His muscles couldn't have moved even if they hadn't been strapped down.

The light within the cargo hold burned his eyes, but he needed to see it. He held one eyelid open and looked down where the pyramid had been strapped. It was there again, cold and unmoving, held to the floor like the rest of the inanimate cargo. He shut his eye quickly to stop from getting sick. He hadn't taken into account that his mind would need to adjust to his changes just as much as his body had.

"Run—Run—Run it again. Run in again," a voice was saying. "Get—Get another scanner."

The wiring in his brain hadn't fully adjusted yet, and the words echoed and shot around his mind, circling past his awareness several times at a hundred miles an hour.

"We only have the one, Nara. I don't see anything wrong with it," the warthog said.

Jax opened his eye a little more. The two Animalis were talking next to the wall screen. An ICT scan of the pyramid rotated in a three-dimensional image on the display. The lioness' head flicked to the side, and she slowly began to turn around. She held her hand up to stop the conversation with the warthog.

"Jax," she said, her voice still echoing off the walls within his skull. "You lived. I lived. You keep making these mistakes. Your enemy, brought helpless before you—helpless before you—again and again, and you don't have the strength to act." She snarled, and started walking to him.

Jax wanted to speak, but he knew he wouldn't be able to make any audible sounds yet.

"Unless you don't think I'm your enemy?" she said. "How did you activate the pyramid, Jax?"

She waited for him to respond. After a moment, he decided to try. The movement burned his lips.

"We're not enemies, Nara." His voice was a gravelly whisper and came out of his mouth in slow motion. The effort sent his head pounding again.

Narasimha waited for more. When Jax remained quiet, she started to laugh. "Humans are always coming up with new ways to flaunt their stupidity," She looked back at the warthog and laughed again; the sound of it seemed to ricochet around the cargo hold. "Why don't you think we're enemies?" She seemed to be asking it for an honest answer.

"Because …" Jax pulled himself from the brink of unconsciousness. "I'm not fighting against you anymore."

"I wasn't sure you were fighting me before. You were scurrying across my path like a cockroach, trying not to be crushed," she said, standing directly in front of him. She looked into his eyes.

Her head jerked back, and her eyes squinted. When she

spoke, her voice caught in her throat. "No. Please. I was helping!" A tear flicked to the floor from with a forceful head shake.

She was seeing the death and destruction that had come to the Animalis because of her militant attacks, Jax knew. When she looked into his eyes it triggered a series of memories Jax had implanted from the pyramid. They were the consequences of her actions. Seeing her face twisted in pain made Jax's heart ache.

"Why is the pyramid different?" she snarled, breaking eye contact with him. "Why isn't the DNA signature showing up in the CT scans anymore?" She pressed her broad nose close to Jax's cheek. Her moist breath warmed his skin.

"I killed it," Jax said. The numbness in his left hand began to sting. He wouldn't last much longer before he would sink into unconsciousness again while his brain adjusted to the change. "It's gone. The DNA inside it is completely destroyed." He felt the breath stop on his cheek. The breath held for a long time, then returned as a growl.

"Don't lie, human," she said.

"I'd tell you how to use it, but it doesn't matter anymore. No one will ever be able to use it again." It was true. As his last act within the pyramid, he had destroyed the machine's power the only way he knew how: by erasing the DNA flowing within it. It wouldn't affect any of the vast history of DNA he had floated through. The pyramid had only served as a window to see all that had happened, combined with tools to change all living DNA.

He had done the right thing, he was sure of it. No one would be creating another machine like it in a million years. At least not until the unearthly creatures wanted someone to create another one.

Jax started to let himself go. There was a sense of falling backward down a deep tunnel as his consciousness drifted away.

He heard a deafening roar that was loud enough to compete with the ringing building in Jax's ears. "It was mine!" As his mind drifted away, the voice was squeezed down to a tinny echo: "I'll tear you apart for all the world to see!"

30
A New Beginning

In his dream, he had been playing the ACTS Animalis ball game with Hodge. All the players kept remarking about what a big smile he had, and he realized he *was* smiling. The muscles in his cheeks pulled the corners of his mouth into the biggest smile he had ever held.

He woke in a confused state inside a cage. The concrete floor was ice cold, and there was no ragged blanket to hold this time. The exhaustion had subsided, all except the numbness in his left hand. It had stopped stinging and was now vibrating with a constant buzz.

Jax heard the rhythmic stomping of the arena crowd accepting two new Animalis combatants onto the floor above him and was relieved that his mind had adjusted to the change.

They weren't stomping for him this time. But they would be soon.

How long did he have before the arena was cleared and prepared for his turn in it? Jax slowly stood, letting himself experience the slightly altered muscle and tendon structures throughout his body.

Once he was able to walk around his cell, he sat with his legs folded in a meditation position. There had been something he'd wanted to test when he had left the pyramid. He closed his eyes and focused on his breathing. In and out. He slowly increased the duration of the intake and exhale.

The crowd cheered loudly above him. What horrible thing were they praising at this moment? Jax found himself thinking. His mind had wandered. He tried to bring it back to his breath. In for fifteen seconds, hold. Exhale for fifteen, hold.

"I don't know what kind of stunt that was you pulled last time, mal'chik, but people went wild over it. I can't believe Nara found you again. And look at you, already have a new one grown." The deep voice of the arena host broke Jax's concentration again.

Jax refused to open his eyes to acknowledge the man. In for sixteen seconds, hold. Exhale for sixteen, hold.

"This time, I'm sorry, mal'chik, but I can't offer you any help." He seemed to think it was big news. "Not unless you want to split Nara's kingdom with me if you win."

Pretend he isn't there. In seventeen seconds, hold. Exhale seventeen seconds, hold. Jax felt a tingle.

"If you kill Nara, it's all yours. Her planes, the printer shops."

Jax tried to hold onto the tingle, spread it around with his awareness.

"But, then, I guess one of the others will come after you. Those Animalis, they'd go to the ends of the Earth for her," he was saying. "Strangest thing. They're not terrified of her, like they should be, of a predator like her. I guess that's why I haven't made any moves against her myself."

The tingle faded. He lost it. Well, it was worth a shot anyways. Jax let his breath return to normal and opened his eyes.

"Aw, there you are," the man said. "Good. Do I need to shock you? Or will you come peacefully this time?"

Jax didn't fight. He let himself be led down to the cage that would spill him out into the arena. The man kept talking along the way, trying to inspire a good, money-earning fight from Jax.

The crowd began to chant. It was a different chant than Jax had heard before: "Na-ra!" Boom, boom. "Sim-ha!" Boom, boom. It was ominous that they already knew what was coming. Inevitably coming, there was nothing Jax could do to stop it. The large man stood in the shadows when Jax's cage started to push him forward.

Sunlight absorbed the darkness as the cage was pushed forward into it. The cage stopped. Narasimha watched him from across the arena. Her clothes revealed the redundant ripples of muscles in her arms, neck, and legs. Her breathing was shallow. The focus of her stare revealed her animal origin. Jax could feel himself being transformed in her eyes, like he was already a chunk of meat waiting to be devoured. The walls of the cages swung open.

Jax took a deep breath. He was getting close to the end of the DNA's projected probable future that he had seen—and that which terrified him more: the time limit before the changes he had made disappeared. He could feel the blood in his veins growing cold with fear, but he had to stay calm. He tried to see through Narasimha the way he had in the pyramid. She was a living house of DNA. They were connected, brother and sister in life.

Narasimha slowly walked out of the cage. Her feet took the delicate steps of a hunt about to begin.

"Stop your attacks on humans, Nara," Jax called out to her. "We're not your enemy. I'm not your enemy!"

She could have been in the vacuum of space. The words hadn't reached her. She continued to inch forward.

Jax flexed his muscles, testing the changes to his body once more before the fight.

In front of him was one of the most deadly predators to walk the Earth. He had seen her devour a man, and now he had to conquer his fear of her. He couldn't be afraid of her terrible jaws, or her razor-sharp hands.

In an instant, her delicate walk burst into a charge. The muscles in her body demonstrated their full potential, launching her across the arena at a terrifying speed.

Jax's heart pounded, and his altered brain worked in overtime. An extra layer of neurons preprocessed the visual information coming in from his eyes and gave him the sense that everything was moving in slow motion. Her claws extended from the tips of her fingers as she dove toward him. He could see her exact trajectory before her legs left the ground.

With a quick dodge to the left, his increased strength propelled him safely away from her lunge. As her hands hit the ground, he leaped several yards away.

She crumpled against the ground where she had been expecting to tackle Jax, and a cloud of dust swirled around her.

Her growl was the first thing to re-emerge. With a fluid convulsion of muscle, she leaped from the dirt and landed on all fours. She shook her head.

"How?" she asked. Her eyes were filled with hate beyond the point of rage. Her skin wrinkled and pulled up in an expression that made Jax want to run for his life.

Jax extended his left arm at her, pointing his fingertips, ready to protect himself from the terrifying beast in front of him. He hesitated, then lowered his arm. He had to save that surprise for a true emergency.

She stood and began another slow approach, more wary of his speed and strength.

The pre-processed visual information showed her muscles in her chest and arms beginning to bulge. Potential energy was building up in her shoulder.

Her hand sliced through the air, almost overcoming Jax's ability to slow the action. Jax shrank backward and felt the tip of a claw pass in front of his nose.

"What have you done?" she hissed, swiping at him again. "You're not human."

Jax easily moved and dodged again and again. With his physical changes, he could survive the fight, but his goal wasn't just to survive. He had to win Narasimha for humanity.

With a disgusted sniff, Narasimha stopped her attack and stepped away from him. "Stun him!" she called to the lip of the arena.

Jax's heart sank. With a quick glance upward, he could see the blue glow of shock sticks lighting up around the arena. The nearest guard jabbed, and Jax twirled to the side. Another guard moved closer and cut the air.

The buzz of electricity carved past his head as he dodged. Jax dove away from the sticks to the center of the ring, where Narasimha waited for him.

He hit the ground in a roll and came to a stop facing Narasimha. Their eyes locked for a moment and she shuddered. With a growl, she began another cautious approach.

"I'm not your enemy, Nara," Jax whispered. He watched where her eyes went and moved to force eye contact again. "Humans are not your enemy."

"Guards!" she bellowed. "This fight is over. Take him back to his cage!"

Ladders sprung up along the walls, and the guards looked ready to enter the arena to capture him.

"Call them back," Jax said.

She growled in response.

"I can kill them, Nara. Call them off, now," he said.

He pointed his left arm into the air. Inside his forearm, Jax pumped the new muscles hidden beneath his skin. The specialized cells contracted and released their stored electric energy.

The air above him exploded as lightning shot out of the tip of his index finger. Fifteen hundred volts instantly expelled from the three condensed electric eel glands in his arm. The blinding light was gone before a shockwave of sound shook the walls of the arena.

Jax felt a sharp sting and yanked his hand back against his chest. His body buzzed from the residual current dancing around his skin. It had worked better than he had expected, but his finger was bursting with pain. He moved his hand to see the tip of his finger charred completely black.

"Stop!" Narasimha called.

The guards were already backing away, shaking their heads. The crowd of Animalis watching the fight shrieked.

"You … I …" she said, trying to avoid eye contact.

Her breathing grew intense. Watching her struggle, Jax found himself wanting to comfort her. This poor creature had given her life for the benefit of other Animalis and was being forced to confront the reality that she had caused far more harm than good.

"Kill me," she said.

"No," Jax said with a rush of sadness. "You can't die, Nara! Not with them depending on you!" Jax gestured to the audience. "I will protect you. I will go to the ends of the earth for you. You keep seeing the death caused by your actions, but you have to have known the pain you were causing. You didn't know there was a better way. There is a better way! I've seen it!"

Jax could see her muscles coiling and bulging. Every fibrous inch of her body called for his blood. He could have moved to avoid it, but he couldn't let himself. He deserved what she was about to do to him, for attacking her, for killing the innocent warehouse workers, for being a part of the mistreatment that had led Narasimha to feel justified in her attacks.

Fur, claws, ferocity, and fatality erupted from the ground. Jax could feel the bottom of his stomach open into an empty void as he watched her come for him. Instead of his life passing before his eyes, he could see Narasimha's life leading up to this moment. Her family's passing, her struggle to survive, then joining the militants and struggling to save other's lives. There was no way she could save them. All she could do was take revenge. Now, her life's work was revealed for what it was, tragedy. She had to kill what was forcing her to confront it. Her mouth opened wide for her accuser.

Jax smiled. Even with all the pain that the world could offer, and what it was about to offer him, he was glad to have something to die for.

She slammed into him and they both crashed against the ground. Her face drew close, snarling and panting. He could see right into her yellow, fireball pupils now. There was more than rage inside her now.

"I'm sorry," Jax said to her. "I'm sorry I killed the people you love, Nara."

Narasimha stopped. She held her body perfectly still, watching him. Her eyes grew narrow and she bit into his throat.

With her head turned sideways, scooping as much of his neck within her jaws as she could, her ear ended up just inches away from his mouth. Jax continued to whisper through the constriction. "I'm sorry I can't do anything to bring them back."

A deep growl started to fill the arena. She hesitated, and pulled her mouth off his neck without crushing it.

Claws slashed down on top of him, splitting his chest in a burst of blood and pain.

"There is no other way!" she cried. "We know what you do to animals that submit to your tyranny!"

The searing heat of the gash in Jax's chest shook his body.

"Why don't you fight me now?" she demanded.

"I have to show you the side of humanity you haven't seen before," he said. He was nearing the end of his ability to affect her. He had one last card to play, one final change he had made within the pyramid. Then it was up to her, whether she would kill him of not. "I can't show you by myself. You are going to see more memories, Nara, with the next two words I say to you." It was another trigger to unleash memories he had planted in her mind. "Hurley Grimshaw."

Narasimha's nails retracted from his skin, and her gaze drifted to images playing in her mind. Her eyes grew wide, and she roared in agony. "Why can I see this woman? The Animalis!" Her eyes were swelling with emotion. "They're killing them!" Her roar was ear splitting.

"I gave you these memories," Jax said through his pain, "so that you could see what I saw inside the pyramid."

She was seeing the wholesale murder of the Animalis that Hurley had been a part of.

"This is life, Nara. This is what happened. But don't give up on us. If you can see her life, don't give up on us."

She released him and backed away, shaking her head and moaning. He had also given her the rest of Hurley's life. Narasimha could see how Hurley had changed, became penitent, and filled with compassion.

Jax painfully pulled himself to his feet. His clothes were heavy with blood.

"Make it stop!" she bellowed. She stepped back, searching for her escape.

"I love you so much," he said. "Your desire to protect your Animalis brothers and sisters is so beautiful."

On top of the pain flooding his body, he began to feel the changes he had made melting away. His body was returning to normal.

Narasimha turned back and charged at Jax. He kept still, his arms open. He let the fear of her brutal approach pass through him in a breath and felt peace take its place.

Tears overtook Narasimha's rage and her attack faded before it had begun.

"This isn't real," she tried to say with force, but it came out in doubt. "How could a human change like this?" She was walking to him now. Her voice was sinking into a whimper. "It doesn't change what they've done to us."

"No," Jax said. He could feel hope building inside his chest. "But there's a better way to make things right." He was within arm's reach of her now. "Help us find a better way, Nara."

The powerful, bold, dominant lioness Jax had known was

gone. A pitiful expression had replaced the ferociousness. Her shoulders rolled forward, and she turned her head down and away from him.

She took another step toward him. She was so close that the fur on the back of her neck bent under his breath. She was waiting for him.

Around them, the audience continued to watch in silence. The guards shifted uneasily. The sweet smell of ozone drifted down and Jax filled his lungs with it.

"Humanity needs you, Nara," he said. He meant it. Jax wanted to hold onto the hope he was feeling. It was a moment that held the promise of a new future, but one that would still be filled with pain and struggle.

Jax brought his hand up and began to stroke the soft fur on the back of her neck. She hadn't killed him. She hadn't ripped him to pieces as she could have easily done. Part of her had wanted to change and was looking for another way.

Something inside the lioness rumbled under his hand and tickled his fingertips. He kept stroking the fur when he realized what it was: her deep, rhythmic purr.

Epilogue

Hank sat on the edge of his bed, letting the weight of his head sink down between his hands. His fingers stroked through his hair, tickling his scalp.

A tremor of pain cascaded through his body, an echo of the drug still making its way out of his system. When he closed his eyes, he could see the lioness standing before him again, her terrifying eyes, and teeth, and snarl.

"Jax," he said out loud to himself. The rescue plane had found the pyramid, but not Jax. This time he couldn't hide from the guilt; he had been blinded by the need to get the machine and use it. So blind that Jax had been taken again because of him.

Hank found his last memory of Jax in his mind. The image was rough, changing as he remembered it. *I've got to keep my focus,* he scolded himself. But the face was there—

There was a sudden explosion within Hank's mind, a supernova of information. Traits, thoughts, whole lifetimes, generations of lifetimes pouring through him.

His subconscious mind went to work, cataloguing and storing the information, while his conscious mind reeled with questions: *What's happening to me? Where is this coming from?*

Connections began to form: all of the new memories

stemmed from Jax. Hank was inside Jax's mind while he looked on at an unfathomable vista of experience. He could see Hurley, Narasimha, himself, and the two little animals, Moxie and Little Hank.

Hank felt another tremor of pain coming on, about to pull his mind away from the glimpse into what had to be eternity.

Once the throbbing had left him, he went back through his mind to review the new memories. Jax had been inside the Ivanovich Machine!

Unlike Jax, Hank locked onto one aspect of the experience, and couldn't let it go: Moxie and Little Hank were not created by the pyramid; they had been there before it was created. They were from somewhere beyond physical reality.

His subconscious mind took the memory and stored it away with a tag. The name of the tag phased from his subconscious into his conscious mind, and he mouthed the word out loud:

"Seraphis."

THE END